THE PLAINS
OF ABRAHAM

BY

JAMES OLIVER CURWOOD

AUTHOR OF

THE ANCIENT HIGHWAY,
THE FLAMING FOREST,
SWIFT LIGHTNING, ETC.

Fredonia Books
Amsterdam, The Netherlands

The Plains of Abraham

by
James Oliver Curwood

ISBN: 1-58963-560-4

Copyright © 2001 by Fredonia Books

Reprinted from the 1928 edition

Fredonia Books
Amsterdam, The Netherlands
http://www.fredoniabooks.com

In order to make original editions of historical works
available to scholars at an economical price, this
facsimile of the original edition of 1928 is
reproduced from the best available copy and has
been digitally enhanced to improve legibility, but the
text remains unaltered to retain historical
authenticity.

FOREWORD

AN opinion I have stated before is that a writer of romance is not an historian, nor can he ever be judged as such, though his pages may carry more of history and truer history of a certain people and time than has been written. For, as there are times in an historical novel when fact insists upon drawing a sombre cloud between romance and its fulfilment, so there are times when the necessities of romance make permissible that poetic licence which writers of fiction have been granted from the remoteness of the ancients, and which will persist further ahead than we can possibly see into the future. In *The Plains of Abraham* I have made an humble effort to "carry on" with the same fidelity to truth that I prescribed for myself in my first historical romance, *The Black Hunter*, and it is probably a deeper satisfaction to me than it is to my readers to know that Marie Antoinette Tonteur and her fierce old father lived and loved as I have described; that Catherine Bulain and her valiant son were flesh and blood of their day; that Tiaoga and Shindas, Silver Heels and Wood Pigeon and Mary Daghlen, the Thrush, are not creatures of fancy, and that *The Plains of Abraham*, like

The Black Hunter, is largely a romance of life as it was lived and not as it might have been lived. It is with a keen sense of my own limitations that I realize I have been only partly successful in bringing back to life those men and women whom I chose from the accumulation of material at hand. The gathering of this material has been the most thrilling adventure of my life; the travelling foot by foot over the hallowed ground, the reading of letters written by hands dead a hundred and fifty years or more, the dreaming over yellow manuscripts written by priests and martyrs, the winning of the friendship of holy nuns of the Ursulines and devout fathers of Quebec who still guard the treasures of the New World pioneers of their faith—and, lastly, the unveiling of loves and hates and tragedies and happiness of the almost forgotten period embracing the very birth of both the American and Canadian peoples, and weighted with happenings that shook the foremost nations of the earth and largely made them what they are to-day.

While *The Plains of Abraham* and *The Black Hunter* are in no way dependent upon each other, it has been my intention that they shall, together, give a more complete picture of the men and women and stirring events of their times than it would be possible for either to do individually. The present novel begins approximately where its predecessor left off, the first terminating with the episodes closely following the battle of Lake St. George and the second finding its finale on the Plains of Abraham. Anne St. Denis and Nancy Lotbinière of *The Black Hunter* play their small parts in the lives of Antoinette Tonteur and Jeems Bulain of *The Plains of Abraham*, so close is the intermingling of the periods.

That we, as a people, know little of the more intimately human side of our history, and that its most picturesque and dramatic incidents are buried under a mass of printed versions which recognize only the great and the near great, is illustrated in no way better than by the forgotten report of an officer who was under Colonel Henry Boquet when he invaded the Hidden Town of the Indians described in this story and "released" the white prisoners there, later assembling them in a camp to which white men and women came from the near-by provinces to find their lost ones. This remarkable document was printed in the provincial correspondence of the Register of Pennsylvania in 1765, and since that time, in so far as I have been able to discover, has rested in oblivion, though it throws more light on Indian character than any other thing that has been written.

A part of this report is as follows:

The Indians at first delivered up twenty prisoners, but promised to restore the remainder. The Colonel, having no faith in their promises, immediately marched into the very heart of their country, where he received a large number, even children born of white mothers, but these little children were so completely savage that they were brought to the camp tied hand and foot; for in no other way could they have been taken from the wigwams. Two hundred were now given up, but it was supposed that at least one hundred yet remained in the interior, scattered among different tribes.

Language cannot describe the joy, terror, disappointment, expectation, horror, and gloom; every face exhibited different emotions. The scene baffled description; husbands found wives, parents children, and sisters brothers. The brother embraced the tender companion of his early years, now the mother of Indian children. Various were the groups thus collected—some, not understanding the language of their new-found relatives, were unable to make their wishes known—others recovered children long supposed dead—some stood in despair, living monuments of wretched uncertainty. Embracing their captives for the last time, the Indians shed torrents of tears and gave up all their little property as an evidence of their affection. They even applied and obtained the consent of Boquet to accompany them to Pittsburgh; and during that journey they hunted and gave venison to the captives on the march. Among the captives was a young Virginian who had captured the heart of a young Mingo. Never was there seen an instance of more real affection, regard, and constancy. The young Mingo was told to beware of the relatives of her he loved. He replied, "I would live in her sight or die in her presence—what pleasure shall the Mingo have—who is to cook the venison—who to thank him for the soft fur? No one! The venison will run—the fur will not be taken—the Mingo can hunt no more." The Colonel dismissed him with a handsome present. Every captive left the Indians with regret. The Indian children shed tears, and considered the whites as barbarians. Several women eloped in the night and ran off to join their Indian friends. One young woman was carried off tied by her friends, to prevent her from joining the Indians. There had not been a solitary instance among them of any woman having her delicacy injured by being compelled to marry. They had been left liberty of choice, and those who chose to remain single were not sufferers on that account. There was one young woman whose relation was such as to excite an unusual degree of interest. It had been her fate to be captured at an early age. She had been captured and taken away to a distant tribe, far from the dwelling of the whites. Years had removed every prospect of restoration to her former home. She had been adopted in the family of an Indian chief. Her delicacy of form and feature made an impression on a young Indian. He would attend and aid her in the performance of her duties; sympathize with her distress, and alleviate her cares—thus by a thousand kind attentions he won her heart. They were married—they had children—they were happy—she felt happy because she possessed the affection of her husband and children. When she heard she was to be delivered up to her former friends her grief knew no bounds. Thus would she reason: "As a wife of an Indian, as a mother of Indian children, can I enter the dwelling of my parents; will my parents be kind; will they receive my children with affection; will my former companions associate with the wife of an Indian Chief; will they not shun my steps? And my Indian husband who has been so kind, so very kind, can I desert him?" No, she would not surrender him—and that night she eloped from the camp, accompanied by her husband and children. When Colonel Boquet was informed of the circumstance, he requested that no pursuit should be made, as she was happier with her Chief than she would be if restored to her home.

Upon his return from this expedition, Colonel Boquet was immediately elected to the rank and pay of Major General, Commander in Chief of His Majesty's forces in the Southern Department of America.

My great-grandmother was a Mohawk, and it is with pardonable pride and satisfaction that I find myself able to present to the public an occasional evidence of the nobler side of Indian character, suppressed through a period of centuries by the white man's egoism and prejudice. The Indian was the greatest of all friends, the greatest of all patriots, the greatest of all lovers of his country. Despoiled, subjugated, annihilated, *he died a savage*.

JAMES OLIVER CURWOOD.

Owosso, Michigan, November 20th, 1926.

THE
PLAINS
OF
ABRAHAM

THE PLAINS OF ABRAHAM

CHAPTER I

ON A sunny afternoon in May, 1749, a dog, a boy, a man, and a woman had crossed the oak opens of Tonteur's Hill and were trailing toward the deeper wilderness of the French frontier westward of the Richelieu and Lake Champlain—the dog first, the boy following, the man next, and the woman last.

It was a reversal of proper form, Tonteur had growled as he watched them go. A fool's way of facing a savage-infested country that had no end. The man should have marched at the head of his precious column with his long gun ready and his questing eyes alert; the woman next, to watch and guard with him; then the boy and the dog, if such nuisances were to be tolerated in travel of this kind, with evening coming on.

Tonteur was the one-legged warrior seigneur from whose grist mill down in the valley the four were going home.

His eyes had followed the woman with a subdued and appraising hunger in them. Henri Bulain was a strange man, he had thought. He might be a little crazy, might even be a fool. But he was also a very lucky husband to possess a woman with the sweet face and form and the divinely chaste heart of Catherine, his wife.

Jeems was a fortunate boy to have her for a mother.

Even the dog was a scoundrel for luck. An Indian dog at that. A sneaking, good-for-nothing dog. A wreck of a dog without a soul, to be fed by her, petted by her, smiled at by her—as he had seen her smile.

Tonteur had prodded the heel of his wooden leg into the soft earth as they disappeared across his meadow bottom lands. The King of France had honoured him, and he was first of the long string of heroic fighting barons settled along the Richelieu to hold the English and their red barbarians back. He was Doorkeeper to the waterway that led straight to the heart of New France. If the English came with their scalping fiends, the Mohawks and the Senecas, they would have to pass over him first of all. No general could be given greater distinction than that. Honour. Wealth. A wide domain over which he was king.

And yet——

He envied Henri Bulain.

It was midafternoon. Maytime shadows were growing longer toward the east. The sun was still a mellow glory over the land, a golden radiance without sting or glare, a lambent sea which spread itself in warm pools and streaming veils over an earth which seemed to be purring gently with peace and joy. It had been like that since morning. It had been like that for days. Sweet rains had come, pulling up green shoots from the soil; there had been winds, dark clouds, and deep thunder, but only at night since two weeks ago this Thursday afternoon. With each dawn had come the glow of the sun, the singing of birds, the building of nests, the

opening of flowers, the deepening a little more of the
plastic greens in the forest.

It was so quiet this afternoon that one could hear
clearly the humming of bees, and with this friendly
and comforting sound the tinkling symphony of running
water finding its way in a hundred little creeks and rills
down to the meadowed lands of the Richelieu. There
was no wind that moved a leaf or twig, yet all about
there seemed to be a living breath of something—a spirit
of growing things, a song of flowers, a perfumed laughter
rioting on the hilltop and in the valley, almost too mysterious for human eyes to see or human ears to hear.

It was the hour when birds were singing softly. Morning had heard their defiance, a glorious and fearless
challenge of feathered minstrelsy to all the spirits of
darkness; but with late afternoon, sunset, evening, these
same slim-throated songsters found a note of gratitude
and of prayer in their chastened voices. A thrush sang
that way now. A catbird's melody joined it. Silver-
throated brush warblers piped their subdued hymns
in the thickets. Flowers crushed underfoot. In the open
spaces they carpeted the earth with white and pink and
blue. Flowers and birds and peace—a world filled with a
declining sun—a smiling heaven of blue over the treetops—and with them a dog, a boy, a man, and a woman
advancing westward.

Three of these, even the dog, Tonteur envied.

This dog had a name which fitted him, Tonteur had
thought. For he was a wreck of a dog—even more a
wreck than the splendid seigneur himself, with his stub of
a shot-off leg and a breast that bore sword marks which

would have killed an ordinary man. The dog, first of all, was big and bony and gaunt, a physical ensemble of rough-edged joints and craggy muscles that came by nature and not because of hunger. He was a homely dog, so hopelessly homely that one could not help loving him at sight. His hair was bristly and unkempt. His paws were huge. His jaws were long and lank, and his ears were relics of many a hard-fought battle with other beasts of his kind. His tail was half gone, which left him only a stub to wag. He walked with a limp, a heavy, never-failing limp that seemed to shake his long body from end to end, for his left fore paw—like Tonteur's foot—was missing. A crooked, cheery, inartistic, lovable dog to whom the woman—in a moment's visioning of the fitness of things—had given the name of Odds-and-Ends.

So Tonteur was half right in thinking of him as a wreck of a dog, but in one other thing he was wrong. The dog did have a soul—a soul that belonged to the boy, his master. That soul had a great scar seared upon it by hunger and abuse in an Indian camp where Henri Bulain had found him four years before, and from which, out of pity for a dying creature, he had taken him home to Jeems. It was a scar cut deep by clubs and kicks, a wound that had never healed and that made the dog what he was—a tireless and suspicious hunter of scents and sounds in the woods.

He was always ahead by a step or two, even when the song of birds and a softly stirring melody of peace filled the day. He was ahead this afternoon. Of the four who were filing westward, he seemed to be the only one who watched and listened for danger to come out of the beauty and stillness of the world about them. Now and then he glanced up at his master. Trouble lay in the boy's face and eyes, and the dog sensed it after a little and whined in a questioning way in his throat.

Daniel James Bulain was the boy's name, but from babyhood his mother had called him Jeems. He was twelve and weighed twenty pounds more than his dog. Odds-and-Ends, called Odd for short, weighted sixty, if the scales in Tonteur's gristmill were right. One would have known the dog and the boy belonged together even had they been in a crowd, for if Odd was a battered old warrior, the boy, on the other hand, gave every evidence of an ambition to achieve a similar physical condition.

"Why, he's dressed up like a bold, bad pirate come to abduct my little girl and hold her for ransom," Tonteur had roared, down in the valley, and Jeems's father had joined the baron in his laughter; then, to make the thing worse, Tonteur had turned him round and round, slowly and appraisingly, with lovely little Marie Antoinette looking on, her dainty nose upturned in patrician disdain—and with Paul Tache, her detestable cousin from the great city of Quebec, openly leering and grimacing at him from behind her back. And this after he had prepared himself with painstaking care for Marie Antoinette's eyes should she happen to see him! That was the tragedy of it. He had put on his new doeskin suit on this day when they were going to Tonteur's mill for a bag of meal. He carried a gun which was two inches longer than himself. A big powderhorn swung at his waist, in his belt was a knife, and over his shoulder hung the most treasured of his possessions, a slim ash bow and a quiver filled with arrows. He had worn his coonskin cap of fur in spite of the warmth of the day, because it looked better than the lighter one, which was stripped, and in this cap was a long turkey feather. Odd, the dog, was proud of his martial-looking master, but he could not understand the change that had come over the boy or why he was going home with such a strangely set and solemn face.

Henri Bulain was aching to describe the little scene to his wife as soon as Jeems was out of hearing. But Henri was always seeing either the bright or the funny side of things. That was one reason why Catherine had married him, and it was why she loved him now even more than fifteen years ago, before Jeems was born. It was the big and all-embracing reason why the wilderness with its trees and flowers and dangers loved Henri Bulain. It was because *he* loved life—loved it in such a vastly inclusive and mysteriously trustful way that Louis Edmond Tonteur, the lion-hearted baron of the seigneurie, had called him a fool for his simplicity and predicted the day when his scalp and those of his wife and boy would adorn the small round hoops of the savages.

From her position behind the dog, the boy, and the man, Catherine Bulain looked upon her world with a joyous and unafraid pride. No boy, in her opinion, could equal Jeems, and no man her husband. That challenge always lay in her dark eyes, rich with sleeping lights because love was there. One could see and feel her happiness, and as Tonteur secretly built up the fire of his yearning when he was alone, so she loved to exult in her own possessions when her men folk were ahead and could not see all that came and went in her face. This desire to hold within herself some small and sacred part of her rejoicing was because she was English and not French. That was why Daniel James had an English name, inherited from her father, who had been a New England schoolmaster and afterward an agent of the Penns down in Pennsylvania. It was on the frontier of that far province that Henri had found and married her two years before her father's death.[1]

"And for fifteen years you have been growing younger and more beautiful," he was fond of telling her. "What a tragedy it will be when I am old and bent and you are still a girl!"

It was true that Catherine did not look her thirty-five years. Her face, as well as her eyes, was young with the softness and radiant changeableness of girlhood, and especially on this Thursday afternoon when she walked behind her boy and her husband from the Richelieu bottom lands. The climb over Tonteur's Hill had brought a flush to her cheeks, and with the glow of the sun in her glossy hair she was a witching picture for Henri to look back on now and then as he shifted the heavy bag of meal from one shoulder to the other.

Tonteur was aware, possibly even more than Henri Bulain, that Catherine's adoration of her men folk and

---

[1] Daniel James Adams, Catherine's father, was killed in a feud between a village of Tuscaroras and a rival village of Delawares, in Pennsylvania, in the summer of 1736.

of everything that went with them, even to the primitive discomforts of the wilderness life which had claimed her, was built up against a background of something more than merely being the mate of a man and the mother of a son. Culture and learning and broadness of vision and thought, nurtured in her first by a gentle mother, and, after her death, developed and strengthened by a schoolmaster father, had given to her a medium of priceless value by which to measure happiness. Sometimes she yearned a little for the things outside this happiness—dreamed of brocades with gold embroidery, of buttercup silks and blue satins, of white moires and dainty Valenciennes, and for that reason in Henri's cabin were roguish caps with pink and lavender ribbons, and cobwebby lace for Catherine's hair, and many simple but pretty things made by her own clever hands. She could make frills and fichus as fine as any that Madame Tonteur ever wore, with all their cost, and to-day her simple gown of sprigged muslin, caught up with blue love-knots, and her cloak and hood of bakneesh red had given her a loveliness in Tonteur's eyes that made his heart thump like a boy's in his battle-scarred breast. Because of her feminine adroitness in fashioning beauty and perfection out of simple and inexpensive things, and also because she was of the spawn of the despicable English, Madame Henriette Tonteur had come to regard her with much the same aversion and dislike with which she would have looked upon a cup of poison.

Tonteur knew this and cursed in his honest heart at the woman who was his wife, with her coldly patrician face, her powdered hair, her jewels and gowns and her platonic ignorance of love—and then thanked his God that little Marie Antoinette was growing less like her with each day that passed over her pretty head. For Marie Antoinette was tempestuous, like himself, a patrician without doubt, but with a warm and ready passion to offset that curse, and for this, too, he blessed the fortune which in one way had been so unkind to him.

Behind her husband and boy Catherine had been thinking of Tonteur and of his wife, the aristocratic Henriette. For a long time she had known of Madame Tonteur's hatred, but it was not until this afternoon that the other discovery had come to her, for, in spite of his most heroic efforts, Tonteur had betrayed himself when suddenly she had caught him looking at her. Catherine had seen the shadow of his secret—like a ghost swiftly disappearing. Up over the Hill she had added many twos and twos together, until, in the sure way of a woman, she knew what Tonteur was thinking and did not fear or distrust him for it.

At the same time her thoughts inspired her with a warm appreciation of her own great fortune, for against another man's unhappiness and another woman's failure as a wife she could see more clearly the things for which she, in the fullness of her felicity, should offer up the devoutest of prayers. The man ahead of her was humming a French tune as he carried his hundred pounds of whole-corn meal, and one could see that he was French in every drop of blood that ran through his veins. Catherine loved the spirit of this blood even more than she did the English which was in herself. Just as she had become French, so Henri in his heart had become as wholly English, and never tired of swearing that he would not trade one tiny breath of the precious life in Catherine's body for all of his beloved New France. From the beginning, his influence had been stronger than his wife's, for while Catherine kept everything that was English alive in her memories, and taught her boy in English as well as in French, and sang her English songs and treasured her English books, she loved New France as she had never loved the more forbidding aspects of her New England home, and she loved the warm-hearted and sunny people in it with a sympathy and devotion which might have come from birth and not adoption.

Yet Madame Tonteur hated her. Disbelieving whatever good might have been said of Catherine, she hated her first as a deadly enemy of her race, and hated her then because she dared hold her head as proudly as a baron's lady, and hated her last of all because, nothing more than the wife of a worthless backwoodsman like Henri Bulain, she was impudent enough to be the prettiest woman anywhere near the Tonteur seigneurie.

And, so far as it was in her power, she had planted and nurtured this hatred to growth in the heart and mind of her proud daughter, Marie Antoinette, until Tonteur, blind to the feline subtlety of a woman in such matters, wondered why it was that his girl, whom he worshipped above all other things on earth, should so openly display unfriendliness and dislike whenever Jeems came to Tonteur Manor.

CHAPTER II

OF THIS same thing Jeems had been thinking as he walked ahead of his father and mother. His mind, at present, was busy with the stress of fighting. Mentally, and physically in a way, he was experiencing the thrill of sanguinary battle. Half a dozen times since beginning the long climb over Tonteur's Hill he had choked and beaten Paul Tache, and in every moment of these mental triumphs Marie Antoinette looked on with wonder and horror as he pitilessly assailed and vanquished her handsome young cousin from the big city of Quebec.[1]

Even in the heat of these vivid imaginings, Jeems was sick at heart, and it was the shadow of this sickness which Odd caught when he looked up into his master's eyes. From the day Jeems had first seen Marie Antoinette, when she was seven and he was nine, he had dreamed of her, and had anticipated through weeks and months the journeys which his father permitted him to make with him to Tonteur Manor. On these rare occasions he had gazed with childish adoration at the little princess of the seigneurie and had made her presents of flowers and feathers and nuts and maple

---

[1] In 1749, the population of Quebec City, metropolis of New France, whose wealth and culture and courtly life made it at that time the Versailles of the New World, was less than seven thousand.

sugar and queer treasures which he brought from the forests. These tokens of his homage had never served to build a bridge across the abyss which lay between them.

He had stood this hurt and still kept Marie Antoinette in his thoughts, for there was no other child to help fill her place. But since last autumn, when Madame Tonteur's sister and her son Paul had come to the seigneurie, his dreams had grown more clouded until, on this Thursday afternoon, they were replaced by grim and merciless visions of a future vengeance on the young man who had laughed at him and humiliated him, and who, without any grace whatever that he could see, basked warmly in the smiles and graciousness of Marie Antoinette's favour.

For all his shattered hopes of friendship with Toinette, he now found an excuse to blame this rich and high-toned youth with his green and crimson velvet suits, his lace ruffles and gold brocades, his silver-handled sword and supercilious, conceited airs. His antagonism was not a thing brewed only in his mind, for Paul Tache, who was the son of a Quebec army officer deep in the intrigues of the Intendant, was the last straw to break down whatever hopes he had possessed of ultimately making an impression on the seigneur's daughter. With the coming of Paul, who was two years older and a head taller than himself, and who paraded all the fine and courtly manners taught to young gentlemen in Quebec, she had regarded him more haughtily than ever, and that very day had made no effort to hide her amusement when Paul said, with a sneer on his dark face, "*Doesn't it make you tired to walk all the way in from the woods, little boy? And does your mother allow you to load that old gun of yours with powder and ball?"*

It was the memory of this moment which rankled in his breast—a moment in which he had stood speechless, his face hot and red, his tongue hopelessly tied, his heart only half beating as the Quebec boy walked away with Toinette, strutting like a turkey cock and looking back contemptuously as he went. It was the knowledge of his own failure to reply or to do anything but stand red-faced and dumb, like a fool, accepting the insult without protest, that deepened his gloom and increased his bitterness.

He was glad when his mother and father paused to rest on the edge of a great rock near the trail, for this interval gave him opportunity to go on alone, and when he was alone he could tear and thrash Toinette's cousin in a much more admirable way than when the others were tramping close at his heels. By the time Odd had preceded him to the edge of a high plateau, which was richly covered with grass and thickly grown with big chestnut trees, his mental orgy of vengeance and bloodshed was beginning to subside.

Suddenly Odd stopped so that his gaunt body made a barrier against Jeems's knees. He stood with his pawless leg off the ground, and when he slowly rested it to earth again it was in a manner which sent a thrill of anticipation through his master. They stood at the edge of a flower-strewn open among the chestnut trees, a dancing place for the wood fairies, his mother had called it that morning, and all about this lovely open was a thick growth of hazel, like a fence put there by the fairies themselves to shut out prying eyes from their frolics. It was a hundred yards across this sun-filled playground of the wild, and on the far side of it, concealed in the bushes, Jeems knew there was game of some kind.

He dropped to the earth and drew himself behind the decaying mass of a monster log that had fallen a hundred years before. Odd crouched at his side with his muzzle level with the top of the log. Thus a minute passed, and after that another, and more on top of them, yet Odd gave no sign of discouragement, nor did Jeems. They were so still and motionless that a red squirrel studied them curiously for a sign of life and a chickadee almost stopped to rest on the end of Jeems's gun. A fragile sweetness of violets and anemones rose from the ground, but Jeems did not look down at the white and pink and blue masses of them crushed under his knees. He watched the far side of the clearing on a line as straight as a die with the pointing of Odd's nose.

Another minute of this rustling stillness, and a magnificent turkey cock strutted majestically out into the sun. He weighed twenty pounds if an ounce, thought Jeems. His head was like blood, his beautiful body a gold and purple bronze, and his gorgeous breast plume touched the ground. He was a proud and immaculate bird, defying all the world in the empty open, and he shuffled his wings and began to swagger about in a circle while the chuckling and clucking sound of his satisfaction clearly reached the watchers' ears. In this moment Jeems thought again of Paul Tache, for the Quebec boy was like this turkey cock, always flaunting his clothes and disporting himself with the importance of a man.

He caught his breath short as a slim brown female bird came out from the bushes to join her red-headed monarch. A flutter of velvety wings followed her and in as many seconds six more females joined the gathering in the open. The turkey cock paraded more proudly than before and puffed himself up until he was twice his honest size, and it seemed to Jeems that the lady turkeys were all crowding about him like so many Marie Antoinettes attracted by his fine clothes and his manner of making himself big in their eyes. At the sight before him, Jeems hated Paul Tache more than ever and was possessed with the inspiring thought of wreaking his first vengeance upon his rival's head by killing the turkey cock.

Slowly he withdrew the long-barrelled gun from the top of the log and tautened the string of his bow. He waited until the big bird stood less than eighty yards away. An inch at a time he rose higher on his knees, and Odd's body grew stiffer with his movement. A choking sound came from the dog's throat as the long bow was bent. The twang of the string was like the ring of a steel tuning fork, and across the open sped a grayish flash. There followed a mellow sound, a great commotion, a leaping of gorgeous colour high into the air, then a wild beating of wings and a speeding away of seven brown forms to the safety of cover. Paul Tache, the turkey cock, was down and dying, and in the space of a dozen seconds his seven Marie Antoinettes were gone.

A moment later, Jeems and Odd stood looking down on the turkey cock, and gladness leapt once more into the boy's face and eyes—for here was not only a splendid dinner for to-morrow, but also, in his imagination, the first blow struck against his enemy.

There was a point on the ancient Indian trail over and beyond Tonteur's Hill where a narrow path made by generations of Caughnawaga, Algonquin, and Ottawa feet ran close to the edge of a precipitous height with miles and miles of glorious country under it. This valley lay to the westward and was rich with deep forests and glimmering lakes, a quietly slumbering land filled with mystery and beauty and with seldom the smoke of an Indian camp fire rising out of it. It was a fortunate valley in many ways, for it was far enough from the Richelieu to escape the desecration of white men's axes, too near to the long-houses of the Mohawks for the safety of the red hunters of their enemies from above the St. Lawrence, and too closely a part of the French and their allies to be more than adventurously invaded by the hunting parties of the Six Nations. So it had lain for many years in peace and silence. Yet countless eyes must have looked upon it in the centuries that had gone by, for on its valleyward side the shelving rock was worn smooth by those who had rested there to gaze down into its forbidden lure, where life would have been so pleasant to live.

Viewed from where Catherine and Henri paused to

rest, the valley under them was a huge oriental rug of greens and golds and blacks and silvers—greens where the meadows ran in and out and the hardwoods were bursting into tender leaf, golds where the slanting sun struck floods of yellow light upon poplars and birch, blacks where the thick evergreens grew in deep masses of darkening gloom, and silvers where the still waters of three small lakes gleamed with the warm splendour of jewels. As they sat on the rock there came to them a faintly exquisite and lulling melody, a droning and unchanging cadence which enchanted and rested the senses, mingling as it rose with sweet air laden with the delicate fragrance of flowers and the gossamery breath of growing things. Only at dawn and at an hour when the sun was poised for its drop behind the curtain of the western forests did this sound rise from the valley—the song of thousands of squirrels. And as it was this afternoon so it must have been from the beginning, for, as far back as the oldest Indian story went, the huge gray stone had been called Squirrel Rock.

As Henri's eyes rested upon the pleasant scene, he told the story of Jeems, and he was still chuckling over the humour of what had happened when he discovered the clouded and serious look in Catherine's face.

"It is what I have been guessing of late," she said, and there was no laughter in her voice. "Madame Tonteur hates me and she has been training Toinette to hate Jeems!"

"What are you saying?" cried her husband. "Madame Tonteur hate you! It is impossible. Of all people in the world not to like——"

"I am the one," said his wife. "And you, poor Henri, with your foolish notion that everyone must love us, have never been able to guess the truth. She hates me so much that she would like to poison me, and not being able to do that, she has turned little Antoinette's mind against Jeems."

"You went in to see her to-day!"

"Yes, because I am a woman."

"She cannot hate you!"

"No more than she can hate bugs and snakes and poison."

"But—Tonteur. It is impossible, I tell you! He does not feel that way."

"No, I am sure he does not," said Catherine.

"If Tonteur likes us and treats us so well, why should his wife dislike you?" he demanded.

"First, because I am English. You must always remember that. Though I have come to love your country as dearly as my own, I am still English, and Jeems is half English. We are of a people who are your country's enemies. That is one reason why she hates me."

"And there is another?"

"Yes. She hates me because her husband sees fit to look upon me in a kindly way," answered Catherine. She was ready to say more, but the glad laugh which she loved came from Henri's lips, and in a moment she was tightly held in his arms.

Then he thrust her from him with playful roughness and pointed down the valley.

"As long as we have that, what do we care about Madame Tonteur or all the rest of the world?" he cried.

"Let it fight, I say, and let women like Tonteur's wife quarrel and hate if they must. So long as you are not unhappy in a land such as this we look upon yonder, I would not trade my place for all the kingdoms on earth!"

"Nor I, as long as I have you and Jeems," said Catherine, and as Henri turned to his corn again she added, "but I am not thinking of you or of myself. I am thinking of Jeems."

They started slowly up the trail.

"Madame Tonteur's dissatisfaction with me has been amusing, and I have had my innocent frolics out of it, like to-day, for instance," she continued in the silence of her husband's pondering thoughtfulness. "With you and Jeems I need no other company to keep me happy, and so Madame Tonteur's dislike has caused me no special pain. I have even liked to tease and plague her, for which I should properly feel shame. To-day I let my braids down, feigning a bit of headache as I did it, but truthfully to let her see how long and thick they are and how skimpy her own hair is, for she is only a little older than I. You should have heard her sniff when her sister from Quebec said my hair was beautiful and that it would be a crime to pomade or powder it. I may be wicked, Henri, but I cannot hold myself from pestering her in these ways, for all the trouble she has taken to make me so distasteful to her own unreasonable self. I tried so hard to be her friend, but when at last there ceased to be a hope, why, I began to see the humour of it, just as you have always taught me to catch the whimsies in unpleasant things. But with

Jeems and Toinette—it is different. He has dreamed of her for a long time and has made her a spirit companion in his adventures and play."

Henri looked at Catherine. "I know—I can see—I was stupid to laugh at him down there. But Tonteur laughed, too. I did not think a boy so young would take it to heart."

"A child is like a woman," said his wife. "Both are more easily hurt than man ever dreams."

"I will hurry to Jeems and tell him how sorry I am," said Henri.

"You will do nothing of the kind," replied Catherine.

"But if I have done wrong——"

"You will keep it to yourself—this once," decided his wife. So he waited discreetly, and after a moment she said, "Henri, I know that Louis Tonteur is a good and noble man and that in his heart is a great loneliness and want of something, although he worships Toinette. No man could love his wife, even with her blue blood and high ways. He is so pitifully lonely that I am going to ask him to come to our place often and bring Toinette with him."

"You think he will come?" asked Henri eagerly.

"I am sure he will," replied his wife, and now that she was thinking only of Jeems, she was glad she had not told her husband what had been at her tongue's end —the secret of her discovery that afternoon. "He will come," she added, "and I am sure, if I ask him, he will bring Toinette."

Henri laughed his pleasure.

"Tonteur is one man I love," he said.

"He is a man made to love," agreed Catherine.

"But—Toinette——" and Henri shifted the bag of milled corn to his other shoulder. "If Madame Tonteur says no, what then?"

"Monsieur Tonteur will still bring her," replied Catherine. "That is, if I tell him it will please me very much," she added, smiling up at him.

"That he will!" cried Henri confidently. "He will bring Toinette if you look at him like that, *ange!* But if he does such a thing, and Madame Tonteur protests, and he dares to do it again——"

"Possibly she will accompany him after that," said Catherine. "It may add to Madame Tonteur's liking for me, Henri." She laid her hand on his arm, for they had come to the edge of the woodland open, and ahead of them Jeems and Odd were standing over their slain turkey cock.

The wild hot pride of youth and achievement possessed the lad as his father and mother came toward him, and like a bristling gargoyle on four legs Odd stood joyously wagging his stump of a tail. Here was triumph, and the boy's eyes lighted up when he saw his mother's interest in what he had done, and the unfeigned amazement in his father's face as he dropped his milled corn to the ground and looked down upon the magnificent turkey cock with the feathered arrow transfixing it.

Catherine regarded her boy unobserved by the two whose hunting instinct drew their eyes to the fallen game. Her own eyes were shining, and after a moment Henri saw what she was seeing and thinking and placed one of his big hands tenderly on his son's slim shoulder. Yes, Jeems was like his mother except for his blond hair and gray eyes, and in these two things he resembled his mother's brother, that worthless, wandering, always fighting and forever lovable vagabond, Hepsibah Adams. Henri's heart was happier at his wife's proud contemplation of her son, and he burst forth in praise of the lad's exploit.

"What a shot!" he cried, bending low to examine the bird and the arrow. "Straight through from wing to wing as clean as a bullet—and right up to the shaft of the feathers! I'd swear you did not have that strength in your arm, lad! Yet the arrow was sped from back there at the edge of the open, you say? I scarce believe it! It is a shot for Captain Pipe and White Eyes and Big Cat, and not for you!"

These three were the Caughnawaga Indian friends who had taught Jeems to shoot, and it was Captain Pipe who had made his bow of choice seasoned ash.

They went on as the sun was setting behind the wilderness, and the golden pools of light grew dimmer about them and shadows grew heavier and more velvety dark among the trees. Because of this approach of evening with all of its stillness and beauty, an instinct born of the solitudes made the four travel so softly that one could scarcely hear the footsteps of the others. The sun was not yet down and would light the western sky with springtime glow for another hour, but the forest through which the old Indian trail wound its way had grown thick and gloomily vast, so that it made a dusk like night within itself. To the boy and the dog this timbered country which lay between the seigneurie and their home was a silent and mysterious realm of adventure, a place filled with whispers of mighty things to happen, and with ghosts—ghosts everywhere—of promising and lureful things of which neither was afraid. To the man and the woman it was different, for to them, with their experience and understanding, the beauty and greatness of God in nature had never grown common or old. In this great forest, with its age-old trees and battlemented tops, Catherine's heart beat faster and her soul rose to the awe and majesty of spirit which she could not see, but which, like a warm presence closing in softly about her, she could clearly feel. Through the woods, though the trail was narrow, she walked with her hand in Henri's, and for half an hour they spoke no word except in whispers. A little more, and there was sky to see again with its glow in the west, and then small opens and scattered maples and chestnuts and beech, with green meadows running like ribbons between them, and at last, coming to a broader meadow that looked down a gentle slope into the forbidden valley which they had viewed from Squirrel Rock, the four saw their home.

It lay in a sheltered dip which was like a diminutive child of the larger valley, a low and cheerful cabin of peeled logs, with more windows in it than a cautious man would have had, and with a huge chimney of clay and stone at the end. It was not a "rolled-up" house, with logs standing endwise in a trench, and possibly built around the stump of a great tree which could be used for a table within, but a home of beauty and comfort and luxury, as those things were measured on the frontier, and the best that Henri Bulain could build. Catherine's love for this home was next to her love for Henri and her boy. From its windows, which were unshuttered against foe of any kind, she could look east, west, north, and south from the knoll in the dip on which it stood—south and east over the forbidden valley, where every morning she could see the sun rising over the Tonteur seigneurie and Squirrel Rock; northward up the slope into the dark depths of the forest; and westward to the sinking sun where lay the vast reaches of unexplored country of which Henri Bulain was always dreaming, and toward which Jeems was beginning to turn wondering and sometimes yearning eyes as he grew older.

But Catherine possessed the feminine glory which would forever hold her men folk back. Close about the cabin was her own domain—her flowers, her gardens of shrubs, her bird houses built of chestnut bark, her box hedges among the thinned-out trees, with pretty paths edged with whitewashed stones winding in and out among them. Her daffodils and wild-flower plots were in bloom, and from this day until the white frosts there would be no end of flowering things. Most of all she loved her kit-run-abouts which Jeems called Johnny-jump-ups, and her sweet Williams and bouncing Bets, the last of which was the plumed ancestor of all the carnations. From daffodil-time until the autumnal marigold there would be hollyhocks, celandine, roses, lewpins and candy-tuff, larkin-spur and sweet-scented pease, sunflowers and catchfly, pinks and Queen Margarets, and a score more of grasses and flowers in her gardens, until a stranger coming upon her wilderness home would scarcely have believed that it lay at the edge of a raw frontier.

Running up to the borders of these gardens were Henri's work fields, beginning first, because of Catherine's artistic eye, with the gentler growths of husbandry —carefully groomed and plotted soil for herbs and vegetables, lettuce, sorrel, parsley, mallows, chervil, burnet, thyme, sage, carrots, parsnips, beets, radishes, purslain, beans, cabbages, squashes, asparagus, musk melons, cucumbers, and pompions; and beyond these marked-out patches lay the broader fields for heavier grains and foods, ten acres of well-tilled land in all, ending up against the hard-maple wood out of which, in the preceding month of April, Henri had taken his year's supply of fifty gallons of maple syrup and four times as many pounds of sugar.

These precious possessions the four saw as they came down the green slope, and not one half of them would Catherine have exchanged for all of Madame Tonteur's riches. Only a pallid glow of the sun was left, and the world was preparing itself for the close of day. Overhead an endless column of pigeons was on its way to a great roost in the forbidden valley, flying crows settled into the gloom of the Big Forest, and black and gray squirrels in the hardwoods ceased their chatter and slipped like shadows from tree to tree. Catherine's chickens were gathered about their shelter, and up from the fenced-in meadow, through which a creek ran to lose itself in the woods, their ox and cow had come to the log-barn gate.

Catherine was smiling at her husband, and in Henri's eyes was an answering light of happiness, when out of the peace and beauty which lay about their home rose a piercing and blood-curdling cry—a cry which seemed to stop every sound that was in the air, which reached the pigeons and swerved them affrightedly, which startled the phlegmatic ox at the gate, a cry of monstrous depth and vastness, and with that cry a wild figure came toward them from its hiding place in the greening shrubbery of Catherine's garden.

With a lurch of his shoulder, Henri sent the bag of corn to the ground, while ahead of him Jeems swung his long gun into the crook of his arm and Odd stiffened and let out a sullen growl. The scraggy and mysterious figure advanced up the slope, and Jeems had looked to his flint and priming and stood with a ready thumb on the hammer of his weapon when from behind her husband and her boy Catherine gave first a startled gasp, then a little scream, and sped past her protectors to meet the advancing stranger with open arms.

"*It's Hepsibah!*" she cried. "*It's Hepsibah!*"

CHAPTER III

THE stirring words had scarcely fallen from his mother's lips when Jeems laid his gun on the ground and ran after her, but with all his haste she was in her brother's arms before he could overtake her, while his father, carrying the turkey cock but without the corn, came hurriedly out of his amazement and down to meet them. When he arrived, Hepsibah Adams was holding Catherine with one arm and with the other had hoisted Jeems halfway to his shoulder. In a moment he freed himself enough to hold out a hand as rough and knotted as the old oak tree which sheltered the cabin from the afternoon sun.

If ever a man bore an affinity to an oak, with its cheer and strength and rugged growth, that man was Hepsibah Adams, the Indian trader. There was also something about him which made one think of Odds-and-Ends. With all this he was as cheerful a creature to look upon as friend or enemy could want to meet. He was not as tall as Henri by half a head, nor did he have his leanness. His shoulders were wide and his body thick, and his face was as round as an apple and almost as red, with marks and mars of stress and battle set upon it, but in such a way that its vivacity and the good humour of its twinkling eyes were enhanced rather than spoiled by the vicissitudes of fortune. He wore no hat, and on the top of his head was a saucer-like space as bald as an egg, but under this beauty spot, as Hepsibah called it, his reddish blond hair grew thick and rampant, with its ends curling up, so that with a small effort of imagination he might have been taken for a shaven friar who had been at hard grips with the disciples of Satan.

When the excitement of first greetings was over, Catherine stood back from her jolly rogue of a brother and viewed him with a pair of eyes bright with affection, but which glowed at the same time with an appraising and speculative questioning which her lips at once put into words.

"Hepsibah, I am so happy to see you that it makes my heart choke, and yet I observe that you have not kept your promise to stop fighting, for one of your ears is nicked and your nose is crooked and there is a mark over your eye which was not there when I saw you two years ago!"

Hepsibah's weather-stained face broke into a smile.

"I can't say as much for your nose, Catherine, for it grows prettier each year," he said. "But if a Dutchman's ham should happen to come against it, as one hit mine in a little joust in Albany Town, why, I'll say there would be a bend in it, or no nose at all. And as for the ear with a nick in it, what can you expect from a Frenchman—excepting your sweet-tempered husband here—when he gets a chance to use his teeth instead of the hands which God gave him to fight with? The slit in the face is only a crease left by an Oneida's knife when he misled himself with the thought that I had got the best of a bargain, which I never do get, or I'm a sinner! But is that all? Do you keep no better account of me than that?"

"The bald spot is larger, Hepsibah, and so even and round it amazes me."

"That is because I gave a Seneca hairdresser a good hatchet and holder to pluck out the hairs in the Indian way and make it so, Sister. I hated that bald patch, which was as uneven as a candle-dripping on the top of my head, but now that it is round I like it."

"And I saw a tooth gone when you laughed."

"Only a second dose from the Dutchman's knuckles. God love me, but you should have seen that Albany Dutchman fight!"

"And your clothes," said Catherine, coming to the main point in her mind at last. "You look as though a bear had played with you. Hepsibah, has anything happened—near here?"

"A mere trifle, Sister. A few miles back I ran into a bunch of Frenchies who said this was a long way from New England and had it in their minds to turn me t'other way. But that was nothing, nothing at all. I am a bit ashamed of you, Catherine, for you have missed the important thing!"

"What is that?"

"My stomach," declared Hepsibah, holding his ample paunch with both knotted hands. "It is sunk and shrunken, as you may clearly observe. It has fallen in on itself until it hurts my backbone, and has withered and wasted itself to the dimensions of a lady's. It is dwarfed, shortened, circumscribed, and reduced—

fairly warped and strangled from lack of food! And if I do not eat very soon——"

The rest was smothered in Catherine's arms and laughter.

"Dear old Heppy!—Hungry—always hungry, and you never will be any other way. So we shall have supper almost as soon as smoke can be made to come out of the chimney. I am so happy you have come!"

"And I," added Henri, getting in a word at last.

Jeems was tugging at the hand of his roving vagabond of an uncle, who was his greatest hero in all the world, and dragged him back to get his gun.

As they went, the happiness in Catherine's face was clouded for an instant.

"Best keep good eyes on our Jeems for a time, Henri," she warned. "Hepsibah, you know very well, is a singularly improvident and thoughtless man, overfilled with foolish tricks and contrivances most alluring to boyish minds, and of which, because of Jeems, I am a bit afraid."

But Henri only chuckled, for the thought was in his mind that it was a fattening of one's good fortune to be taught tricks by a man like Hepsibah Adams.

Then Catherine saw that a film of smoke was rising from the top of the big stone chimney.

"Hepsibah has already started a fire," she said.

When they came through the wide double door of the kitchen, Henri drew a deep breath of satisfaction and Catherine gave a pleased cry of surprise. It was a great kitchen, thirty feet from end to end and twenty in width, with the last light of day coming through its western windows. To this fading illumination was added the rosier glow of a flaming back log and a huge mass of hard-maple coals which faced them as they entered. Henri had spent a month in the building of their fireplace, and the proudest seigneurie along the Richelieu could not boast a finer one. He had housed Catherine and Jeems with an aunt in Three Rivers while constructing their home, and when Catherine first saw the fireplace she walked straight into it without bending her head, and so wide was it, as well as high, that Henri had built seats within the chimney-place on either side, and over these were hooks on which to hang firearms, and even small drawers set into the stone for his pipes and tobacco; and farther back, never in the way of smoke or soot, were many other hooks for Catherine's treasures of pots and kettles and pans, so that the chimney-place was a kitchen in itself and a cozy snug-corner for wild wintry nights as well. The problem of getting fuel, which at first had somewhat frightened Catherine, had never worried Henri at all, for in the winter he dragged up with his ox hardwood logs six feet in length and two feet thick, which he ran on rollers through the door to the firepot, and with one timber such as this for a back log and two or three smaller ones with which to cuddle it, he had a fire that would last a day and night, and not only was he rewarded with greater comfort than if he had burned smaller logs, but he was also saved a vast amount of cutting.

It was the aliveness of this fireplace which had drawn an expression of surprise and pleasure from

Catherine—that and the aroma of cooking things which greeted them. Since Catherine's earliest memories, her brother had boasted of his excellence as a cook, and most assuredly he had been busy since his unexpected arrival. Half a dozen chains were dropped from their bolts in the thick oak lug-bar seven feet above the fire, and from the pothooks at the end of these chains were suspended as many pots and kettles, steaming and boiling and giving forth a cheerful sound of dancing pewter lids against which the bubbling water was playing an animated and pleasing melody. But to Henri, who always loved the sound of these busy pots with their lively cheer and promise of supper, a still more delectable thing was the great roast of venison which Hepsibah had hung before the fire. He had ignored Catherine's Dutch oven, or roasting kitchen, of which she was exceedingly proud, and had replaced that household device with the more primitive arrangement of a stout hempen string tied to a wooden peg in the ceiling, to the end of which, in the glowing heat of the fire, he had securely fastened a haunch of young venison. By giving this string a twist now and then, the meat was made to turn slowly for an interval of several minutes while its juices dripped into the basting pan under it. That Hepsibah had been watchful of his roast, basting it so frequently that there was not an inch of dry surface upon it, was evident from its richly brown and savoury appearance as it swung slowly before the fire as if unseen hands were attending it.

Housewifely instinct made Catherine give the hempen string a twist before she took off her cape and hood and patted her hair more properly into place before a mirror hanging on the wall. Then she glanced down the long table which Hepsibah had laid with her pewter in preparedness for the roast. Henri knew how fast her heart was tripping as he took her hands and held them for a moment and saw a mist of tears behind her lashes. It had been two years since she had seen Hepsibah, two years of yearning and praying and hoping for this irresponsible brother, the last of her close blood ties, who came and went with the inconstancy of the winds and yet had never succeeded in spoiling her dream of having him some day as a permanent member of her little family. Each time he came to them, Hepsibah was full of promise, swearing upon his soul that he had made up his mind to remain with them forever, as Catherine pleaded with him to do; and then, some day or night, he would disappear with all his belongings, and no one would see or hear him go, and it might be six months, or a year, or, as in this instance, even longer before he returned, ready to promise and swear upon his soul all over again but sure to steal away in the end as before. Once he had confided to Henri, "I can't say good-bye, not even to an Indian, and I surely can't say it to Catherine. I'd rather leave her smiling and laughing than crying."

Each time that he came, he bore a huge pack on his shoulders, as if partly in penance, and the opening of this pack and the distributing of its contents had come to be the biggest event in Jeems's life, and also in his mother's in a slightly less degree. But Jeems had no trespassing thought of the never-failing bundle as he went back for his gun in the company of his beloved Uncle Hep. At the most providential of moments, his hero of all heroes was at his side, and securing this mighty personage's pledge of secrecy he lost no time in telling him about the boy he hated. Marking the grip of Jeems's hand, and catching the telltale tremble in his voice, Hepsibah sat down upon the bag of ground corn and did not leave it until by shrewd questioning and sympathetic interest he had drawn from Jeems's heart a large part of what it had withheld from his parents that afternoon. At a second loud blowing of Henri's dinner horn they rose to their feet, and as Hepsibah shouldered the corn, his round red face was like a full moon of promise and cheer.

"It doesn't take *size* to win a fight, Jeemsy," he said, speaking in a confidential way. "Barring this Dutchman at Albany, I've never been rib-roasted by a big man yet, and I'm only tolerable sized, you observe. I've always had a reasonable preference for the big ones, come as come can, for they are slower to move and fall harder, and nine out of ten of them carry fat. This Paul Tache, now—I know by your telling of him that you can cob and comb him until he begs for mercy, which is the proper time, if he's down, to give him a few whops for good measure and memory. It's all what you've got your mind made up to, Jeemsy—nothing more and nothing less. And you've got your mind made up to warm him, so go and do it, I say."

Catherine came around the corner of the cabin to meet the plotters, and Hepsibah discreetly held back further words as he winked broadly at Jeems.

It was the great night of two long years in the Bulian cabin, and Catherine's three Betty lamps and her Phœbe lamp and a dozen candles as well were lighted in honour of it, so that when darkness fell thick and starless about the wilderness, with masses of rain clouds gathering overhead, the home at the edge of Forbidden Valley was bright with glow and cheer. Even the crash of thunder and a deluge of rain on the chestnut-barked roof, and hatfuls of wind that rattled the windowpanes, seemed to pass unnoticed in the joy that was within. The roast was cut open, and with attendant dishes of sukquttahhash, Johnnycake, potatoes, and carrots, and hasty pudding with maple syrup, gave opportunity for such feasting that an hour was well gone before Hepsibah Adams thrust back his end of the long table bench and brought forth his fat pack from under the stairs which led up to Jeems's sleeping loft.

As long as Jeems could remember, this had been a signal to clear the table of every dish and crumb that was on it, and while his father smoked a long Dutch pipe and his Uncle Hepsibah fumbled with mock clumsiness at the tyings of his pack, he ran a race with his mother to see whose side would be cleaned up first. When it was done, his mother put a Betty lamp at each end of the table and then seated herself so that she was facing her brother, with delight and expectancy equal to Jeems's flushing her cheeks and brightening her eyes.

Hepsibah buried his hands in the mysterious depths of his bundle.

"Just a few little trinkets," he began, using the identical words he had employed one year after another.

"A few whim-whams and baubles for the boy, a bit of trumpery for Sister, and a farthing's worth of nothing in particular for you, Henri—all picked up at small cost and no trouble in the town of Albany, where lives a Dutchman with two of the biggest and heaviest skull-breakers in the Colonies. Ah, here we have the first package, with writing on it in the hand of the scholar who sold me the goods—a cap, a ruffle, a tucker, and a bolt of lace at five shillings a yard! Now who in this room can such sillies be for—unless——" and at Catherine's delighted exclamation he tossed the bundle to her. But scarce had she opened it, with her eyes intent upon her business, than Hepsibah unfurled a red silk petticoat in the candle glow, and this time Catherine sprang to her feet with an amazed intake of breath, for so well had Hepsibah arranged his surprise that, one after another, he had a white love-hood, a black love-hood, and three more petticoats on the table—one of scarlet with black lace, one of coloured drugget with pointed lace, and a third of black silk with ash-gray lining; and as Catherine stood gazing upon these treasures fit for a queen he added to them two pairs of stays for an eighteen-inch waist, and then showered over them such an array of lace drowlas, gorgets, piccadillies, and other neckerchiefs that Catherine closed her eyes for a moment and then opened them wide as if there might be a chance of some clever trickery in it.

"Dear Mother in heaven!" she cried. "Are all of these ravishing things for me?"

"Of course not," said Hepsibah drily. "The stays

are for Jeems and the drugget skirt is for Henri, to be worn when he goes to church on Sunday."

But Catherine paid no attention to his fun, if she heard at all, for her slim fingers were running swiftly over her gifts, caressing one and then another, until Henri forgot to puff at his pipe, and Jeems stood up better to see the excitement in his mother's face.

"They must have cost a fortune!" she exclaimed, pausing to look at her smiling brother and at the same time holding up the scarlet petticoat with black lace. "This one, for instance——"

"Two pounds fifteen shillings," said Hepsibah, opening his pack wider and working his hands quickly. "But an ounce or two of trumpery like this, *ma cherry*, costs more," he added, trying to speak a bit of French. "A bonnet, and the best in Albany, at four pounds ten, and here half a bolt of tamboured muslin at eighteen shillings a yard, some lutestring at twelve shillings, calico at six shillings threepence, and durant with the figures turned t'other side around, at three shillings sixpence—enough cloth, the scholars who sold it to me swore, to build dresses and pretties for as fine a lady as there is in the land. And to go with these dresses I have here ruffles and tuckers and threads and buttons and ribbons, and four pairs of the nicest shoes that ever came up the Hudson," and placing these last-named articles on the table with a flourish of his arms, Hepsibah gave a gloating chuckle and paused to fill his pipe.

Jeems's heart was near breaking with suspense, and it seemed to give an audible crack when his Uncle

Hep's gnarled hands went into the pack again. The method of procedure had always been the same—his mother coming first, and then he, with his father looking on until the last. But this year Hepsibah had decided upon a change, for he drew a bulky package from his store and passed it to Jeems's father.

"Three of the finest pipes I ever laid my eyes on," he announced. "One made in Holland, one in London, and one in America, and five pounds of Virginia tobacco to go with them, Henri, along with a hat, a coat, and a pair o' boots that may take you with honour to any swoirree or gentry merry-making this side of the sea. Now, how's that?" And he stepped back as if his pack were entirely empty and held nothing at all for Jeems.

For an eternity, it seemed to Jeems, his uncle remained in this terrifying posture. Then, with deliberate and aggravating slowness, Hepsibah Adams returned to his pack.

No one of the three who were watching him would ever have guessed that Hepsibah's act was one weighted heavily with the force of destiny, nor that with dramatic inevitableness it was to change the course of human lives, bringing the high down to earth, and the earthly to great heights, loosing passions and hatreds and loves, breeding tragedies and joys, and ending, at last, in what it is the purpose of this humble chronicle of human events to narrate.

A swift-coming thought, a deft return into the pack of a small bundle which he had intended for Catherine, and Hepsibah had changed a world. On such trivial happenings do the most powerful of the fates sometimes rest. Out of the farthest corner of the collapsing pack he brought this bundle to light once more and unwrapped it as he turned toward Jeems's big-eyed, anxious face.

"Jeemsy," he said, "if I've put the notches in my memory right, you were born on the coldest January day I ever saw, and that makes you just twelve years and four months old this evening, which means, if you figure it right, that only three years and eight months lie betwixt you and the day when you can be counted a man. According to law, you are a King's subject of maturity from that day and can take life and all its belongings into your own hands, so long as you are honest about it, and can stand up in equality before the stiffest periwigged judge in the Colonies or New France. In other words, Jeemsy, I mean that in less than three short years you will be a full-fledged man!"[1]

Having delivered himself of this introductory peroration Hepsibah finished unwrapping the package, and never had Catherine beheld such a handsome piece of velvet as that which her brother displayed in the candle glow. It was, *par excellence*, the finest of the treasures he had brought, a cloth of matchless beauty, a crimson glory so filled with changing humours and colours that it seemed to be alive in his hands. Surely this was another present for his mother, Jeems thought. But to

---

[1] In the middle of the Eighteenth Century both male and female youth ripened early in its capacities. Boys became men by law when sixteen, girls' best marriageable years were from fifteen to seventeen, and a young lady of ten was deemed no longer a child. Experience and education so swiftly developed youth to its maturity that Governor Winthrop's son became executor of his father's will when he was only fourteen years of age.

his amazement and Catherine's surprise Hepsibah thrust the cloth into Jeems's hands.

"For Mademoiselle Marie Antoinette Tonteur from her devoted admirer, Daniel James Bulain," he announced. "Jeemsy, don't blush. Twelve and ten are not far from sixteen and fourteen, when you will be man and woman, and if ever a seigneur's daughter finds herself lucky it will be on the day she marries a son of the tribe of Adams. The writing on it, Jeemsy, tells where't came from and how much it cost; and along with it I have brought you some nankeen for britches and clothes, four shirts, and a three-cornered hat with a black ribbon, six handkerchiefs, and a jackknife, two pairs o' serge britches, as many of new shoes, and—this," and from the now completely emptied pack he drew forth a beautiful long-barrelled pistol, his eyes aglow with a fighting man's pride as he fondled it in the light of the candles and pointed out its merits to Jeems. "As long as you live, you must never part with this pistol, Jeemsy," he said. "It isn't new, you see, but its record is one of glory as long as my arm, and I'll tell you about it some day. It's a killer, lad, a killer deadly and sure, good for a hundred paces with less than an inch of drop," and he gave the weapon into Jeems's hands.

An instant of disapproval gathered in Catherine's eyes.

"It was kind of you to bring the cloth for Antoinette but I do not care for the pistol, Hepsibah," she said. "A pistol makes me think of—men fighting men. And here we are at peace, having need only of the rifle and of Jeemsy's bow and arrows to bring us meat. I feel it is not best!"

As she spoke thus confidently of peace, a cloud came over Hepsibah's face, but in a moment he had laughed it away and was telling her that within a week she would be as proud of her boy's marksmanship as she now seemed fearful of the pistol's influence upon his future.

An hour later, when Jeems went to his bed in the loft, it was of neither pistol nor marksmanship he was thinking, but of the piece of red velvet which he placed close to his pillow before he snuffed his candle and laid himself down for the night. If his heart beat less swiftly now, he was even more joyously thrilled than when he had been with his people. The rumbling of thunder and flashing of lightning had passed, and the soft spring rain fell steadily on the roof a few feet over his head, drowning in its drowsy and musical rhythm whatever sound of voices might have come to him from the fireplace room. He could hear the running of water off the roof in a hundred busy trickles and streams, and caught the mellower sound of it pouring from the chestnut-bark trough at the edge of the eaves into the wooden barrel below.

Jeems loved this music of falling water. It soothed and comforted him and made his dreams more vivid. He loved the foot-wide rills in the forests at snow-melting time; he loved the dark and hidden creeks stealing their way among the cool and shaded places in summer; he loved the bigger streams, the lakes, and even the still ponds which in August were covered with green "frog scum." But most of all he loved the rain. And now, with his hand resting against his present for Toinette, and with the comradely beating of the rain above him, the world that had gone to pieces for him that day reassembled itself swiftly in his mind. Here, at last, was the kind of gift he had tried to build in his dreams. Flowers and feathers and nuts and maple-sugar bars could not equal one square inch of its beauty. It was lovelier than anything he had ever seen Antoinette wear, and his spirit rose in such increasing exultation that in the darkness of his room his eyes opened wide and sleep was miles away.

To-morrow was the day of the auction sale at Lussan's place. Lussan was a wealthy farmer at the edge of the next seigneurie, ten miles away. He was returning to his old home near the Isle of Orleans, a country he liked better than the Richelieu, and was selling most of his goods. Among these were a plough with an iron point, a forty-gallon soap kettle, and a loom which Jeems's father wanted, so he had planned to start with the ox early in the morning. Jeems had heard Tonteur say he intended to buy Lussan's three slaves, a mother and father and daughter, and that the young wench was for Toinette. Toinette would be with her father. He would take his treasure package with him to Lussan's and find an opportunity to give it to her.

Should Paul Tache be there and dare to overlord him again, or laugh in his meanly suggestive way, or speak sneeringly, or so much as say a word against his gift for Toinette. . . .

A rumble of fresh-growing thunder was advancing out

of the west, and preceding it came a roar of wind and a deluge of rain. Lightning cut once more in vivid flashings across the narrow panes of the bedroom window, and the roof seemed to bend and groan under a sudden torrential bombardment. Jeems fought in unison with the elements. His spirit mounted savagely with the turmoil. He had his enemy down and was thrusting his head into wet and slimy mud. He was beating his face and eyes, and spoiling his splendid raiment, and pulling out his hair. And Marie Antoinette was looking on. With the gorgeous red velvet in her hands and her eyes big and starry, she was watching him as he choked and kicked and pummelled the life out of Paul Tache!

The outburst of thunder and wind and deluge, a whim of playful spring, passed as swiftly as it had come, and, in passing, it left Jeems breathing quickly and fiercely in his bed.

He had risen in these moments to reckless heights, and his mind, hot with its desire for action, had settled with grim assurance upon what would happen the next day.

First he would present his gift to Toinette.

Then he would do what his Uncle Hep had told him to do. *He would whip Paul Tache.*

CHAPTER IV

HENRI and his wife sat up late with Hepsibah Adams, for this time Hepsibah had come with a set and determined purpose to his sister's home. Had Jeems crept down the stairs toward the end of the evening's talk, he would have discovered the happiness of earlier hours mellowed by a tense and almost tragic seriousness that lay in the faces of his mother and Uncle Hepsibah. The trader's countenance had grown stern, and Catherine's cheeks were like those of a pale nun in the candlelight. The rich gifts from her prodigal brother were heaped on the table, but something of deeper import than a contemplation of their beauty and the thrill of possessing them had gathered in her eyes. In Henri Bulain's face were still the cheer and good-humour and unruffled equanimity of confidence and faith that Hepsibah, with the darkest pictures he had painted, had been unable to disturb.

They were talking about war. As early as this spring of 1749, the American wilderness had begun to stir with whispers of the impending conflagration which was destined soon to turn the eastern part of the continent into a seething pot of fury and death.

While George the Second of England and Louis the Fifteenth of France were playing at friendship after the peace of Aix-la-Chapelle, France gasping for breath with the flower of her armies buried on European battle-fields, and England with her fighting forces reduced on land to eighteen thousand men and to less than seventeen thousand on the sea, the vast colonies of the two countries, working out their own salvations, were steadily and surely and with deadly intent encroaching upon each other. While the two greatest monarchies in Europe were disguising their weaknesses under a screen of clever politics and a shambles of court orgies which transformed their capitals into gorgeous carnivals of extravagance and sensuality, these rival colonies in America had learned to distrust, to hate, and to look forward to a day of extermination and vengeance.

The stage was already set for the writing of the bloodiest and most picturesque pages in American history. Southward from the Richelieu were the bitterest of all the white men's enemies, the warriors of the Six Nations, and northward, sweeping east and west through the Canadas, were the forty scattered tribes who bore allegiance to New France. Behind these savage vassals, on one side, were eleven hundred thousand English colonists holding the sea-coast lands from Maine to Georgia, and on the other less than eighty thousand souls, counting women and children as well as men, to defend and hold the illimitable domains of New France, which reached from the upper Canadas to the Gulf of Mexico and from the Alleghanies to the Rocky Mountains.

Of this alarming disparity in power of fighting men, and of the pitiless scourge which he swore would some day sweep through all the country of Lake Champlain and the Richelieu, Hepsibah Adams had spoken at length but with small effect on Henri Bulain.

"Let war come if it must," said Henri. "The heart of New France is set behind an impenetrable wall of rock and forest, and with these ramparts in our favour, eighty thousand will be a match for the million English if they come this way. But why talk of war, Brother, when there is peace and plenty and a beautiful world about us to enjoy? Let kings fight or play, just as they will, but as for me, should fighting chance to come—why, I shall be a friend to both sides and strike at neither. For no matter what cause should bring about the strife, I could not strike at the people of my Catherine's blood, nor would she have me turn against my own. So why move from here? This is a glorious place. It is neutral ground, and we, being neutral, are fitly placed here. Oneidas and Mohawks have eaten under our roof as well as Hurons and Algonquins, and when deadly enemies such as these meet thus on common ground, what cause have we for fear?"

A light of pride glowed in Catherine's eyes as she listened to her husband's words, and she added:

"Henri loves the Indians, and I have grown to love them, too. They are all our friends."

"Friends!" sniffed Hepsibah. "Henri, it is because of Catherine and Jeems that I call you a fool. Take them where this danger does not hang day and night along the edges of the frontiers. Take them to the St. Lawrence, if you will, or bring them south into Catherine's country. But do one or t'other, for God's sake, or the day will come when Christ Himself cannot save you," and his voice shook with earnestness.

"There will be no war," insisted Henri stubbornly. "England and France have bled themselves white on Continental battlefields, and the peace which was signed only last October will surely not be broken again while you and I are living, for Hanover and Austria have had their fill, as well as the others, and are like two dead men on their backs."

"That is right," nodded Catherine, with a shudder. "I think all fighting is over for many years."

Hepsibah blew out his cheeks like a balloon, then sucked them in with a smack. It was a childhood trick he had never outgrown, a way of telling the world he was fully out of temper, and remembering it as such Catherine smiled, though her fingers twined uneasily in her lap.

"Fools—innocents!" her brother growled. "I tell you neither George nor Louis will have anything to do with the running of this war until every mile of woods between our Colonies and your city of Quebec is red with fire and blood.[1] God love me, it has already begun! French and English traders are fighting wherever they come together along the frontiers, and the hired Indians of one are taking scalps for t'other. Even white men have joined in that pretty game, for Massachusetts has sent out Lovewell and his fifty men to hunt

[1]This prophecy of Hepsibah Adams came strictly true. England and France did not declare war upon each other until May and June of 1756, although for several years preceding this date many wilderness massacres and bloody battles occurred, including Braddock's defeat and the battle of Lake George.

the heads of Indians and French—it makes no difference which, though the order says redskins only!—at a price of five shillings a day plus a bounty for every scalp that is taken; and down in New York country Sir William Johnson counts out English money for human hair, while the French—and you know it, Henri!—are paying a hundred crowns apiece for white scalps as well as red. It's hair the Indians are bringing in instead o' fur, because the prices are bigger and the market surer, and our own blood, both French and English, is working harder each day with whisky and money and guns to turn them into devils. And here you sit like a couple of foolish doves with a young one in the nest, your scalps worth fifty pounds apiece, your windows open, your door unlocked, your senses gone, while over the hill a few miles away this Tonteur neighbour of yours loopholes his houses, trains his farmers with guns, barricades his windows, builds his doors of oak, and makes a fort of his meeting house. *He* knows what is coming up from the Mohawk country and is preparing himself for it as well as he can."

"His business is soldiering," replied Henri, his serenity still undisturbed by the grim and forbidding future which Hepsibah had drawn in his argument, "and it is stipulated in his grant from the King that he fortress his place whether it be in peace or war."

"And besides," said Catherine, "he keeps his women folk with him, and surely, if danger were threatening, he would send them away." She rose from her seat and came around to her brother so that she stood behind him with her arms about his shoulders. "Hepsibah, we know this you have told us is true," she said, pressing her cheek against his face. "There is terrible murder along the frontiers from which you have come, and that is why Henri has brought Jeems and me into this country of his where are only peace and friendship and no thought of the hideous killings and ugly traffickings you speak about. You have argued against yourself, Brother, for it is you who should move out of strife and danger and come to live with us. Then our happiness would be complete. I have prayed for many years that you would come—and never go away again!"

"Together we will have a paradise here," urged Henri.

"And I will find you a wife," added Catherine. "A wife who will love you greatly, and until you have children of your own we will give you half of Jeems."

Hepsibah rose gently out of her arms.

"For Jeems you should change your home to a place where there is a schoolmaster and more for him to learn," he said, catching desperately at a last argument where all others had failed.

"In all of New France and the English Colonies there is no better teacher than our Catherine," answered Henri proudly. "In English and French she has given to Jeems more than he could ever have learned in your town of Albany or our college in Quebec; for there, in one place, he would have been English, and in the other, French, while here he is both, like his father and mother, and will never strike at either of the two bloods that are in his veins."

"Of that I am sure," agreed Catherine. "I pray God my Jeems will never be a fighting man."

When Hepsibah went to his cot in the loft, he stood for a moment with his lighted candle beside Jeems's bed where the boy lay sleeping with the cloth of velvet close to his hands, a smile on his lips. Jeems was dreaming, and the dream took the smile away and put a grimmer thing in its place, and looking down on it Hepsibah thought of Henri Bulain's last words and his sister's prayer, and his lips moved whisperingly to himself, "They can't keep it from you, lad—hope nor prayer nor all their faith. It's coming, and when it comes you'll strike and strike hard, and it's then you'll be what you're bound t'be, Jeems—a fighting man!"

In the candle glow the piece of red velvet seemed to answer Hepsibah Adams, but seeing no farther with his eyes, and going no deeper with his thoughts, the trader undressed himself quietly, snuffed his candle, and went to bed.

Catherine's breakfast was on the table with the break of sunrise, and Jeems was even ahead of that, helping his father with the chores. The ox was fed and the cart ready for a day's rough travel before his Uncle Hepsibah came down from his sleep. Talk of war and massacre and death had left no shadow in Catherine's heart, and Hepsibah could hear her singing as he went with naked arms and shoulders to the spring near the cabin and doused himself in its ice-cold water. The sound of her voice made him pause and face the south, where the dusk and mists of early morning were lifting quickly over the wilderness. His wide shoulders twitched as if the chill of the water had sent a shock through them, and he marked the swellings and dips of the timbered solitudes of Forbidden Valley, and saw where the Mohawks would enter it and where they would come out if his prediction and his fears came true. Then he heard Henri and Jeems laughing near the barn as if one or the other had turned a joke or found something humorous in his work. With the shiver still in his blood, he turned to the water of the spring again and found Odd standing close behind him, also facing the stillness and mystery of the valley, his nose sniffing the air, and his eyes— as the man's had been a moment before—filled with a steadiness and tenseness of look which had in it a sombre and voiceless foreboding. Hepsibah stared, for about them birds were singing, gray wings of pigeons were whirring through the air, crows were cawing in the edge of the woods, and cheerful voices were coming from the barn—all with the red glow of day breaking over the forests in the east—yet the dog was stiffly alert and unresponsive, looking past him into Forbidden Valley.

At the touch of Hepsibah's hand the strain seemed to leave Odd's body.

"It'll bear watching, boy," commended the man. "It'll bear watching day and night, but 'specially in that hour of darkness which comes just before the crack o' dawn. Not now, *but soon!*"—and he turned to his bath again.

When Jeems went ahead of his father and uncle to Lussan's place, he did not burden himself with unnecessary habiliments of either peace or war. He wore his old suit of brown homespun cloth, with Indian-made moccasins and leggings of doeskin, and on his head was a frontiersman's cap with an eagle feather in it. From under this cap his blond hair fell with its ends touching his shoulders, and with only his bow for a weapon his slim young body was free and buoyant and much handsomer than it had been the previous day with its carefully chosen raiment and warlike accoutrements.

A part of Jeems's very soul was his love for nature, a passion which was claiming him even more completely than it had his father and mother, though he had not begun to express it clearly even to them. From his earliest days, both Henri and Catherine had sown in him the seeds which had now sprung up to shape the future of the man, and in the example of their own tolerant and nature-loving lives they had implanted in him convictions and truths which back in Catherine's puritanical New England home would have been regarded as blasphemous. Catherine had taught him that all things had souls and language, even flowers and trees and the birds and beasts they slew for food, and that while destruction of life for the achievement of necessities was neither wrong nor to be condemned, *wanton* destruction was a sin which only God Himself could forgive. In further proof that God had intended one form of life to exist upon another, and yet within reason and judgment and charity, Henri Bulain never lost an opportunity to unveil for his boy the hidden and fascinating manifestations of life in the wilderness. Thus Jeems had come to understand that, from the smallest insect to the largest beast, living things were ceaselessly nourishing themselves upon other living things in such a balanced and intelligent way that no one thing in nature ever completely destroyed another.

In New France, where freedom of speech and the poetry and gentler side of life had found a soil in which to grow, such beliefs as these could be publicly expressed without fear or danger; but had Catherine been in her girlhood home she would have shielded Jeems in a cloak of ignorance, for the days were not gone in the Colonies when the powers of Satan were accredited to those whose new ideas or broader visions struck at the deeply rooted and narrowly prescribed laws of religious thought.

But with this presence of language and the power of heaven in the forests there were also other interests for Jeems. The blood in his veins demanded excitement and activity, and his was only an intermittent success in living up to what had been so basically a part of the teachings of his parents. There were many times when he killed sheerly for the thrill of slaughter, for the temptations about him were without number and exceedingly great. The woods and hills and meadows were alive with game. It was so plentiful that wild turkeys were selling for a shilling apiece in Boston, pigeons a penny a dozen, and fat young deer as cheaply as sixpence each, while in the town of Albany the prices were even lower and turkeys were selling for fourpence, and a stag for a cheap jackknife or a few iron nails. Squirrels were so numerous that in this same year of 1749

Pennsylvania paid threepence a head for six hundred thousand that were killed as pests.[1]

But this morning Jeems had brought his bow and quiver of arrows only because they were as much a part of him as the clothes he wore and he had no desire to inflict his might upon bird or beast. He was filled with exultation mingled with a determined eagerness. He knew he would fight if Paul Tache was at Lussan's place, and what was going to happen in that fight was as definitely fixed in his mind. He was on his way to elevate himself to supreme heights in the opinion of Marie Antoinette Tonteur—after he had given her the piece of velvet. The glory of the morning itself was in his blood. The sweetness of the hills and opens, the song of birds, the beauty of blue sky and green earth all combined in a responsive chord to the song that was in his heart, a song of emancipation almost—of deliverance from the oppression of a mind bullied and subdued until this hour. And now that he was on the point of achieving the fulfilment of a positively settled act, he wondered why it had not happened before.

No one was ahead of him when he arrived at Lussan's place. It was nine o'clock, and the sale was not until eleven. Lussan and his wife and daughter and two sons, and the three slaves who were to be sold, had been busy since dawn, and Jeems immediately found ways in which to help them. Half of a young ox was already

<hr>

[1] Indians have always been conservationists. But it was at this period in American history that the frightful slaughter of wild life by white people began. As many as a thousand deer were killed in a single drive by a merciless system of fire-hunting. The carcasses were left to rot, for the animals were taken for their hides alone, which were worth from ten to forty cents each.

spitted on a long iron bar and slowly roasting over a red-hot mass of hickory coals. The outside Dutch oven was filled with a huge baking of bread, and benches were set with pewter and snow-white dishes of poplar wood. Lussan was a famous maker of whisky and flip and beer, and three barrels were ready, hoisted on chunks of wood with their spigots down, waiting for the willing hands of his friends and neighbours to turn them. His brewing apparatus and still, for which there was bound to be high bidding, lay close behind the barrels, all polished and bright in the sunlight to tempt the eyes and purses of the buyers. About his prosperous home were the things which were to be sold, and the three slaves were working among these, their uneasy and aching hearts strengthened by their master's promise that they would be sold together and not singly.

After a time Jeems found himself with nothing to do and hunted out the plough and kettle and loom which his father wanted to buy. While occupied in this way, he came upon a table piled with a hotchpot of articles, and his heart gave a jump when he saw a number of books printed in English. How Lussan had come into possession of them, reading only French as he did, Jeems did not try to conjecture, for his mind was filled with the thought of his mother's joy if he could take these treasures home to her. There were five of the books, *Malvern Dale*, *Evelina*, *Telemachus*, *Eloiza*, and *Joseph Andrews*, a thrilling list of titles it seemed to him, and as quickly as he could he approached Lussan upon the subject of their worth and purchase. Seeing no merit in printed English and small chance for their sale, and being as well a free-hearted man and already warmed by his own excellent beer, Lussan gave them to Jeems in return for the hour of service he had rendered.

Overjoyed by this unexpected windfall of fortune, Jeems began to watch anxiously for the coming of his father and Uncle Hepsibah and for the appearance of the seigneur Tonteur and whoever might be with him. Nearer neighbours arrived before his father and uncle came out of the forest, and he lost no time in depositing his bundle of books in the cart, after which he fastened Odd with a buckskin thong to one of its wheels. He did not have to guess what Odd would do if free when it came to his fight with Paul Tache.

The hour for the sale drew near, and fully half a hundred men and women and a score of children had gathered, yet Toinette and her father had not arrived. Jeems placed himself where he could see down the road that came from the Tonteur seigneurie, and when at last he heard the auctioneer's voice bellowing forth his announcement that the sale was about to begin, he felt a sombre sinking of his hopes. They livened instantly when three figures on horseback appeared at the end of the half mile of road. The foremost rider was Tonteur, the second Paul Tache, and in the third saddle rode a slim, wide-hatted little person who was none other than Marie Antoinette Tonteur herself.

Concealing himself behind the bole of a tree, Jeems watched them as they passed, so near that a pebble flung by a hoof of one of the horses fell at his side. His courage almost failed him then, for while his hands clenched at the sight of Paul Tache, his heart faltered in its

beating as his attention turned from his enemy to
Toinette. She had become, all at once, a young lady
whom he could easily believe he had never seen before,
and the change in her held him for a few moments so
forgetful of his own existence that he would have been
discovered had one of the three happened to glance in
his direction. Toinette was equally unconscious of a
certain ten-year-old miss of yesterday, for one of her
dearest anticipations had become reality, and she was
wearing her first riding suit, a gorgeous blue camlet
trimmed with silver, just arrived from Quebec. With
this she wore a smartly cocked beaver hat which bore a
rakish feather, and from under this hat her long dark
hair fell in a cascade of carefully made curls, partly
restrained in their freedom by two or three red ribbons
enmeshed among them. She was superbly aware of the
lovely figure she made, and every inch of her body was
at a dignified tension as she rode past the place where
Jeems was hidden.

After she had gone, Jeems felt an overwhelming sense
of littleness and unimportance. For Toinette was no
longer Toinette, but a real princess, grown up. And Paul
Tache, riding close beside her, with hair powdered and
tied and with a red velvet coat that could be seen a
mile away, seemed now to be infinitely removed from
the plottings which he had conceived against him. He
stepped from behind the tree and stooped to pick up
the pebble which Toinette's horse had flung at him.
He could hear the auctioneer's voice, and others bidding for Lussan's properties. Then came a burst of
laughter which rose with unrestrained abandon above

all other sound, a blast of merriment which he would have recognized anywhere in the world. Only his Uncle Hepsibah could laugh like that.

His spirit leapt like the flare of powder in response to the cheerful sound of his uncle's voice, and what he had lost for a few moments became a part of him again, stronger than before. He returned to the grass-covered open in front of Lussan's house as Paul helped Toinette from her horse; and then, to his amazement and increasing admiration, he observed his Uncle Hep approach the baron boldly and offer his hand. Tonteur accepted it, and a little later Jeems saw them drinking flip together. These matters he made note of as he stood at the outer edge of the throng gathered about the auctioneer, who was making the welkin ring with his descriptions of Lussan's goods and his exhortations for people to buy. This man, who possessed a huge pair of lungs, had an ally as well as a competitor in the barrels of whisky and flip and beer, between which and the table whereon he stood men began to pass back and forth with increasing frequency; for while these barrels drew his customers away for a time, they were sure to send them back—as Lussan had planned— mellower in disposition and heart and with purse strings looser at every imbibition.

The sights and excitements of the scene about him would have made for Jeems one of the most thrilling events of his forest-rimmed world, had his heart not been choked with the emotions of impending drama. Even the aroma of many good things to eat held no interest for him. The voices of the auctioneer and the bidders, the loud banging of a wooden mallet which put a note of legality to every sale, the hubbub of men and women about him, the play of children, the fighting of a couple of dogs, all seemed outside the things he had come to seek. Yet he did not press his desires by undue haste, and it was half an hour before he found himself close to the one who occupied his thoughts. This happened in such a fortuitous way that Toinette, concealed by the ample forms of Lussan's wife and daughter, was within a foot of his shoulder before he knew it. She did not see him, and he stood with wildly beating heart, breathing the faint perfume from her person, his senses dazed by the nearness of her splendour and his world of vision filled only with a great broad-brimmed hat, an enravishing mass of lustrous curls, a sunset of crimson ribbons, a pair of slim shoulders—and then, his paradise broken by the ugliness of reality, he discovered Paul Tache. The young man was returning from a journey to the barrels, and, when he saw Jeems, a contemptuous smile twisted his lips. It was this look which turned Toinette so that she found Jeems standing beside her, his cap and a package in his hands, his face tensely set as he fought himself into obliviousness of his rival's presence.

He held out his gift to her.

"My Uncle Hepsibah has just come from the English Colonies, and he brought me this that I might in turn give it to you. Will you accept it, Toinette?"

He forgot Paul Tache. Spots of red came into his cheeks as Toinette's surprised eyes greeted him. She almost smiled, and as if something made her forgetful of her magnificence and the dignity it imposed, she extended her hand to receive the package. He felt the embroidered doeskin of her glove against his flesh, and the touch of it, the gathering colour in her face, the manner in which she accepted his gift, sent the blood racing through his body. He had scarcely hoped for this graciousness after the way she had treated him yesterday, and Toinette, won by the unexpectedness of his act, was conscious of her forgetfulness and of the embarrassing nearness of other eyes and ears about them. The colour deepened in her cheeks, and, mistaking this for still greater evidence of the pleasurable thrill he had given her, Jeems was sure she was about to thank him for his gift, when Paul stood beside them. Ignoring Jeems, Toinette's cousin led her away, politely relieving her of the package as they went. It was then Toinette turned to smile at Jeems, in spite of the eyes she knew were watching her. In this same moment her escort allowed the package to drop surreptitiously from his hand.

This act, inspired by a contempt for the forest boy, and urged by a meanness of spirit hidden under a display of wealth and fine clothes, swept Jeems's thought from Toinette, whose nearness of person, surprising beauty, and sweetness of disposition had almost made him forget his one reason for being at Lussan's sale. This weakness in the armour of his intentions was sealed when he saw his present fall to the ground. Toinette became instantly immaterial in the path of a storm of emotion which caught and held him fiercely. He saw only one person where there were two, and that one was Paul Tache. In half a dozen seconds, as many years added themselves to his shoulders, and with these years came a fuller capacity for hurt, for hate, and for a desire to avenge. In a brain white with the heat of these things, and in eyes blinded to the presence of all living forms except that of the youth who had darkened his mind with bitterness, Toinette ceased to exist for him, and when he sprang forward to recover the bundle, it was not with the thought that he was rescuing it for her, but that it was to be his reason for glorious war when the moment was at hand for him to hurl it in his rival's face.

That this moment should arrive as if inspired by a genius intent on guiding his destiny did not strike Jeems as unusual. Detaching themselves from the shifting groups of which they had been a part, Toinette and young Tache strolled to their horses, knowing that many glances followed their elegant departure. Giving themselves a brief time in which to be admired, they sauntered into the gardens back of Lussan's house.

From the flip barrel, where their newly made friendship had been growing apace, Tonteur and Hepsibah watched the pretty pair, with broad grins on their faces; and nudging the well-covered ribs of the man he should have regarded as an hereditary enemy, but in whom he had found a convivial comrade well suited to his own humours and disposition, the baron chuckled loudly.

"There they go, friend Adams, a couple of young peacocks on parade! My fine lady has grown into a young woman since she put on that costume and the big hat, and as for the *petit maître* who thinks himself a blood and a buck—why, I say, if this skinny little nephew of yours——"

"Sh-h-h! There goes Jeems!" interrupted Hepsibah.

Unaware of the attention of the old war dogs, Jeems was only a few steps from Paul and Toinette when they disappeared behind Lussan's house. He held back with a feeling of satisfaction when he saw the two going down a path which took them out of sight of any curious eyes that might have watched them. Not until the last flutter of Toinette's skirt was gone did he proceed with the business of following them, and then, like an Indian, he slipped noiselessly along the path and found them standing, somewhat perplexed, at the edge of a soggy and ill-smelling open space where Lussan had built his barn and wherein his cattle and pigs had gathered for so long that one was sure of a precarious and unpleasant footing. Toinette, her chin tilted, a flash of indignation in her eyes as she held up her skirt with both hands, was on the point of loosing her wrath upon her escort for daring to bring her to such a place of defilement when Jeems stepped out from a rim of bushes and confronted them.

His face was pale. His slim body was as taut as a bowstring. His eyes were almost black. He did not see Toinette, scarcely knew that she was in his world, even as her anger gave place to an exclamation of surprise when she saw in his hand the package which he had given her a few minutes before. He approached Paul Tache, and that youth, misinterpreting the slowness of his movement and the bloodless pallor of his face as signs of embarrassment and fear, sought to cover his disgrace in Toinette's eyes by an explosion of haughty protest at being followed and spied upon in this way. Jeems made no reply except to hold out the package. Sight of it choked the words in the other's throat. Jeems's silence and the way in which he continued to extend the package brought a deep colour into Paul's face. He and not Jeems was conscious of the amazement in Toinette's countenance and of the intensity of her interest in the situation. He recovered himself swiftly and, with a guileful change of manner, held out his hand.

"Pardon me," he apologized. "It is good of you to bring the package—which I accidentally dropped."

Jeems came a step nearer.

"You lie!" he cried, and with a furious movement he hurled the bundle at Tache's face.

The force of the blow sent Paul reeling backward, and Jeems was at him with the quickness and passion of one suddenly transformed by madness. He had never fought with another boy. But he knew how animals clawed and disembowelled. He had seen owls tear each other to pieces. He had watched a duel between two mighty bucks until one gasped out its life with a broken neck. He had looked on the hunter-wasps as they tore off the heads of their prey. In a hundred ways he had viewed strife and death as the wilderness knew these things. And all that he had witnessed, all that he knew of torture and violence and the desire to maim and kill gave to his action a character of such lively ferocity that it drew a howl of pain from Paul Tache and a shrill little scream from Toinette.

Jeems heard the scream, but it held no significance for him now. His dreams were gone, and Toinette, her presence close to him, her eyes upon the battle just as he had imagined in the thrill of his mental visionings, was forgotten in the more vital depths of his interest in the flesh and blood of Paul. In the first attack, his fingers clutched like small iron claws in the folds of Tache's cravat and coat, and the rending of cloth, a splitting asunder of gorgeous material almost to the other's waist, was evidence of the strength behind his assault. He followed this with a fury of scratching and tearing and both went down in the mêlée. When they rose, Paul heaving himself up with an effort which flung Jeems from him, they were such a sight of muck and stain that Toinette forgot her precious dress and covered her eyes in horror. But she was looking again in an instant, for the spectacle fascinated even as it appalled her. Jeems had landed on his feet with a fist loaded with mud, and this he projected with an aim so accurate that half of Paul's face was obliterated by it, and as he leapt with a roar of rage at his smaller assailant, he was such a shocking contrast to his usual immaculate self that Toinette nearly ceased to breathe. Then she saw and heard what her feminine eyes and instincts could not understand or keep proper count of, a mad twisting and tumbling of bodies, panting breaths, grunts, and finally a clearly audible curse from Paul Tache. With that sound Jeems flew backward and landed on his back.

He was up almost before he had struck, and with his head ducked low like a ram's in a charge, he hurled himself at Tache. This individual, having cleared his eyes sufficiently to perceive the blindness of the other's rush, stepped aside and swung a well-directed blow which again sent Jeems down into the muck. His hand filled itself with this sticky substance a second time, and as he returned to battle he let it fly at Paul. Profiting by experience, Paul dodged skillfully, and the volley passed over his head, spreading in its flight, and fell in its contaminating virulence upon Toinette. She saw her raiment spotted and defiled, and such a sudden fury rose in her that she sprang upon Jeems as he clawed and kicked in a clinch with Paul, and assailed him with all the strength and bitterness of her small fists and biting tongue.

Jeems had seen the tragedy of the misdirected mud, and he knew that Toinette's hands and not Paul's were pulling viciously at his hair. There is a hurt which bears with it a sting of satisfaction, and this emotion pressed upon Jeems as he fought desperately in front and felt himself attacked treacherously from behind. For Paul was accountable for the mishap to Toinette. Had the other not dodged in a cowardly fashion, allowing the stuff to pass on to her, the thing would not have happened. It did not take more than a few seconds for the inspiration of this thought with its apparent justice and truth to fire him with a determination beside which his former resolution sank to insignificance. He was no longer fighting for Toinette's approval, but against her, against Paul Tache, against all the world. Toinette, pulling at his hair, beating at his back, had raised his struggle to epic heights. The strength of martyrdom filled his lean arms and body, and he fought with a renewed fierceness that made his heavier but softer antagonist give way before the punishment, and both went down to earth again. Toinette fell with them, her long skirt impeding the activity of their legs, her big hat hanging like a sunshade over her face, her beautifully made curls tangled and spotted with mud, her hands beating angrily at whichever of the two chanced to come in her way.

Jeems was aware of her presence and physically sensible of her combativeness, but in the complexity of action which surged over and about him he could afford no discrimination in the manner of using his arms, legs, teeth, and head, and at last, finding herself disentangled, Toinette scrambled to her feet considerably bruised and in such disorder that no one would have recognized her as the splendid little lady of the seigneurie who had come so proudly to Lussan's place a short time before. Her handsome hat was a crumpled wreck in the mud. Her dress was twisted and bedraggled. Her hands and face were discoloured with soil, and her hair was so tangled about her that she was almost smothered in it. Despite this physical condition, her mental self was more than ever inflamed with the desire to fight, and seizing upon the hard and woodlike stalk of a last year's sunflower which lay in the dirt, she succeeded in bringing it down with such force that, missing Jeems, it caught Paul on the side of the head and laid him sprawling flat on his face. This terminated the conflict for Toinette, who gave a cry of apprehension when she saw what she had done.

During the half minute or so preceding Toinette's well-intended but mismanaged blow, Jeems had felt the discomfort of an increasing lack of wind, and would have made testimony that either Paul or Toinette, or both, were hammering him with wooden mallets similar to the one he had seen employed by the auctioneer. This impression was created solely by Paul's fist, animated to redoubled strength and action by the fact that Jeems's teeth were fixed in a vulnerable part of his anatomy. Paul had recovered from Toinette's blow before Jeems could take advantage of it, and what happened during the final round of contention remained largely a matter of speculation in Jeems's mind. He was sitting up, after a little, and there was no one to strike at. Paul and Toinette were out of his reach yet he heard their voices, and, turning his head, he discovered them, oddly indistinct, moving in the direction of Lussan's house. He tried to call out, thinking that Tache was escaping like a coward, but something in his throat choked him until it was impossible for him to get breath enough to make a sound. He made an effort to rise that he might pursue his beaten enemy. The earth about him swam dizzily. He was gasping, sick at his stomach, and blood was dripping from his nose.

A horrifying thought leapt upon him, and so sudden was the shock of it that he sat staring straight ahead, barely conscious of two figures emerging from the concealment of a thick growth of brushwood twenty paces away. The thought became conviction. He had not whipped Paul Tache! Paul had whipped him—and his enemy's accomplishment had been so thorough that he could still feel the unstability of the world about him as he drew himself to his feet.

His eyes and head cleared as the realization of defeat swept over him. Then he recognized the two who had appeared in the edge of the open. One was his Uncle Hepsibah, the other Toinette's father. Both were grinning broadly at the spectacle which he made, and as they drew nearer he heard Tonteur's voice in what was meant to be a confidential whisper.

"Is it really your *petit-neveu*, friend Adams, or one of Lussan's pigs come out of its wallow? Hold me, or what I have seen will make me split!"

But Jeems heard no response from Hepsibah, for the trader's face suddenly lost its humour, and in place of it came a look which had no glint of smile or laughter in it.

CHAPTER V

H ALF an hour later, Jeems was scrubbing himself in a hidden pool of creek water not far from Lussan's place while close to him his uncle cleaned his battle-stained clothes.

Hepsibah Adams talked as he worked.

"I say it again—that with a few tricks o' the trade you'd have cleaned his batter good, Jeemsy. And those are the tricks I'm going to make you acquainted with from this day on. It's fists you want to use and not so much the Frenchy woman's way o' teeth and nails. Biting is all right if you can get hold of an ear or some other killing thing, but when you set out to bite off a leg or an arm, why, Jeemsy, you're likely going to die at that post of duty, unless the other fellow has lost the use of his driving hams. And that's mostly what you were doing, lad, biting when you weren't kicking or scratching, and a mighty good job you made of it, too! If that little cat Toinette hadn't jumped in after she got your handful of mud, you'd have had more to your credit still, for if ever your hair got a tugging it was the little lady herself who did the job, and pulled your head back so that Paul had good driving space and something to hit each time. You got a good roasting, Jeems, a trouncing and basting as good as I ever saw, especially the last part of it; but it's a matter of education to be fustigated like that and nothing for which you need blush with shame. Why, when I came to my senses I gave that Albany Dutchman the primest beaverskin west of the Hudson for walloping me! It was a joy I shall never forget, and taught me a lot. A man must be flayed now and then to keep him in shape. For that reason, you're a better man now than you were an hour ago."

Jeems was doubtful of this final statement as he drew himself from the pool. Cool water had refreshed and strengthened him, but one eye was closed, there were bruises and scratches on his face, and his body was lame in many joints and parts. His anger, however, had subsided, and there was something different about him as he came from the water, a change that was slight, but one which his uncle's shrewd eyes did not fail to perceive. The lad was not crumpled by his defeat, nor was there a suspicion of humiliation or embarrassment in his attitude. The cold and steady light which gleamed in his good eye delighted Hepsibah. To that individual, exultant over the Adams spirit which he had seen displayed so energetically in the fight, Jeems seemed to have grown an inch or two in height and to have added twice as many years to his age. Even Odd, who was in their company, appeared to regard his master with a new and inquisitively analytical respect.

Jeems was drying himself in the air and Hepsibah was absorbed in his monologue on the art of fighting when a distant crash in the underbrush drew them to attention. This interruption to the solitude of the pool continued until, through a disruption of bushes, ap-

peared Tonteur, who came down to them with such a
wild flourish of an object in his hand that Odd gave a
contemplative growl. Jeems stared with all the power
that was left of his vision, and a shiver ran through him,
for he beheld in the almost unrecognizable thing in
Tonteur's hand what was once the beautiful hat worn
by Toinette.

"Look upon it, friend Adams!" cried Tonteur. "*Her
hat!* And every inch of her is like that from the tips of
her toes to the top of her head. They're combing and
cleaning her now, Madame Lussan and her girl, and my
Antoinette screaming all the time for this little monster
of yours that she may scratch out his eyes! It is so funny
I can only look at her and laugh—and she must go home
bundled up in Jeanne Lussan's clothes, which are seven
sizes too large! I swear you have missed the sight of
your life in not seeing her at close range, so messed and
tangled that she has commanded Madame Lussan to
burn her riding suit and everything that goes with it.
But if you have missed this spectacle, which I would
not exchange for the half of a seigneurie, you have at
least won our wager, for it is true your *petit-neveu* is
the greatest fighting man of his size and weight I have
ever seen, and has placed my daughter *hors de combat*
for many a day, though her spirit yearns for a new trial
at him!"

Taking notice of Jeems's bruised face and the distress
which had come into it, he stumped quickly to him and
laid a friendly hand on his shoulder.

"Tut, tut, my man, don't look so blank and miser-
able! It isn't entirely your fault this fiery minx of mine

got into the fight, and a lot of her ego has been lost in her dishevelment, if you know what I mean. If you don't, just bear in mind that her young stalwart is also rigging himself in homespuns, and that you've left marks of equal merit all along the battle line. Some day you'll put him in the mud and keep him there, and when that day comes, if you'll let my eyes have proof of it, I'll give you a horse to ride home from Tonteur Manor, and you may keep him for your own."

Whereupon, holding the wreck of Toinette's hat before his eyes, Tonteur broke into laughter.

"If only her mother could have seen it," he said, calming himself at the thought and heaving a deep breath of regret. "The patrician blood of the *ancien régime* mingling with the ignoble dirt of a barnyard! The exalted brought to earth at the hands of the lowly Goth and Vandal! The daughter of a noble dame cleaned of her pride and vainglory by a backwoods cub like Jeems Bulain! A peasant and a princess in a battle royal, with the salt of the earth on top, to say nothing of the three-tailed bashaw who is the pet of her sister's eyes—all down in the muck at the same time! Could *she* have seen that, I would willingly pay the price of being buried alive along with this!"

Hepsibah Adams had given a grunt midway of this speech and now gazed upon the seigneur with a sombre eye.

"I don't make it clear just what you mean by Goth and Vandal, and I can't remember what the Bible says about the salt of the earth, but when you call Jeems a backwoods cub and a peasant, and in the same breath ride him along with the dirt of a barnyard, your language comes nearer to my understanding," he growled. "And that being the case, I'm telling you there never was another tribe like the tribe of Adams, in spite o' what you're saying about the noble dames in your family, and this Jeems you are tongue-tying into hard knots is an Adams, and a good one, too, though his mother had the misfortune to marry a Frenchman when I wasn't looking. From the day Old Nick put his hoof into the Garden of Eden, the Adamses have been the flower of the human flock. We've been fighters from the time fighting began, and when the contention of man gives way to everlasting peace there'll be an Adams, and not a Frenchman, somewhere about to put a period to the story we've helped to write. So if there is any doubt in your mind as to the quality of this lad you're talking about, you'd best set yourself straight or take a measure or two with me to test the truth of the things I've said!"

Tonteur's face had grown red with indignation.

"What! You dare to insinuate that Jeems's mother dishonoured herself by marrying a Frenchman?" he demanded.

"I didn't go quite that far," said Hepsibah, "but I might make it clear by saying that any Frenchman is a dog for luck when he marries into the tribe of Adams, and this holds good for all and sundry princesses who may go by the name of Tonteur."

Tonteur dropped Toinette's hat to the ground.

"No Frenchman would stand for such insult, sir," he retorted. "And, to drive it deeper, are you inferring that my daughter was responsible for the disgraceful scene in Lussan's barnyard?"

"Not entirely responsible," said Hepsibah, "but subscribing to and largely abetting. That is what I would truthfully say."

"Your nephew forced the fight without pretext or excuse!"

"And your daughter jumped in where she had no business to be, just to set the fur flying faster!"

"Jeems struck her with a handful of mud!"

"Which was an accident!"

"It was deliberate, sir! I saw it!"

"It wasn't!" shrieked Jeems. "I didn't mean to hit her!"

But the two men, their fervour inspired by persistent attention to the barrels of flip and strong beer, scarcely heard his protest. They had drawn close to each other, and the seigneur was swelling as if on the point of bursting his waistcoat, while Hepsibah Adams, his round face lighted by a grin of anticipation, began to roll up his sleeves.

"You call me a liar, then?"

"Yes, and all of your tribe of Adams!"

Jeems gave a cry and Odd a fierce howl, for something happened so suddenly that both were startled by it. Hepsibah had made a pugnacious lunge, but faster than his movement, and infinitely more skillful, was that of Tonteur's wooden peg, which rose with vigour and precision and smote him a resounding thwack on the side of the head that knocked him off his feet. With such celerity had the friendliness of the two men transrormed itself into belligerency that Jeems stood aghast as he heard the sound which he thought must either be the cracking of his uncle's skull, or the rending of the wood in Tonteur's leg. To see his intrepid relative spread out like this robbed him for a time of the power to move or breathe; but when he saw this fallen idol half on his feet and witnessed Tonteur's hickory peg as it made another vicious assault upon Hepsibah's pate, knocking him flat again, Jeems's pent-up breath released itself in a yell and he began to hunt for a club. By the time he had armed himself, Hepsibah, half stunned, had contrived to avoid a third swing of Tonteur's underhung weapon, and the two men were hugged in a fierce embrace, choking and gouging each other at the sheer edge of the pool. Desperately Jeems manœuvred to employ his club, but before he could get in a blow the soil gave way and the combatants plunged into the water, out of which, after a turmoil in which Jeems thought that both must drown, Hepsibah came floundering and puffing ashore dragging the baron after him.

Then to Jeems's amazement his uncle stood back and, surveying Tonteur, who had also clambered to his feet, doubled himself over with laughter. With his brain cooled by the chill of the water, Toinette's father seemed in no way resentful of this; and while Jeems stood with his stick half poised, ready to deliver a *coup de grâce*, he was treated to the spectacle of the two men, so recently at each other's throats, closely gripping hands.

Dropping his club he hurried to his clothes and began to put them on, while Odd stood beside him, sensing the presence of a situation which was beyond his comprehension. The merriment of the two who had been fighting became greater until, at last, seizing upon an inspiration, Tonteur proclaimed that only one thing could fittingly put a cap to the incident and that was a bottle of Madame Lussan's wild plum brandy.

Jeems waited until they were gone in the direction of Lussan's house, having made no answer to the recommendation that he remain where he was until his uncle returned. This he had no intention of doing. Even the comradely praise which Hepsibah had given him before Tonteur's arrival, and afterward the unexpected embroilment which resulted from their meeting, had not abated the painful sensations in his breast. That his uncle had commended him for the valiancy of his fight with Paul Tache and had championed him to the point of blows with their neighbour filled him with courage and pride. At the same time, there was an ache within him that overshadowed these things and that became a poignant misery as he looked upon Toinette's battered and desecrated wreck of a hat. A vision rose before him of an hour ago, when under this hat he had seen a glory of soft curls, a face of pink loveliness, and a pair of bright eyes smiling with a new friendliness upon him. In the heat of his battle with Paul, these details had gone out of his mind, but now they came back and pressed themselves upon him more vividly than when they had existed in the presence of Toinette.

Dejectedly he gazed upon her hat. For him it stood as the tragic end of all his hopes, and nothing in its forlorn wretchedness roused in him a desire to smile or laugh. It was more than a crumpled bit of finery. It

was Toinette herself, a part of her crushed and broken
at his feet, a token of the bitter hatred which she must
forever hold against him after this. He stooped and
picked it up. The jaunty feather was gone. The rim
was broken. In the scuffle between his uncle and the
baron, Tonteur's wooden peg had put a great hole
through it. It was caked with dirt and mud that was
beginning to dry. Yet Jeems's fingers had never thrilled
as they did when he held it in his hands and looked
cautiously about to make sure no prying eyes were
watching his act. A lump came in his throat, and Odd,
standing quietly with his eyes on his master's face, saw
the starting of tears. Jeems blinked these away. Then
he knelt at the edge of the pool and washed the hat until
it was a shapeless mass in his hands, but with some of
its softness and lustre revealed again. Completing his
task, he returned to his father's cart for his bow and
arrows. He did not feel he was running away when he
left on the homeward trail without letting his father or
uncle know.

He disappeared into the woods and walked swiftly
through the deep aisles of the forest with Odd at his
side. A new emotion burned in him, one of change, of
spiritual transformation, of physical growth. The world
about him was not the world through which he had
travelled this trail in the early morning, nor was he the
same Jeems. Had Jeems's mother known what had
happened, she would have understood the story un-
folding slowly in the boy's face, and it would have frightened her, for a mother dreads the day when childhood
draws itself away, like a beautiful shadow, to be re-

placed by the sterner form of maturity in her offspring. Catherine had held this day back from Jeems as long as she could, even in a time and place where the ruggedness of life and its social conditions schooled plastic youth to early duties and responsibilities. Now it had come in spite of her. Jeems was unaware of the fact, though he felt the new sensations pressing upon him. The events of an hour had made him older. It was an hour in which he had lost, and yet in losing trivial things he had unconsciously achieved greater ones. Paul Tache had whipped him. Toinette's cool friendship had turned to hatred. His dreams were wrecked, his rose-hued hopes sunk into oblivion.

Yet a different poise was in his chin as he walked through the solitude, a different swing in his step. Morning had sent him on an errand of hysterical desire, now he was returning home vaguely appraising the folly of an act which seemed to have been born a long time ago, in a period of uncertainty, of half faith, of ill-defined and divided yearnings. Through Paul and Toinette and his defeat at their hands, he was beginning to see the wider horizons of the world that was shaping itself in his brain and in which the vital factor was *himself*. When he fought Paul Tache again, he would not be the Jeems of Lussan's barnyard, and when that time came, as it surely would, he would not throw mud into the face of Toinette Tonteur!

Hepsibah would have rejoiced greatly in this breaking down and building up of fabrics in Jeems's visionings, and would have sworn it was the blood of the Adamses rising in him, a fighting strain, an unconquerable spirit, the beginning of a sure and steady resolution born of the lad's first contact with strife and adversity. Even Catherine had not guessed the depth of affection which the adventurous Indian trader held for her boy, nor the fear that lived with it, the jealous and yet unspoken apprehension that a caprice of fate, like her marriage to Henri Bulain, would at last turn an Adams into a Frenchman. But within the few hours he had been at Catherine's home, this misgiving had subsided in his breast, for Jeems was more than ever like his mother, with something in his face and a quietness of manner which her brother failed to discover in Henri Bulain, with his foolish confidence and dreams of enduring peace. Jeems's battle with Paul Tache had cemented Hepsibah's conviction that he was every inch an Adams, and his happiness, with the opportunity so near at hand, had found expression in a triumphant return with Tonteur to the barrels of flip and beer. Could Catherine have beheld the fight which gave to Jeems's uncle such pride and satisfaction, she would, like Toinette in a moment of awful suspense, have shut her eyes with horror. For she sometimes recalled with a shudder Hepsibah's frequent and bloody battles in the days of his early boyhood, when to engage in physical combat was his greatest joy, and when—though one would never have guessed it now—he had been so much like Jeems in his thinness and fury of action that in a scrimmage the two could scarcely have been told apart.

It was not long after Jeems's departure from Lussan's place that Hepsibah discovered he was gone, and with

a quick adieu to Tonteur and a word to Henri he set
out after him. Sharp walking and the cool earthy smells
of the forest cleared his mind of the mellowing effects
of Lussan's brews, and he began to feel certain qualms
rising in him as he progressed. He did not like the
thought of Jeems going off alone in this way, which had
the appearance of retreat, and under his breath he
swore at the baron for luring him from the pool and at
himself for yielding to temptation. Few men could keep
pace with the trader on a trail, despite the rotundity of
his bulk, and at the end of an hour he came to a halt,
with Jeems stepping from behind a bush half a dozen
paces away, an arrow fixed to his bow.

If Hepsibah had a doubt of his nephew's courage, it
was dispelled by this watchfulness and the lad's readi-
ness for action.

"I'm dead, looking at the theory o' the thing," he
commented. "Jeemsy, I'm ashamed o' my carelessness
and proud o' your discretion. At that distance you could
stick an arrow half through me!"

"Clear through you," corrected Jeems. "I've done it
with a buck."

Hepsibah's eyes glowed with pleasure at the note of
calm boastfulness in the boy's voice.

"Why did you run away?" he demanded.

"I didn't," replied Jeems, meeting his uncle's look
with a flash of resentment. "You ran away from me—
with Tonteur. I wouldn't go like that with Paul Tache!"

They continued along the trail, and in the boy's
steady silence Hepsibah's face wore a pondering serious-

ness. Then he said, laying a hand tenderly on Jeems's arm:

"Son, what do you think of me for doing that?"

"I wouldn't do it—with someone I hated," answered Jeems, looking straight ahead.

"But I don't hate Tonteur. I like him."

"Then why did you fight him? And why did he almost kill you with his wooden leg?"

Hepsibah was not quick in answering such a fine point of logic, and the hardness in the voice at his side, so unlike that of the boy whom he had comforted and encouraged at the pool, drew his gaze casually, and yet more shrewdly, to the other's face. Twice he started to speak, and each time his lips were closed by the memory of his sister and of the talk which had passed between them when Jeems was in bed. Then the thoughts in his mind burst forth in spite of his worship for Catherine and his desire not to overstep the importunities she had placed upon him in respect to the use of his tongue when in the presence of Jeems.

"Fighting," he began in a subdued voice, treading softly upon the forbidden subject as if Catherine might be near and listening, "is the breath o' life, the spice of existence, and the most reasonable thing ever invented. Without fighting the earth might as well turn up its toes and die. It's a sort o' medicine, you'll see in time, lad. It clears the complexions o' nations, makes religion what it is, and irons out the troubles o' people just as the Lord o' Hosts intended it should. By which I mean, Jeems, that the biggest and best friendships are made through fighting, with nations as well as men, and that when you shake hands with a man you've fought, granting the grip is a good and honest one, you've made a friend forever."

"I wouldn't shake hands with Paul Tache," said Jeems. "Not ever. Some day I am going to kill him."

The quietness of his voice stirred Hepsibah with a feeling of uneasiness. He was thinking of Catherine again as he continued his measurement of the boy.

"Killing, except in the case o' war, is not a good thing to have on your mind," he remonstrated. "And there will be plenty of that before you're much older, Jeems. Until then, learn the tricks I'm going to show you, whip this young Tache, and then offer him your hand to shake. That's the glory o' the game."

The tenseness in Jeems's face gave way a little before his uncle's words and the good-natured laugh which followed them.

"I'll never shake hands with Paul Tache," he repeated. "I'm going to whip him. Some day I may kill him."

"That's better," approved Hepsibah. "You *may* kill him, which doesn't set the mark o' surety on your intention. But if you ever find it necessary to put an end to his days, don't do it in a spirit o' hatred, lad. Fighting, if jolly and well intended, lifts the soul to glorious heights; it makes you laugh as well as cry, and cleans out all the thistles and weeds in the back yards o' your life, making you broader-minded and stronger o' blood. But when that fighting is poisoned by hatred and you reach a point where you can't laugh at the cracking o' your own pate as well as the other fellow's, then it's a *dee*structive thing and the worst that can empty its vials o' desolation upon the earth. Jeemsy, that's what is spreading like a plague over the land right now, the same poison o' hatred with which you fought young Tache, and the time is coming—it's almost here—when it's going to burn up this world of yours in flames so red and terrible that God A'mighty Himself won't be able to stop them!"

Hepsibah let his voice rise with the emotion which was never entirely quiet within him, and at the astounding words he was saying, Jeems's thoughts lost their hold of Tache and he stared wide-eyed and wondering. Hepsibah went on, seeing the visions of impending events which he had described to Catherine and Henri the night before, and Jeems's blood ran fast at the pictures his uncle painted of their wilderness world in the grip of massacre and war.

"All this you should know," said Hepsibah defiantly, thinking of the futility of his arguments with his sister and her husband. "You're coming to manhood, Jeems, and if your mother and father won't look after themselves, you must do it for them. There's fighting in your future, and you might as well make yourself ready for it, though I can't see any reason why you should tell your mother about it or what I've said. She'd punish me, I swear, and your mother's sweetness is no sweeter than the bitterness of her reproach when she doesn't say a word, but just looks at me as if I'd struck her with my fist. You won't tell her, will you?"

Jeems shook his head and promised.

"Then I'll go to the end of what I had in my mind," continued Hepsibah. "It begins with this thing we call hate. When you say you hate Paul Tache, you're simply giving evidence o' the fact that you've been bitten by a snake you can't see or feel or hear, a snake beside which the copperhead o' the swamps is a gentle and kindly creature and one we should look in the eye with friendship and love. This snake lives in our own blood, Jeemsy, and it's a cuss for brewing trouble. It has been hard at work for years in this country of ours until hate is becoming the biggest part o' the air we breathe. White men like you and me set this snake at work. First, down there, we began hating the French and the French began hating us; and then we set the Indians to hating our enemies and our enemies did the same; and after that, not being content with the deviltry we'd done, we started the Indians to hating among themselves. *We* did that, lad, we white descendants o' the Son o' God, with our greater wisdom, our whisky, our guns and lies, until in a hundred tribes o' redskins between the Upper Canadas and the Ohio there isn't a tribe that doesn't hate some other tribe, and all because we hate the French and the French hate us. Jeemsy, bear this in mind—it wasn't the Indians who brought hair to us—*we sent them out to get it*. We wanted proof of their killings, so we asked for the scalps and paid cash money for them, and the French did likewise; until, with prices for the hair of men and women and children rising steadily, white men took to the dirty trade they had taught the savages. And this has brought about such a competition in the taking of human blood that the cover won't keep the pot down much longer, and when the cover blows off, the sky itself won't be big enough to hold what comes from under it. That is what hate will do, the hate o' two breeds o' white men for each other; and when it's over—mark me, Jeems!—they'll blame the Indian for it. There's no hate like a white man's hate, not even an Indian's, for it's deadlier because o' the power and knowledge behind it, which have taken advantage of simpler folk from the beginning of time. So I say it is a point in your disfavour to go on hating Paul Tache."

For a little while Jeems had forgotten Paul. It seemed to him the world of peace which he had always known was suddenly gone. In vague and scarcely believed whisperings and rumours he had heard of dark happenings along the farther frontiers. But his father and mother, living their lives of persistent hopefulness, had smoothed away the thoughts to which his uncle's unleashed tongue now gave freedom. As Hepsibah Adams went on with what his conscience urged him to say, even pausing to trace with a stick in a spot of open sand a map of the countries which would soon be at grips in war, pointing out their places of weakness and strength, Jeems's soul had entered another life and world. And when, after making tiny trails to mark the paths of invasion and greatest danger, Hepsibah put a finger on what he called Forbidden Valley and stated his conviction that the Mohawks would come that way with fire and tomahawk, Jeems caught his breath with a throb of suspense.

"Again I'm telling you that you have reached a time

in your years when you should know these things,
continued Hepsibah, rising from the plot of sand. "And
now that I've unburdened my mind and set you straight
in spite o' your father and mother, I'm ready for that
first lesson in the art o' defence and offence which will
show you why you didn't whip young Tache. There is
much to learn, the fine points o' sparring and squaring
away, the justle-holds and grapple, knee-gouging and
choking, and the proper way to kick when down as
well as up—so we might as well begin."

To this suggestion Jeems willingly acquiesced, and
for half an hour Hepsibah trained his pupil in a little
open near their path.

The sun was slanting well to the westward when they
came out of the Big Forest and looked down the slope
upon Jeems's home. Peace and happiness seemed to
have spread their golden wings over Forbidden Valley,
and as Jeems gazed upon its stillness and beauty, its
never-ending lure and tranquil friendliness, his uncle's
words of warning faded before the more pleasant things
in his mind. Smoke was rising in a silvery spiral from
the big stone chimney, and forgetting the tragic oc-
currences of the day, his heart throbbed with the
thrill which would never grow old as he saw his mother
among her flowers. He raised his eyes to the face of the
man beside him as if to challenge the truth of the foreboding things he had said, and he found that Hepsibah
Adams was not looking at the woman or the cabin
below him, but straight out over the broken roofs and
pinnacles of the great forest which ended in an azure
haze on the far side of Forbidden Valley.

And Odd, standing between them, was also gazing steadily beyond the green and brown opens as if in the vast distances were an unsolvable mystery which his soul was struggling to understand.

Breaking from his thought and smiling with good-humoured cheer, Hepsibah put his hand on Jeems's shoulder. A pair of culprits conscious of their duty, they descended slowly to explain to Catherine why Jeems had one closed eye and a puffed-up lip and his uncle a swollen jowl,

ON SATURDAY, Henri Bulain and Catherine took up the regular routine of their springtime work again. This had been interrupted in several ways of late. Heavy rains at night had impeded planting and the little ploughing which remained to be done, and time had been lost in the trips to Tonteur Manor and Lussan's place. At the breakfast table, where Catherine presided with a formality which assured Hepsibah and Jeems that she had not forgiven them for the embroilments they had brought upon themselves, Henri said that Saturday was as good a day as any on which to resume his work, and Hepsibah eagerly agreed with him and offered his assistance.

That her brother, of all men, should have engaged in a common brawl with the baron of the seigneurie, whom she had planned to bring into closer intimacy with her home and family, filled Catherine's sensitive soul with a shock the effect of which it was impossible for her to conceal. She placed small credence in Hepsibah's assurance that he and Tonteur had parted the best of friends; and when Jeems declared this to be true and testified that he had seen them shake hands, lack of convincement still lay in her eyes and with it a deeper suspicion of the one whom she believed was leading Jeems astray in the telling of the truth. Hepsibah knew he was in disgrace and probably would remain so for some time, and his discomfort was increased by the fact that his head had swollen larger during the night, so that every time his sister looked at him she was reminded of the shame he had brought upon her. Yet her displeasure was less than she permitted him to believe, for she could never hold resentment long against her brother, whose genial recklessness and irresponsibility made her regard him with almost the same mothering tenderness with which she looked upon her boy.

On this day the little clearing at the edge of the valley hummed with industry. So filled with beauty and freshness were the sky and air, so glorious was all the world about them, that Catherine sang at her tasks in spite of her wounded feelings. Her outdoor oven of clay and stones breathed fragrantly of baking things, and in one end of it, apart from her bread and cakes, was Hepsibah's favourite dish, a huge meat pie with thick upper and lower crusts between which were the choicest parts of Jeems's turkey. Her laying hens were cackling cheerfully about the barn, and to make the morning a greater success, a family of chicks had come triumphantly out of their shells during the night. There was little left for Catherine to desire as she looked out over their fields. At the end of them she could see Henri and his ox turning over the rich brown soil, and not far from him, in a clearing filled with stumps, Hepsibah and Jeems were at work with grub hoes and axes. A gentler spirit of grace and indulgence filled her bosom as her eyes rested on these toiling members of her family, and when she called them to dinner she had made up her mind to forgive her brother for what he had done.

When he had washed himself and his ruddy face was before her, she put an arm about his neck and kissed his cheek.

"I am sorry I had to be cross with you," she said, and the day was brighter for Hepsibah.

In the stump field that afternoon he came in closer intercourse than ever with Jeems, and the two dug and pried and pulled together, triumphing a little at a time over the tough snags and roots, and finding breath in their labour to talk of many things filled with lively interest for the younger of the two. As Hepsibah's powerful muscles strained and sweat rolled from his face, Jeems found a new thrill in putting his own body to work, for in this toil at his uncle's side there seemed to be a greater thing than the mere act of exertion, a building up of something within him which gave him increasing satisfaction. Hepsibah talked and worked with him as if he were a man, and discoursed on so many things foreign to his life, from politics and his own adventurings to the opportunities awaiting young men along the frontiers, that Jeems's head at times had difficulty with the matters which he was struggling to absorb. Hepsibah was also discovering in his nephew qualities of comradeship and understanding which answered a yearning that had long been in him.

In the evening, when housework and chores were done, Henri and Catherine often strolled about the clearings enjoying the contemplation of achievement and pointing out to-morrow's work, and always looking ahead to the day when the Bulain farm would reach far and wide on all sides of them, with two hundred acres of cleared land in it instead of thirty. In their mind the fields and meadows and orchards of the future were painted as vividly as though they already existed, and so often had they gone over their plans together that Catherine had placed the fences with their gates and stiles and had marked the groves and trees which she did not want an axe to touch. To-night their gladness was heightened by Hepsibah's presence, and Catherine told him of her dream of a great orchard of apple trees covering the sunny slope southward from the Big Forest, and named her favourites among the trees to be planted—the Newton pippin and the spitzenburgh, the Poughkeepsie swaar, the red streak, and the Guelder-ing, with a few russets and costards for eating out of hand. Where they had a dozen trees now, just coming into juvenilish bearing, they would have a hundred or more within a few years, she said. Seeing the nearer and hardier things to be done, Henri pointed out the acres of forest to be cut and stumped, the lowlands to be cleared and ditched, and the stretch of swamp land beyond the maple hardwoods which he would some day drain and turn into a meadow. There were five arpents, or seven and a half English acres, in the stump-filled field where Hepsibah and Jeems had worked, and he planned to have this cleared and ready for the plough by another spring. Five arpents a year was what he had set for himself, which would give him more than a hundred acres in crops at the end of another ten years. Neither of the two was afraid of work. Their faces glowed with the joy of an imaginative building of their little world.

"No place in New France will be more beautiful than ours at the end of that time," exclaimed Catherine. "Jeems will have a wife then, and little children to play and laugh in this paradise—and there, Hepsibah, where you see the great oaks and the two big chestnuts, is the spot we have set aside for Jeems's home."

Later, before he went to bed, Hepsibah stood smoking his pipe under a sky that was an arch of glowing stars. A great silence lay about him, a stillness made deeper by the little sounds of life which came out of it, the breathing movement and pulse which were of the earth itself, the whispering of growing things, the faint and ever-present melody of air stirring softly among seas of forest tops. He could hear the homelike sound of Henri's ox in the barn and the purling of water in the creek. Not far away, a whippoorwill swelled its throat in lonely, beautiful song, and from the edge of the distant swamp another answered it. More than all other birds of night or day Hepsibah loved the whippoorwills. Their solitariness and brooding melancholy touched a sympathetic chord somewhere in his nature, and when the humour was on him he imitated their notes so perfectly that the birds called back to him in a friendly way. But to-night he scarcely heard their cry, nor did his blood react with pleasant thrill to the beauty of the star-filled heavens with their touch of silvery flush in the east where the moon was about to thrust itself over the top of Squirrel Rock. His eyes saw only one thing, and that was the pit of darkness which hung over

Forbidden Valley, and his ears were tensed even now for that which he believed would come out of it some day. He was thinking of the plans Catherine had made for the years ahead, of her dreams impossible for him to break down, of her faith and happiness which he could not darken with his warnings. He felt his failure. He knew he was powerless against all that he had seen growing up about him. Forbidden Valley, treacherous in its beauty, brewing horror behind its smiling mask of peace, had conquered him, and he sensed something almost physical in its triumph.

He thought he was alone, but when he turned toward the cabin he found Jeems standing near him. The boy had come so quietly that Hepsibah's skilled ears had caught no sign of his presence, and for a moment he stared in silence at his face, illumined by the star glow. There was a strange beauty about the lad as he stood there which even the wilderness man's eyes could not fail to see, a thing more fragile than flesh and blood, something built up of a haunting vision of other years when in the empty days that had followed their mother's death he had seen that same questing, yearning light in Catherine's face that he now saw in her boy's.

It was Jeems who broke the spell by coming nearer to his side.

Then Hepsibah thrust an arm toward the submerging sea of darkness before them.

"Do you know that valley well?"

"As far as the lakes, where we go for berries and to shoot wildfowl in season," said Jeems.

"No farther?"

"A little. Hunting is nearer and easier between here and the seigneurie, but we get our candle fat there because it is a good feeding place for bears and the lakes are full of fish with which to bait our deadfalls."

"And you have seen no trails except those made by deer and bear and porcupine?"

"Yes, we have found moccasin tracks."

The flush of moonrise had grown into a flaming ball climbing over Squirrel Rock, and Jeems's eyes were on it.

"I am making a trip to the lakes to-morrow," said his uncle, "and it is my intention to find what lies beyond them. Do you want to go?"

"I am going over there," said Jeems, and he nodded toward the rising moon. "I want to see Toinette and tell her I am sorry for what happened yesterday."

Hepsibah thumbed fresh tobacco upon the spark still left in the bowl of his pipe. He looked sidewise at Jeems, and in the boy's profile, so like his mother's in the soft radiance of the night, he saw a resoluteness of purpose as unimpassioned as the voice in which Jeems had answered him.

"That's a decision born o' the Adams blood, lad," he approved. "There never was a day when an Adams failed to be a gentleman in the vicissitudes of either love or war. It's a fine and inspiring thought to want to apologize to Toinette—even though you were right. I'll go with you and leave the valley for a later day."

"I'm not going to fight," said Jeems. "I'm going to see Toinette—and I want to go alone."

On Sunday morning, when he set out for Tonteur Manor, this was the thought deeply entrenched in Jeems's mind—that he would not fight Paul Tache that day no matter what temptation might be placed in his path. He had told his mother where he was going and what he was planning to do, and with her encouragement to spur him on he felt eager and hopeful as he made his way toward the seigneurie.

This feeling was unlike the one with which he had set out to fight Paul Tache, and what he had to do loomed even more important than any physical vanquishment which he might bring upon his rival. To soften Toinette's heart, now so bitterly against him, to bring back the friendliness of her smile, and to see her eyes alight with the sweetness which she had been on the point of yielding to him at Lussan's place were foremost in his mind. His memory of her and of the greeting which had flashed in her face made him forget her blows and the fury of her tongue. A little at a time, it had been growing stronger in him from the moment he had washed her hat at the edge of the pool. It had not left him during the day he had chopped and dug with his uncle. Now it seemed a part of the sunlight about him, a part of the song of birds, a part of the cool fragrance of the forest through whose soft shadows he travelled. He was anxious to see Toinette again and to offer her all that his small world held, if thereby he could make amends for the ruin and humiliation he had brought upon her. A spirit of chivalry in him, older than his years, rose above the lowly consideration of rights and wrongs. He was sure he was right. Yet he wanted to say he was wrong. Though he did not know it, years had passed since two days ago, and he was a new Jeems going to a new Toinette. His fear of her had vanished. He was no longer borne down by a feeling of littleness and unimportance, and for the first time he was visiting Tonteur Manor without the thought of inferiority sending its misgivings through his soul. In some mysterious way which he did not understand, but which he strongly felt, he had passed away from yesterday forever.

When he came to the open where he had shot the turkey cock, he scarcely thought of the part it had played as a stage for his emotions three days before. Paul Tache had become an unimportant factor for the moment, except as he might seek to interfere with the directness and purpose of his mission. Even if this happened, he was sure that he would not fight. Both pride and courage were strong in him as he neared the seigneurie, and if the blood of knights ever ran through the veins of the Adamses, it was stirring in his own when he saw Tonteur Hill ahead of him.

On the crest of this hill he paused, and no knight ever looked on a lovelier kingdom than the wide domain which lay below him. Until to-day it had filled him with a kind of awe, and when trespassing upon it he had felt like a trivial creature treading the realm of a princess who was farther away from him than the sun. Tonteur's power and riches had frightened him. The length and breadth of his fertile acres. His fortressed church and manor. The great river which he guarded for the King of France. The miles upon miles of wilderness terrain,

Lake Champlain agleam in a blue haze of distance, mystery, romance, the thrill of things he had never lived or known, all forcing themselves upon him and oppressing him with a sense of his smallness. It was here, a long time ago, as they rested before making the descent, that he had first heard his mother and father talk of the wars in which Tonteur had fought—how he had won the favour of the King, and why it was, through her mother's side, that Toinette had in her a drop of blood inherited from a queen of France. His mother had laughed merrily at that, and he had wondered, just as he had wondered at her quickened seriousness when in almost the same breath, his father had told of the days when Tonteur's great-grandfather, Abraham Martin, was a King's Pilot at Quebec and a friend of the great Champlain.[1] So his heart had never been confident, no matter how bravely he tried to make it so, when he came into the bottom lands where his princess lived.

Now it was different. It was as if he had been on a long journey and had returned in every way an equal of those who lived in the valley of the Richelieu. With Odd, he sat for a time on the hilltop gazing upon the proud glory of the seigneurie. A strange fantasy grew in his brain. He saw himself fighting, as his uncle had predicted he would fight, and as Tonteur had fought to make himself a powerful lord of the land. Ambition clutched tightly at his heart. He was seeing a world

[1] Toinette's great-great-grandfather, Abraham Martin, allowed his cattle to wander at will over the fields adjoining his farm where a part of the city of Quebec now stands, and to this tract was later given the name of the Plains of Abraham, on which was fought the battle that changed the history of the world.

larger than he had ever conceived a world could be, and everywhere in it was Toinette. For her he would make himself what her father was—a great man!

But first he must tell her he was sorry. This had ceased to be a duty. It was the flame behind his newly awakened consciousness, an act which had raised itself to the level of a crusade filled with possibilities which set his imagination aglow.

He was about to descend the winding path when a horseman rode across the bottom lands and started up the narrow trail. It was Tonteur. Concealed in a thicket Jeems watched him pass and wondered why he was riding in the direction of Forbidden Valley with such a dour and unpleasant look on his face.

He went down the hill, and at the foot of it made Odd understand that he was to remain there until he returned. Then he struck out boldly for the manor house. This building was made of logs, for Tonteur had a love for trees which was stronger than any temptation to build of stone, as other seigneurs up and down the Richelieu and St. Lawrence had done. It was a palace of giant timbers richly darkened by age and weather, and in Jeems's eyes it might have been the home of a king. It was loopholed for defence, and its windows were protected by huge oaken shutters which could be closed and barred. Not far from it was the church, even more a fortress than the dwelling, for its windows were higher, its one door heavier, and under the eaves was a long bevelled slit through which fifty men might fire down upon a foe. From both the church and the house, defenders could sweep the river with their guns. In the

other direction were the gristmill and barns, and as far
as Jeems could see through the clearings were the loopholed and window-shuttered homes of the vassal farmers of the seigneurie.

Soon his feet were in the path which led to the
manor. It was so still he could have believed that everyone was asleep as he courageously mounted the wide
steps to the door of Toinette's home. On this door was
a great black knocker of battered iron. The face of the
knocker was a grinning ogre, a gargoylish head which,
from his earliest memory of it, had fixed itself upon him
as a symbol of the grim and unapproachable spirit that
guarded the rooms within. Only twice had he heard
its resounding summons to the inhabitants of the house.
Now his hand reached out to awaken the dull thunder
of its voice.

His fingers touched the cold iron. He hesitated in the
moment he was lifting it, for he observed that the door
was open by a space of a few inches. Through this
aperture a voice came to him clearly. It was a high,
biting, angry voice, and he recognized it as Madame
Tonteur's. He raised the weight from its metal panel
and would have knocked when he heard a name which
made him pause in rigid silence. It was his own. Without trying to listen, yet with the discomfort of an eaves-
dropping position forced upon him, he learned why
Tonteur had ridden up the Hill with such stern displeasure in his face.

"It is no fit place for a gentleman of New France to
be going," he heard Toinette's mother say. "Henri
Bulain was a fool for marrying this good-for-nothing

Englishwoman, and Edmond is a greater fool for not driving her from the country when her breed is murdering and killing almost at our doors. The woman was made for a spy, despite the pretty face which has softened Edmond's silly heart, and that boy of hers is no less English than she. The two should not be allowed to live so near to us, yet Tonteur brazenly sets forth to visit them and maintains they are his friends. The place they have built should be burned and the Englishwoman and her boy sent where they belong. Let Henri Bulain go with them if he chooses to be a renegade instead of a Frenchman!"

"Fie upon you for such thoughts, Henriette," chided the milder voice of Madame Tache. "I despise the English as much as you or Toinette, but it is unfair to voice such invective against these two, even though the woman is proud of her pretty face and her boy is a mudslinging little wretch. Edmond is a big-souled man and simply befriends them out of pity!"

"Pity!" sniffed the other. "His pity, then, is an insult to Toinette and me. This English person has become so bold at his favour that she smiles and laughs in my face as freely as any fine lady in the land, and like a charlatan she lets down her hair for you to rave about!"

"Because I asked her to," said Madame Tache. "Are you angry because of that, Henriette?"

"I am angry because she is English, and her boy is English, and yet they are allowed to live among us as if they were French. I tell you they will be traitors when the time for treachery comes!"

Jeems had stood with his fingers clenched at the unyielding iron of the knocker. Now he heard another voice and knew it was Toinette's.

"I think Jeems's mother is nice," she said. "But Jeems is a detestable little English beast!"

"And some day that beast will help to cut our throats," added her mother unpleasantly.

Madame Tache laughed softly.

"It is too bad the woman is so pretty," she said good-humouredly. "Otherwise, I am sure she would have less of your disfavour. As for the boy, we should not blame him for what he cannot help. I have sympathy for the unfortunate little vagabond."

"Which is not a reason why my husband should degrade himself and humiliate me by going to see his mother!" snapped the baron's wife. "If her indecency attracts him there——"

The great iron knocker fell with a crash, and almost before the sound of it reached a servant's ears, the door swung open and Jeems stalked in. The women were speechless as he stood in the wide opening to the room in which they were seated. He scarcely seemed to realize they were there and looked only at Toinette. He remained for a moment without movement or speech, his slim figure tense and gripped. Then he bowed his head in a courtesy which Catherine had carefully taught him. When he spoke, his words were as calm as those of Madame Tache had been.

"I have come to tell you I am sorry because of what happened at Lussan's place, Toinette," he said, and he bent his head a little lower toward her. "I ask you to forgive me."

Even Henriette Tonteur could not have thought of him as a beast after that, for pride and fearlessness were in his bearing in spite of the whiteness of his face. As the occupants of the room stared at him, unable to find their voices, he drew back quietly and was gone as suddenly as he had appeared. The big door closed behind him, and turning to a window near her Toinette saw him go down the steps. An exclamation of indignation and amazement came at last from her mother, but this she did not hear. Her eyes were following Jeems.

He went across the open and into the fields. As he drew near the foot of Tonteur Hill, Odd came cautiously forth to meet him, but not until they reached their old resting place at the crest of the ascent did he pause or seem to notice the dog. Then he looked back upon the seigneurie. A bit of iron had sunk into his soul. The sun was still shining, the birds were singing, the miles of wilderness were golden in their beauty, but his eyes were seeing with a new and darker vision. From the rich valley which had been the fount of all his dreams they turned to the faint gleam of distant water in the south where lay Lake Champlain, and beyond which, not far away, were the Mohawks and the English and the land of his mother's people. It was the blood of that land, running red and strong in his veins, which Toinette and her mother hated.

He dropped a hand upon Odd's head, and the two started over the homeward trail. The dog watched the forest and caught its scents, but he watched and guarded alone, for Jeems gave small heed to the passing interests of the woods and thickets. In many places the hoofprints of Tonteur's horse were left clearly in the earth, and Jeems noted these, for Tonteur and his visit to Forbidden Valley were a part of the thoughts burning in his head.

He walked more slowly through the Big Forest and approached his home from its eastern edge. He could not see Tonteur or his horse or any life about the cabin, but when he came near to it, he heard an alarming sound through the open door. His mother was crying. He ran in and found her with her head bowed upon her arms and her shoulders shaking with sobs. In response to his startled voice, Catherine raised a face wet with tears and, seeing the effect of her grief upon him, tried to smile. The effort fell halfway and in a moment she was almost weeping again, with her face pressed to his shoulder as if he were a man in whose strength she was seeking comfort.

Her words came brokenly, and Jeems's mind was a turmoil of misgiving and fear as he listened.

First he gathered that his mother had been very happy at the beginning of the day. Holding him in an hysterical embrace, and weeping afresh by turns, she told him that his departure to ask for Toinette's friendship, together with Hepsibah's presence in the bosom of her family, had filled her with joy and pride. In addition to these things, Tonteur had come over from the seigneurie, and with that event her morning had overflowed with gladness.

"They seemed delighted to see each other—your

uncle and the baron," she said, with a moan that sent increasing apprehension through him. "We talked about Toinette and you—and they laughed and joked together—and he was so pleased when I asked him to stay and have dinner with us—and they walked off —arm-in-arm—and then—oh, Jeems, Jeems, they went down into the stump field and had a terrible fight!"

Her arms relaxed and, as she dabbed at her eyes with a wet and crumpled handkerchief, she gave a little wail of despair.

"Your father is going now—with the ox and cart— *to get Monsieur Tonteur!*"

Through the window Jeems caught a glimpse of the farm conveyance plodding in the direction of the stump field, with his father flourishing a long whip beside it. Excitement replaced the suspense under which his mother's condition had placed him, and without waiting to see whether she continued the drying of her eyes or fell to weeping again, he darted out of the cabin and ran toward the scene of battle. He took a short cut across the planted ground and arrived ahead of his father, his wind half gone. It was Odd who told him the field was not empty, for nowhere could he see his uncle or the baron. Following the dog's lead, he found them both at the end of the clearing close to the pile of stumps which he had helped to tear from the earth the preceding day. Before he could see them, he heard a voice and knew that Tonteur was not dead.

"I'll cut the liver out of the dishonest scoundrel who made me this leg!" the seigneur was crying in a great rage. "He should be quartered and hung for using a hickory stick with a crack in it! With a sound leg, sir, I've have sent you over that pile of stumps, for it was as clever a blow as I ever struck!"

Jeems stopped, and as he gasped for breath he thought it was strange that he did not hear a reply.

Then he ventured a few steps nearer and beheld Hepsibah Adams sitting on the ground with his back against a stump, his arms hanging limply at his sides, his round eyes wide open, and with a set and stupid look in his face.

"It's a damnable outrage!" came Tonteur's voice again. "*Hickory*, sir—not ash or elm or chestnut—seasoned a year, he told me—and here it is with a crack half the length of it, and an old crack, as you can see with half an eye! I'll murder him!"

Jeems stared at his uncle. Hepsibah was rolling his eyes and making an effort to answer. A sickly grin spread over his countenance.

"I'll make you a leg—that'll last—friend," he said weakly. "A good leg—better leg than that—hickory, too—an honest leg—carrying no hidden crack in it."

"With a leg like that, no crown in Christendom could have stood the blow I gave you," Tonteur answered from a point which Jeems could not see. "A blow having just the right slant to it, and catching you properly as you lunged. It wrenched my backbone, sir—the sheer force of it! Do you declare yourself vanquished, or will you take advantage of my condition, with only one pin to stand on and none whatever to fight with?"

"I'm a little stunned, brother," acknowledged Hepsibah, managing at last to get a hand to his head. "But atop o' your luck I don't like this bit o' vainglory in your talk. I've been harder hit, but never before with wood. You couldn't do it again in a brace o' years, and as soon as I've made you another leg I'll prove it to you!"

Jeems heard the rattle of the approaching cart and advanced into the presence of his uncle and the baron. Toinette's father, like Hepsibah, was on the ground. His clothes were awry and stained with earth, a great lump was rising on the side of his face, and, as Jeems quickly observed, his wooden leg was broken off close to the knee. Upon this scene, over which a profound silence had fallen at his appearance, his father came with the cart.

Henri first gave his assistance to Tonteur.

"If this humiliation and disgrace becomes known, sir, I'm ruined," the baron declared, allowing himself to be lifted until, with Henri's support, he stood balanced on his one good leg. "To hop like a frog, and be carried behind an ox like a bag of wheat—my God, sir, it makes me blush with shame!"

Jeems went to his uncle, and with his aid Hepsibah climbed to his feet and stood dizzily, watching with cheerful appreciation as Henri Bulain hoisted Tonteur into the cart.

"He's a most ree-markable liar, Jeemsy, this man Tonteur," he said. "I'll swear it wasn't his wooden leg that hit me, but a jemmy of iron wielded by the devil himself, or one o' these stumps flying on its own account. It was a mighty blow!"

He made an effort to walk and would have fallen if

Jeems had not exerted his strength to hold him up. Henri, having successfully loaded Tonteur, returned to assist Hepsibah; and the trader, struggling like a drunken man to maintain an appearance of proper equilibrium, permitted himself to be lifted in beside the baron.

From the window of her cabin, Catherine saw the cart coming with its human load.

CHAPTER VII

NEVER had any period in Catherine's life been filled with such a variety of incidents as this Sunday in May. How men could fight and batter each other and at the same time declare themselves the best of friends, she could not understand even with her eyes beholding the truth of it. When Henri unloaded his cargo of damaged humanity, she was faint from shock. The first break in her despair came when the presence of an affectionate good cheer between the two men forced itself on her attention. Hepsibah, whose dizziness still made it difficult for him to stand, insisted that he would not lose a minute in making a new leg for Tonteur and suggested for this article a hickory bar, dried hard as bone, which Henri was saving for a shaft in the grist-mill he was planning to build another year. When this stick was brought to him, the baron burst forth in a pæan of enthusiasm and declared that in all his experience he had never seen a more admirable piece of material. This Catherine observed and overheard as she looked from the corner of a curtained window, and somewhat relieved by the humour the two were in and seeing no serious damage had been done she made up her mind to act as if nothing had happened to mar the amity of the day. That her deception might be less burdened with the danger of exposure, she contrived to get Henri and Jeems into the cabin, and impressed her resolution on them.

So Tonteur was their guest at dinner, and with a great lie, which was whole-heartedly endorsed by Hepsibah, he explained the reason for their facial disturbances, their ride in the cart, and his broken peg, unconscious of the fact that Henri had rushed in to tell his wife about the combat and its results when he came for the ox.

"Wrestling, madam, is a sport of the gods," he said to Catherine, as she cut open the huge turkey pie. "I've had a passion for it since boyhood, and it ran in my family long before the day when Abraham Martin, in Quebec, offered the finest cow in his herd to any man who could put him on his back. It's my fault, and not your brother's, this mess we are in. We were wrestling fair and doing it in a gentlemanly way, as your husband will make oath if you ask him, when my accursed peg-leg caught in one of the stumps in a big pile out there, and down they all came on us, until it is a wonder we are left alive! My good friend, Monsieur Adams, was caught with a hundred pounds of green oak in the pit of his stomach, and with the sickness which came of it and my having only one leg to hop on, we were compelled to avail ourselves of the services of the cart. To-morrow, Jeems, when you dig out stumps, don't make the piles so confoundedly high!"

"Why?" asked Catherine gravely. "Are you and Hepsibah going to wrestle there again?"

"It may be, madam. I am teaching him something new!"

"The devil you are!" exclaimed Hepsibah, then caught himself. "I mean," he added apologetically,"it isn't so new as it was."

When the baron left for home late in the afternoon, equipped with a new peg which pleased him greatly, he promised that he would return soon and bring Toinette with him if he could, and went off merrily with Hepsibah and Jeems, who accompanied him up the long slope to the edge of the Big Forest. There Tonteur turned and waved his hat at Henri and his wife, and after that Catherine saw him lean over to give Hepsibah a jolly thump on the shoulder and to shake hands with Jeems. While her eyes were shining at these signs of friend-ship, which she believed would be permanent, the seigneur, unmindful of Jeems's presence, was saying to Hepsibah,

"I'll give your head a few days' rest, sir. Then, if you don't mind, I shall be grateful for the opportunity of trying out this new leg of mine on it. That is, if you have further desire to compete with me and we can meet where Madam Bulain will know nothing of our *rencontre*. But if you have had enough——"

"I haven't begun," growled Hepsibah. "The luck o' the devil has been in that scoundrelly stick o' yours. To be struck by such a low-down instrument o' war is an insult to my nature, and in our next debate, it's my in-tention to lay you so cold that you'll be satisfied for-ever!"

Tonteur rode into the shadows of the woods, laughing as he went. When he had disappeared, Hepsibah turned to Jeems.

"I want no better friend than a man like that!" he exclaimed. "A fighting man after my own heart, lad, and one it is a pleasure to debate with. If there were only more Frenchmen like him and more of our blood like myself, what pleasure we would find along the frontiers!" A thought coming to him of his nephew's adventure, he asked, "What happened when you went to Toinette? Did you see young Tache? And what did Toinette have to say?"

"I didn't see Paul Tache," replied Jeems, still looking in the direction Tonteur had gone. "Toinette called me an English beast."

What he had decided to keep from his mother he told to Hepsibah, repeating all that he had heard at the door of the manor, in such a quiet way that he might have been recounting an incident which had occurred in another life than his own.

"They hate us because my mother is English," he finished. "Madame Tonteur said that some day we would be cutting their throats."

A few moments passed before Hepsibah spoke. In that time his face had grown dark and thoughtful.

"They were harsh words to use against neighbours, Jeems," he said then, "and hard ones to stand when pointed at those we love. But it's the nature o' the human race when divided against itself, and which mostly worships God for spite. And maybe they were right. Some day we may cut their throats!"

"Are the English—as bad—as that?" asked Jeems, seeing quickly what the other had meant.

"Yes, that bad," nodded Hepsibah, an almost imperceptible note of menace in his voice. "For more than half a century they have been hunting Frenchmen's throats to cut, and, likewise, over that same period o' time the Frenchmen have been hunting ours for the same purpose. That's why, down in the Colonies, some of us are getting tired of a game so bloody and vile and are beginning to call ourselves Americans.[1] It's a new and wholesome name, Jeems, and one that is bound to grow. And for a like reason, because the shortcomings of a parent sometimes give birth to pride in a child, a lot of the people of your father's race are beginning to call themselves Canadians. It's six to one and half dozen to the other when it comes to counting the blame for all the killing and burning that's going on along the frontiers, and the Indians, who started out as brave and honourable men who wanted to be our friends, have been made the instruments o' these two God-worshipping devils named France and England, who have been spattering the world with gore and hate until no mile o' land or sea is free o' the stench of their discord. So while it may be hard to bear, lad, you mustn't condemn Toinette for what she said, for you are a beast in her eyes, painted by her mother and all the French before them, but I'm predicting the time when she will see the truth as she has never been al-

---

[1]British intolerance of this early day, which had already begun to plant the seeds of American independence, was epitomized within five years of Hepsibah's utterance by General Wolfe, who wrote from Louisbourg, "The Americans are the dirtiest, most contemptible, cowardly dogs that you can conceive. They fall down dead in their own dirt, and desert by battalions, officers and all. Such rascals as these are rather an incumbrance than any real strength to an army."

lowed to see it yet. Youth like yours and Toinette's is bound to hold the glory o' this great country in the hollow of its hand!"

Jeems's eyes were filled with a slow-burning fire, as if he were looking ahead to a vision of that day.

"If war comes, on which side are you going to fight?" he demanded. "Will you help cut the throats of Tonteur and his people?"

"God knows!" replied Hepsibah, startled by the bluntness of his nephew's question. "I've asked myself that question many a time, lad, when I've lain alone o' nights in the deep woods. As I've said before, fighting is the breath o' life when it's done with honour and discretion, but no Adams this side o' the sea has ever sunk to murder and massacre, and that's what this is going to be—until the horror of it wipes out hate and brings back reason to our brains. And so, answering you as an Adams should, Jeemsy, I'd say we must watch the ones we love and fight for them if we have to, no matter where our bullets go," and his gaze travelled sombrely over the wide expanse of Forbidden Valley.

After a brief silence, he added:

"I've asked myself who is right and who is wrong, the French or the English, and there isn't any answer, except to say that one is as black as the other. I've roved the frontiers for twenty years now, and no matter what others may say or history may write in days to come, I know the facts. I've lived and slept and fought with these facts until the truth is as clear to me as the sun out there. It's the Indian part o' what's coming that fills me with fear, and one half o' you is as much to blame for that as t'other half, Jeems, you being equally split by birth. Down in the Colonies we use money and whisky and dishonesty of every kind to stir the Indians to madness against the French, and the French work this same evil and to the same bloody end mostly through the use o' the Word o' God. If there is anything to be said in favour of either, it's on the side o' the Jesuit Fathers, for they're a brave and courageous lot o' men, and we can't place a sermon on a level with a keg o' whisky even though it stirs up the same hell. But a scalp ripped from a human head because o' the urge o' religion is just as red as one taken through the influence of a quart o' rum. It isn't the priests' fault. They preach first and are patriots after that. But the result is identical, and so we have a mess of it, with all the Indians in the country prostituted to the selfish and criminal ambitions o' two white peoples who go to church and sing psalms and claim there is a heaven. As one who loves to fight when the fighting is clean, I can't answer your question any better than I have, Jeems. When the time comes, we'll both find our work to do."

In the days and weeks that followed, the spirit of comradeship between Jeems and his uncle grew stronger. This closer consociation with a man whose knowledge of the frontiers and their conditions was excelled by few, and who had supplemented his enlightenment by an acquaintance with the history and political strength and weaknesses of the mother countries that controlled them, gave to Jeems a scope for thought that every hour helped to broaden. With his illimitable resources of information about the wilderness world of half a continent, Hepsibah also possessed a kindly and homely philosophy which, striking deeply at the truth of many things, planted in Jeems's widening viewpoints of life constructive guideposts to the future which he was determined not to forget. To Hepsibah the intimate nearness of a growing mind and body which he loved held a greater appeal for him to remain in Forbidden Valley than his sister's pleadings, and with each day that they went out to the stump field to hew and dig, their affection became more settled and satisfying, until at last it made Jeems almost forgetful of his feud with Paul Tache and helped to heal the aching wound which had come with the certainty that Toinette despised him. Unknown to him, the question he had asked his uncle at the edge of the Big Forest and his disclosure of what he had overheard at Tonteur Manor had struck a significant note in the leather-stocking's heart, and from that time his friendship for the baron assumed a different aspect, not less warm and appreciative but free from the abandonment of personal desire which had already brought about two conflicts between them. After an open challenge and its refusal by Hepsibah on the point of his sister's feelings in the matter, Tonteur, like the chivalrous soldier he was, put a muzzle to his inclinations, and thereafter the intrepid veterans disported themselves, for a time at least, like brothers. But Toinette did not come with her father to the valley, nor did Jeems expect she ever would.

Late spring, then the beginning of summer, followed Hepsibah's arrival at the Bulain home, and still he gave no betrayal of the restlessness which presaged his usual disappearance for another long period into the fastnesses of the wild. This season of the year was always one of torment for the forest dwellers because of the winged pests which crawled the earth and filled the air, and Jeems had come to dread it as an indescribable nightmare of discomfort and suffering. From the first of June until the middle of August, such plagues of mos-quitoes bred and multiplied in the swamps and lowlands and woods that beasts were half devoured alive and the pioneers literally fought for their own existence, smok-ing their cabins incessantly, covering their flesh with hog fat and bear grease, and resorting to every known subtlety that they might snatch a little sleep at night. Within a few days, it seemed to Jeems, a world that had been a paradise of flowers, of sweet scents, of ripen-ing fruits and delicious air was transformed into a hell of insect life which shut out travel in all directions and which invested with poisonous torture every spot where it was not partly subjugated by fire and smoke. The timber was heavy and dark, swamps were un-drained, rivers and lakes were shadowed by dense vege-tation, and in the humid, sweating mould of these places, the malevolent pestilence was born and rose in clouds that sometimes obscured the face of the moon. During these weeks a cordon of decayed stumps and logs smouldered night and day about the Bulain cabin, screening it in pungent smoke, and outside this small haven, work on the farm was continued at a price of physical martyrdom, except under a burning sun, when the insects sought refuge from the glare and heat.

But this summer Jeems's body as well as his mind had found something new with which to grapple, and instead of remaining in the shelter of smoking logs, he greased himself like an Indian and worked shoulder to shoulder with his father and uncle. The trader's leathery skin was toughened by years of exposure until it was immune to the discomfort of mosquito venom, and Jeems struggled to keep in his company and succeeded in doing it, though on close and sultry days or when a storm was brewing, his father advised him to leave the fields. Hepsibah exulted in this fortitude of his young companion, and when the trying weeks were over and late August brought relief, he had put Jeems through a course of training which he swore would make it easy for him to defeat Paul Tache when they came together again, and had taught him the tricks of small-arm loading and firing until at thirty paces his pupil could send a pistol ball into a four-inch target three times out of five. Jeems's pride in this weapon was almost as great as that which he took in his bow, in the use of which his expertness in sending an arrow to its mark never failed to draw expressions of amazement and approbation from his uncle.

Jeems did not go to Tonteur Manor, though occasionally he heard news from the seigneurie. Twice Henri and Hepsibah made journeys there during July and August, and twice the baron rode over to eat Sunday dinner with the Bulains. It was quite comfortable at the big house, their visitor said, as he had cleared and drained the land adjoining it and, in addition to this, he had brought some newfangled cloth from Quebec with which they had made tentlike protections for their beds. Everyone was in high humour there because of the activities going on in preparation for the exit of the entire family for Quebec early in September. Toinette was going to school at the convent of the Ursulines, and now that her ambitious mother was about to launch her upon a fashionable career, fortified by the devout teaching of the nuns, Tonteur declared that he was losing the little spitfire he adored and would have returned to him in three or four years a splendid young lady all ready for marriage to some lucky blade who would not half deserve her. Jeems listened with a feeling of loss which his countenance did not betray. It was as if the fire of his dreams had not only burned itself out, but even the ash were being cleared away. For with an emotion which he made no effort to conceal, Tonteur let it be known that Toinette would not spend much of her time on the Richelieu after this, with so many things to attract and hold her in Quebec, which was one of the fashion spots of the world. Soon there would be plenty of smart young gentlemen at her feet, and he was sure that Madame Tonteur would bag the finest one of the lot for her daughter.

"You are lucky in having a boy instead of a girl," he said to Catherine. "When Jeems marries, he will bring his wife to live near you."

Autumn came, and with it a great glory in the wilderness. Jeems loved these maturer days of golden ripeness, of first frosts, of painted hardwood forests, and of crisp, tangy air when all life seemed rejuvenated and his own veins danced to the thrill of unending promises and expectations. But this year a heaviness of heart was in him with the changing of the seasons. Toinette and her people left for Quebec, and one evening, a week later, Hepsibah gravely announced that he could no longer delay his departure for the far frontiers of Pennsylvania and the Ohio, where his obligations as a trader called him. Catherine was silent for a while, then cried softly to herself. Jeems drew back where his uncle would not see him clearly. Henri's cheerfulness died out like a lighted candle extinguished by a breath of wind. Hepsibah's face was grimly set, so hard was he fighting to hold a grip on his emotion. He promised that he would never again remain away long at a time. He would return during the winter. If he failed to come, they would know he was dead.

When Henri got out of his bed to build the fire the next morning Hepsibah was gone. He had stolen off like a shadow in some still hour of the night.

CHAPTER VIII

MORE determinedly than when his uncle had been with him, Jeems continued at his work and at the mental efforts with which he was struggling to reach out into the mountains and valleys of experience ahead of him. His father came to depend upon him in many ways, and with eyes which were constantly discovering some new change in him, Catherine put greater effort into her tutoring.

Through the fall and winter the Bulain cabin was visited by wandering Indians who had learned that food, warmth, and a welcome were always there. Jeems's friendship for them was tempered by the things Hepsibah had told him, and while he brought himself closer into intimacy with these uninvited guests, winning their confidence and making himself more efficient in their speech, he was also watching and listening for the signs of hidden dangers against which his uncle had repeatedly warned him. Most of the Indians were from the Canada tribes, and among them he found no cause for unrest, but when occasionally an Onondaga or an Oneida came, he detected in their manner a quiet and sleepless caution which told him these visitors from the Six Nations considered themselves over the dead line which marked the country of their enemies. And he made note that they always came through that part of Forbidden Valley which Hepsibah had predicted would be a future warpath for the Mohawks. Still, there seemed to be no sinister thought behind the visits of the savages, and now that his powers of observation had increased, he was impressed by the reverence and devotion with which they regarded his parents, and especially his mother. With a granary filled to the roof and dugout cellars choked with products of the soil, Henri had more than enough for his family and these wilderness guests, and never did Catherine see a brown face turn from her place that its owner did not carry a burden of food on his shoulders. This spirit of sympathy and brotherhood had its effect on the Indians until at times Jeems doubted the suspicions of his uncle and found his own mind in accord with the deeply rooted faith which was the abiding and regulative principle of his home.

This winter he went farther in his adventurings. Captain Pipe, the old Caughnawaga, had a habit of spending several of the hardest weeks near the Bulains, and with his two sons, White Eyes and Big Cat, Jeems travelled to the shores of Lake Champlain for the first time. He was gone a week and planned with his friends to make a longer expedition the following year, as far as Crown Point and a place called Ticonderoga, where the French were going to build a fort some day. On this excursion he experienced the real thrill of danger, for White Eyes and Big Cat, both of whom were young braves who had won their spurs, moved with a caution which was eloquent in its significance.

True to his word, Hepsibah returned in January, coming up from the English forts on Lake George.

He remained only a week and then was off again for an important consignment of goods in Albany, from which point he was going to trade among the Oneidas, if weather conditions permitted him to reach the upper waters of the Mohawk River. This visit, though a brief one, was a relief from the monotony of Jeems's winter and added to the desire which was growing in him to accompany his uncle on one of his journeys.

With Toinette and her people away from the seigneurie, he had no hesitation in going to the Richelieu, and made trips there with his father on snowshoes; and in March, during a break in a spell of intense cold, he went alone and remained overnight in the house of the baron's overseer with whose young people he had become acquainted. This overseer was Peter Lubeck, an old veteran for whom Tonteur held a warm affection, and through his son, Peter the younger, Jeems had his first news of Toinette. She was at the Ursuline school, and her parents had taken a fashionable house in St. Louis Street. Peter said Tonteur wrote in every letter to his father that he was homesick to get back to the Richelieu.

As another spring and summer followed those which had gone before, Jeems knew he was fighting something that had to be conquered, a yearning for Toinette which filled him with a bitter loneliness when its hold was strongest. With this feeling was curiously mingled an increasing sense of pride and resentment which at times made him hear Toinette's clear voice calling him a detestable beast and Madame Tonteur condemning his mother as unfit to be her neighbour.

For two years Toinette remained in Quebec without making a visit to the Richelieu. During these years, the tragedy of his divided birth was forced upon Jeems. There was no doubt that the English in him was uppermost or that the urge in his blood was toward the southern frontiers and the colonies of Hepsibah Adams. Yet he loved the place where he lived with a sincere passion —the Big Forest, Forbidden Valley, all the miles of wilderness about him as far as he could look to the horizons. This was New France. It was his father's country and not his mother's. Between his father and himself a comradeship had grown up which nothing could break, but his worship for his mother was a different thing, as if something besides motherhood bound him to her. His friends had increased in number. He came to know people along the Richelieu but was always conscious he was not entirely one of them. Toinette's words and her hatred for him persisted in his memory and kept recalling this truth.

Catherine did not guess that a shadow was gathering in his mind. Now that she had reconciled herself to the period of rapid development in her boy's life she was proud of his growth, both physical and mental, and her happiness continued as she saw those maturing qualities which left him no longer dependent upon her but made him a factor of protective strength which she had found only in her husband. No span of her life had been filled with such a fruition of hopes and dreams. Hepsibah was away for only a few months at a time. Henri and Jeems had improved the farm beyond their expectations. and in the second year half of the big slope was planted to apple trees. The creek was dammed and its pent-up force turned the wheel of a small gristmill. The chief treasure in her home, her books, had grown with every trip her brother made from the South. No mother or wife in the Colonies or New France was happier than she, and this love of life and its blessings gave to her a spirit of youth which never seemed to grow older and of which Jeems became almost as proud as his father. For them Catherine was more than a wife and a mother. She was a sweetheart and a comrade.

Late in August of the second year of her absence, Toinette returned to Tonteur Manor for a month. Jeems's heart ached with the old yearning, but he did not go to the seigneurie. The days dragged as if weighted with lead, and a hundred times he subdued the desire to make a visit to Peter Lubeck that he might catch a glimpse of her. Paul and his mother were also at the baron's and he felt a sense of relief when he learned that all of them were on their way to Quebec with the exception of Tonteur, who remained for the harvesting of crops. A fortnight after they had gone, Peter told him about Toinette and Paul Tache. He had scarcely recognized Toinette, he said. She had grown taller and more beautiful. His mother declared the nuns had accounted for a great change in her, but Peter was sure that Toinette, with all her loveliness, was still ready for a fight if one urged her to it. Peter was several years older than Jeems, and as he was to be married in December, he spoke with the assurance of one who had gained through experience a definite understanding of ladies. Tache was a full-grown man and dressed like a young noble. One with half an eye could see that he was desperately in love with Toinette, Peter avowed. But if he were a judge of such affairs, and he considered himself to be that, Tache was a long way from a realization of his desires, even taking Toinette's tender years into consideration. She granted him no favours. There had actually seemed to be a little coolness in her attitude toward him. When Jeems smiled at this information and gave it as his opinion that Toinette would marry Tache as soon as she was old enough, Peter shrugged his shoulders and declared that he possessed good eyes and ears, and that he was not ordinarily taken for a fool.

Peter's words stirred Jeems with a satisfaction which he did not let the other see, and not until he was on his way home did he pull himself from the folly of his thoughts about Toinette. Even if she were not smiling on Tache as warmly as he had supposed, he knew she was as far removed from him now as the sun was from the earth. Yet, as time went on, this fresh contact with her presence, though he had not seen her, gave a determined impetus to his plans for the future. His memories and visionings of her inspired him with a force which was frequently hostile instead of friendly, and this force demanded more of him for that reason. It was a challenge as well as an urge, something which roused his pride. It provided a furtive nourishment for the English side of the two opposing parts of him, and there were hours in which he saw himself a splendid enemy where fate had ordained that he could not be a friend. With increasing maturity giving to him a deeper and more understanding passion for his mother, and a fuller comprehension of the noble qualities in his father, he was harassed by a confliction of emotions which he revealed to neither, and confided only in Hepsibah Adams. The difficulty of solving the problem which confronted Jeems was as great for Catherine's brother as it would have been for Catherine herself, for as early as the spring of 1753, when Jeems had passed his sixteenth year, there was no longer a doubt in the minds of the people of the Colonies and New France as to the surety of the struggle which was impending. While France and England were officially at peace, the forces of the two countries in America were on the verge of open war and were instigating the Indians to a strife of extermination. Celoron had been ordered to attack the English at Pickawillanay in retaliation for the activities at Detroit. Marquis Duquesne, the new Governor at Quebec, had reviewed the troops and militia of New France and was sending fifteen hundred Canadians and French colonists to drive the English from the upper waters of the Ohio. Everywhere along the unprotected frontiers the Indians were killing and burning and such vast sums were being expended by both sides for human hair that scores of white men had taken up the lucrative business of hunting for scalps.[1]

---

[1]Until 1637 scalping was unknown in New England. The church-loving Puritans began by offering cash for the heads of their enemies. Later these God-fearing people accepted scalps if both ears were attached. Bounties differed over a period of one hundred and fifty years, and in different parts of the country. The French were first to offer bounties for the scalps of white people, the English quickly following suit. At the time of this story, the English were offering as high as $500 for a warrior's scalp, and from $150 to $50 for those of women and children, including the scalps of unborn babes

Almost at the door to Jeems's home, war preparations were in progress, for every landed baron along the Richelieu was training his vassal farmers, and when the wind was right the Bulains could hear faintly the twice-a-week firing of muskets at Tonteur Manor. Being free of the seigneurial protection and laws, Henri did not go to drill. Nor did Jeems. Yet Tonteur rode frequently to their home, especially when Hepsibah was there. He was in better spirits than usual, and it was all on account of Toinette, he said. After all, there was a lot of himself in Toinette, and he thanked God for that blessing. She was homesick for the Richelieu. Her letters to him were filled with a longing for it, and she declared that, in another twelve months, when her schooling would be finished, she wanted to live at the Manor and not in Quebec. That was enough to make him happy, and he laughed at the thought of danger for womenfolk along the Richelieu—in the fortified places. The English and their savages would not get nearer than the lower end of Lake Champlain when war came; and they would be driven from there very shortly, and also from Lake George. But on such an outlying farm as the Bulain place, which had no protection whatever, there was the possible peril of wandering scalp hunters and he never tired of urging Henri and Catherine to make their home within the safety of the seigneurie.

---

torn from their mother's wombs. French prices were somewhat lower than the English. Over a long period of years, human hair was a larger item of traffic than fur, and *in one lot* the Senecas delivered and received payment for *ten hundred and fifty scalps* taken from the heads of white men, women, and children along the frontiers. Christian races, not savage ones, were the inspiration behind these horrible deeds in that bloody dawn of our history when the United States was about to be born.

He asked Jeems and Henri to come to his drill, and that they did not respond made no difference in his friendship. He could understand how hard it would be for Henri to prepare for war against his wife's country, and his secret adoration for Catherine was greater because of her courage and her faith in both peoples with the catastrophe so near. It delighted him to think that his own confidence was a comfort to her, and the eagerness with which she accepted his opinions as a soldier encouraged him to go beyond what Hepsibah considered intelligent bounds in giving easement to her mind. He did not guess what was in Jeems's heart, nor did the boy's father or mother. Only Hepsibah knew fully what was there.

Early in the autumn, the trader took Jeems on a journey to the English fort on Lake George, thence travelling into the New York country, returning in November. They found a change in Catherine. She was not less confident or less contented in the paradise she was helping to build, but something had come into her life which she was accepting bravely and courageously and even with pride. One evening, she spoke of the military activities along the Richelieu. Many river youths were training with their elders, she said, and it did not seem right that Jeems should not be among them. While killing was wicked and inexcusable, it was a God-given privilege to defend one's home and family. She quoted Tonteur to substantiate her belief that war would never reach them, and she knew that Jeems would not seek it any more than his father. But she thought it would do no harm for Jeems to prepare himself along with the other young men of the seigneurie.

To this suggestion Hepsibah's homely philosophy made objection. He told Catherine the day was coming when Jeems would be compelled to fight and that he would have to choose one side or the other to champion. When that day arrived, sentiment would not stand in the way, for, with a world in turmoil about them, one could not be English and French at the same time. He declared that even Henri would be drawn into the struggle, unless the scalp hunters came to solve the problem for them all. No man could tell on which side they would be when forced to it, and as he despised a traitor more than anything else, it was his opinion that Jeems should not be taught the ways of war under the flag of France and then, it might be, fight for the English. As a frontiersman, he maintained that the finest fighting man was the Long Rifle, a free wanderer of the forests, a leather-stocking trained to a hundred greater things than the firing of a musket in company with a score of others. That was what Jeems should be. He was already fitted for it, lacking only a wider experience. As a Long Rifle he could serve where honour and duty called him when the act became necessary.

This discussion was the beginning of another phase in Jeems's life. It placed before him certain definite obligations of manhood which even his mother had to recognize, though she wanted to hold him as long as possible in his boyhood years. During the next year he made several trips with Hepsibah, going to Albany and as far as the country of Pennsylvania. Each time he returned to his home something held him more closely to it.

In the autumn of 1754, after four years at school, Toinette returned to Tonteur Manor.

In this same month of September the seventieth acre of land was cleared on the Bulain place.

Peace and happiness lay over the Richelieu. It had been a splendid year for France along the far frontiers. Washington had surrendered at Fort Necessity, and Villiers was triumphant at Fort Duquesne. England and France were still playing at the hypocrisy of friendship. While they played, thrusting at each other secretly and in the dark, not an English flag was left waving beyond the Alleghanies. French arms and Indian diplomacy were victorious along the Ohio and westward to the plains. The policies of the British Royal Governors were alienating their Indian allies, and in spite of their million and a half population against eighty thousand in New France, Dinwiddie had frantically called upon England for help. In response, England was sending General Braddock.

Pæans of gratitude and triumph were sung in the churches throughout New France because of the beneficence of this year, and in a double rejoicing over Toinette's homecoming and his country's success at arms, Tonteur planned a levee and barbecue at the seigneurie. Hepsibah was away at the time, which disappointed the baron, who insisted that Henri and his family must attend the celebration or he would never call them friends again.

Jeems felt a thrill growing in him as the day drew near. With it was no apprehension or thought that it would be easier not to go than to go. He was no longer the Jeems of Lussan's place as he set out in the company of his father and mother with Odd pegging along faithfully at his side. In January he would be eighteen. The alert and sinuous grace of one of the wild things of the forest was in his movements. Catherine was more than ever proud of him and rejoiced in the cleanness of his build, in his love of nature and God, and in the directness with which his eyes looked at one. But she was not more proud than Hepsibah Adams, who had seen in this pupil of his flesh and blood the qualities and courage, the lock, stock, and barrel, as he called it, of a fighting man.

Yet, on the morning when they started for the levee, much of the boy of years ago was in Jeems's heart, though it did not reveal itself in his face and actions— not the boy who had thrown mud but the boy largely moulded by the Indian trader. To this part of him Toinette would remain a living memory forever, no matter what happened—the Toinette of his earliest days, the Toinette to whom he had carried his presents from the woods, the Toinette who had accepted his gift at Lussan's sale. He had wondered at the fate of the piece of red velvet, and once, a long time ago, when hunting near Lussan's, he had dug the old barnyard half over in search of the unrecognizable rag into which its glory must have fallen, if, as he believed, it had been trampled into the mire by the conflict of that day.

He was anxious to see Toinette, but with this desire

there remained none of the old yearnings which had once oppressed him. She whom he was going to regard to-day was a stranger, one into whose presence he was determined not to force himself again. This resolution was not inspired in him by a lack of boldness or an uncertainty as to his own social fitness. An immense pride upheld him. The spirit and freedom of the forests were in his blood, and behind these things was also the spirit of Hepsibah Adams. He knew that he could meet Toinette coolly and without embarrassment should they chance to stand face to face, no matter how splendid she had grown. And he realized there must be a great change in her. She was fifteen now. A young lady. At this period of his life, five years seemed a long time, and he thought it was possible he might not recognize her.

An overwhelming moment of shock seized him when at last he saw her.

It was as if a yesterday of long ago had come back into this to-day, as if a picture which had been burned and scattered into ash had miraculously been restored.

She was taller, of course. Perhaps she was lovelier. But she was the same Toinette. His dazed senses almost resented the startling fact, which broke down the barriers he had built up about his dreams and castles as the walls of a pearl build themselves about a hurt. He could see no change in her except that she had become more a woman. Hepsibah's work, his own, his freedom, and his courage were dissipated like dust as he looked at her, and once more he felt himself the inferior being offering her nuts and feathers and maple sugar and praying in his childish way that she might smile on him. This was not a new Toinette removed another million miles away from him, as he had supposed she would be, but the old Toinette, commanding him to slavery again, stirring anew the rubbish heap of his broken and discarded hopes, touching fire to half-burned-out desires, challenging him, dragging him from his pride and his strength and making his blood run hot in his body.

Yet she had not seen him!

At least, he thought she had not. With a group of young ladies from the neighbouring seigneurie, she had come down from the big house, and he was almost in her path, with Peter Lubeck at his side. It was Peter who advanced a step or two toward them. Except for his action, Toinette would not have turned, Jeems thought. He pulled himself together and stood with his head bared, as cold and impassive in appearance as a soldier at attention, while his heart beat like a hammer. Toinette had to face him to return his companion's greeting.

It was impossible for her not to see him when she made this movement. But there was a slowness in her discovery, an effort to keep from looking at him which was more eloquent than words. Toinette had known he was there. And it had not been her desire to speak to him.

If he needed courage, it was this enlightenment which gave it to him. He inclined his head when she met his gaze. Her face was flushed, her eyes darkly aglow, while his own cheeks bore only the colour of sun and wind. He might never have known her, so unmoved did he stand as she went on her way.

She had slightly nodded, her lips had barely formed *a* name.

In spite of all his uncle had said, there were hatreds which would not die!

Later, after the feast on the green, came Tonteur's spectacular feature of the day, a military review of his tenants, with wives and children witnessing the martial display. The male guests, who had drilled in their own seigneuries, joined Tonteur's men. Only Henri Bulain and Jeems were not among them. Henri, sensitive to the fact, and to save Catherine from the hurt which might arise because of it, had started with her over the homeward trail half an hour before. Jeems had remained. This was his answer to Toinette's contempt— that he was not of her people, that his world was not circumscribed by the petty boundaries of the seigneurie. He stood with his long rifle in the crook of his arm, conscious that she was looking at him, and the invisible shafts from her eyes, poisoned with their disdain, stirred him with the thrill of a painful triumph. He could almost hear her calling him an English beast again. A coward. One to be distrusted and watched. He did not sense humiliation or regret, but only a final widening of what had always lain between them.

He bore this feeling home with him. It grew as time went on, and with its growth an increasing restlessness came over him. The nearness of Tonteur's princely possessions to Forbidden Valley cast a shadow which sometimes repelled him and at others drew him toward it, until in one way or another he was beginning to find himself never quite free from its influence. Events of the winter added to its effect upon him. From the sharp, frosty days when the chestnuts began to fall from their opening burrs, Tonteur Manor became a place of life and gaiety. Toinette seemed always to have friends about her after this, young gentlemen as well as ladies. They came from the seigneuries along the two big rivers, and also from Quebec and Montreal, and the parties they held, the nightly dances at the Manor, the presence of wealth and fashion almost at the doors of his own humble home set for him more vividly the dead lines over which even his thoughts might not pass without punishment to his soul. The gulf between reality and the visions of his childhood became so vast that in a little while he was scarcely able to see across it. As this happened, his eyes turned the other way as if drawn by a gentle and yet irresistible force which was determined to impress on him more and more the fact that down there, in his mother's country, were freedom and happiness and equality among men which the growing shadow of the Tonteur seigneurie was holding back from him here. Against this call of a new motherland to which he was a stranger fought his love for the things to which he had been born, and so twisted did his thoughts become with the conflicts within him that only hard, long miles of travel through the forests could subdue the fires they built.

News creeping through the wilderness and reaching every corner, like the whispering winds, kept an unquenchable heat under the ash of these fires, fanning the embers into flame in spite of him. Secrets were no longer secrets. Rumours had grown into facts. Fears had become realities. England and France were still playing at peace in their mighty courts. In the sunlight they were friends, in the dark they were seeking each other's lives like common cutthroats. Their catspaws, New France and the Colonies, had been prepared for their immolation—Wilderness Children, plastic, moved by youth, inspired by faith, filled with courage, urged to destroy and to pile destruction on destruction by two scoundrels aged in their cleverness, France and England. Two freebooters of the sea, two footpads on solid ground, deep in the mire of their plottings, and, unconsciously, building the foundation for a nation greater than themselves.

But New France, with a child's blindness to the faults of its parent, loved the rotten court of Louis XV, which it called home.

And the thirteen little Colonial governments of the English, quarrelling like small boys among themselves, just beginning to walk alone, feeling the significance of the new word *American*, cheated by their parent, laughed at by their parent, hated by their parent, still yearned for the love of that parent as children have wanted love from the beginning of time, and were loyal to it.

So tragedy began to move, to build out of death, out of betrayed confidence, out of dishonour and fraud and pitiless murder the American and Canadian nations of the future.

Without declaring war, England was sending General Braddock and an army to kill off the French and their Indians in the American wilderness; and, trying to outdo the other hypocrite, France was sending Baron Dieskau and an army to reap the waiting crop of Colonial lives.

Glorious France!

Honourable England!

Eighty thousand French and more than a million English in the New World cried these untruths as they made ready for the sacrifice. Massachusetts enlisted one man out of eight of her male population. Connecticut, New Hampshire, Rhode Island, New York, and the others followed her example.

Children, loyal, proud to fight—and hating the French ferociously!

Then came Braddock, preceding Wolfe, to call them worthless trash.

And New France, a glory of sun and land even now gutted of her prosperity by corruptions brought from Louis and La Pompadour, sent out her own sons to fight and kill, valiant, glad, confident—and hating the English implacably!

With them, on both sides, went Indians from almost a hundred tribes—red men who had once found honour in fighting, but who, now, skulking and murderous and vengeful, found their souls in pawn to the great White Fathers across the sea who had prostituted them with whisky, bought them with guns, maddened them with hatreds, and who paid them for human hair.

Proud old England!

Chivalrous France!

Pride and chivalry and love—of these things Jeems was thinking as winter grew into spring and spring into summer. Only love held him from leaping to the temptations which were drawing closer about him, love for his mother whose happiness marked the beginning and the end of all action on the part of her men folk. And in this hour, when three out of four of the fighting men along the Richelieu were preparing to join Dieskau, when half of his acquaintances at the Tonteur seigneurie had already gone to fight Braddock, when the forests trembled at the stealthy tread of painted savages, and when the Frenchman who did not rise to his country's call was no longer a Frenchman, Jeems observed that the strain upon his father was more difficult to bear than his own. For Henri, in spite of his worship of Catherine, was of New France to the bottom of his soul, and now that other men were making a bulwark of their bodies against her enemies, his own desire to make the same sacrifice was almost beyond the power of his strong will to control. In their years of comradeship, Jeems and his father had never come so near to each other as in these weeks of tension.

Almost as painful to them as the sting of a wound was the day when Dieskau came up the Richelieu with a host of three thousand five hundred men and made forever a hollowed ground at the Tonteur seigneurie by camping there overnight.

When she knew they were coming, Catherine had said:

"If your hearts tell you it is right, *go with them!*"

But they remained. For Henri it was a struggle greater than Dieskau fought, greater than that in which Braddock died. For Jeems it was less a torment and more the mysterious madness of youth to tramp to the clash of arms. For Catherine it was the gehenna of her life, a siege of darkness and uncertainty in her soul which gave way suddenly before news which swept like a whirlwind over the land.

God had been with New France!

Braddock and his English invaders were destroyed!

No triumph of French arms in the New World had been so complete, and Dieskau, the great German baron who was fighting for France, moved southward to crush Sir William Johnson and his Colonials and Indians, planning not to stop until he had driven them to the doors of Albany.

With him were six hundred and eighty-four of the loyal men who were beginning to call themselves Canadians.

Tonteur rode over to bring the news to Henri Bulain. To Catherine he recalled his prediction that the English would never get into this paradise of theirs. Now the whole thing was settled for many years to come, for Dieskau would sweep their last enemy from the Champlain country as completely as a new broom swept her home. A dozen times he insisted on shaking hands with Hepsibah, who was with the Bulains this summer, repeating that he loved him personally and that no ill thought could exist between them. But he was frank in his avowal that he held a mighty grudge against the encroaching English. He had sent almost every man he had to the scene of fighting, and only his wooden leg had kept him from joining Dieskau.

Even Toinette had wanted to go!

This recalled an imporatnt matter to his mind.

Toinette had entrusted him with a letter for Jeems. Boiling over with his own selfish exultations, he had forgotten it. He hoped it was an invitation for Jeems to come to the seigneurie. He had often told his girl she should be more friendly with the lad.

Jeems took the letter and went off by himself. It was the first recognition from Toinette since the day of the levee. He had not seen her and had tried not to think of her. Alone, he read the words she had wirteen him.

With pitiless coldness and brevity, they called him a renegade and a coward.

On a September morning some days later, Jeems stood watching his uncle as he disappeared into the frost-tinted woods of Forbidden Valley. It seemed to him that Hepsibah's suspicions and guardianship of the valley had become greater with the growing news of French triumphs in the south which so positively assured their safety. Only yesterday Tonteur had brought the latest word from Dieskau. The German had been on the eve of smashing Sir William Johnson and his mob of Colonials and Indians when his messenger had left. By this time the event had probably happened, Jeems thought. Yet his uncle was going into Forbidden Valley with a look in his face which puzzled him.

Restlessness possessed Odd after Hepsibah had gone. Years were beginning to leave their mark on the dog. He was past the prime of his splendid strength, and the hair about his muzzle was graying a little. He was gaunter, shaggier, limped a bit more heavily, and some.

of his habits had changed. He was not as eager for the long and tireless hunts in the forest, and liked the warm sun. He was growing content to watch life with Jeems instead of ceaselessly pursuing it. He was not old, and yet he was no longer young. With increasing age, which was leading him down into the shadows slowly, had come a deeper wisdom, sharper instincts, keener visionings even where he did not see so far or so clearly. There remained one thing which did not fail to stir in him the tense fierceness of his youth. This was the Indian smell. He always told Jeems when one of their wilderness visitors was near, sometimes many minutes before the savage appeared from the woods. And he never tired of watching Forbidden Valley. In the dawn he faced it. At midday he dozed with his half-closed eyes turned toward it. In the evening he sniffed its scents. Yet he did not go down into the valley unless Jeems or Henri was with him.

During the morning, Odd's uneasiness began to reflect itself in Jeems. Soon after noon, he left his work and told his mother he was going in the direction of Lussan's place. Catherine walked with him through the young orchard and up the slope. Never had she seemed more beautiful to Jeems. The glory of the day, its warm blue skies, the tinted forests, the golden pools of sunlight over the earth all seemed a part of her. His father was right—this mother of his would always be a girl. From above the orchard, standing on a little plateau that overlooked the Bulain farm, they called to Henri, who was in his turnip field, and waved at him. Jeems stood for a few moments with his arm about his mother. Then he kissed her, and Catherine watched him until he was lost to her sight in the Big Forest.

Jeems did not have the desire to hunt, nor did Odd. Unexplainable impulses were pulling at them both. Odd's restlessness was unlike his master's. Whenever Jeems paused, the dog turned and sniffed the air of their trail, facing Forbidden Valley in an attitude of suspicion and doubt. Jeems observed his companion's enigmatic actions. Odd was not giving the Indian signal. It was as if something without form or substance, a thing bewildering and unintelligible, *lay behind them*.

The counter impulse in Jeems was to go on. Without a reason or a purpose, except that the disquiet in his mind demanded it, he was heading for Lussan's place. The air was crisp. Fallen leaves rustled under his feet. From the hilltops the country lay about him in sweeping panoramas of reds and golds and yellows and browns, and he began to look back from these hilltops —far into the Indian summer haze which hung like a gossamery veil between him and the adventure-filled country of Lake Champlain and Lake George, where so many things were happening. It was the kind of day, trembling with promise and lure, to stir more deeply and with almost a savage insistence the yearnings that had for so long been smouldering in his breast. Off there was where he wanted to be, where dramas such as he had heard about but had never seen were being played, where men were fighting and where the chivalry and courage of which he had dreamed himself a part were painting themselves in colours of triumph and glory in the history of his world. And there was where he should be.

They came to Lussan's, nine miles from their home. Since Lussan's departure, the place had been abandoned, and in those five years the wilderness had largely reclaimed what man had taken from it. The big green open in which the crowd had assembled and where Toinette and Paul Tache had walked so proudly was overgrown with sumacs and blackberry bushes. Tall grass flourished about the house. Where the gardens had been was a tangle of weeds and briars. A few rose bushes struggled against the inundation, and a single sunflower, a last survival of propagation through many seasons, stood with its black-seeded face toward the western sun. Porcupines had eaten at the doors of the house. Shutterless windows gaped to the winds and rains. The path leading to the barn was cluttered with growth, and at the end of it the barn itself was a dead thing hidden from the sun. A tree had fallen, crushing in its roof; poison ivy festooned its rotting foundations, and shadows were all about it. The cow yard was rank with burdock, ragweed, and thistles. Sections of the pole fence about it had slumped to the ground.

Jeems stood where he had fought Paul Tache, and ghostly whispers crept about him in the stillness. They stirred an aching loneliness in his heart, as if this desertion and ruin were all that remained of his own hopes and ambitions. Then came a feeling of dread, almost of fear. He turned back to the house and to the open, where long ago he had stood with Toinette and all her loveliness so near to him.

The sun had set and dusk was gathering over the land before he drew himself away from the ghosts which haunted Lussan's place. Night could add nothing more to his gloom.

Odd whined frequently in his eagerness to reach home. Sometimes he showed impatience at his master's slowness by running ahead. Jeems did not hurry. He unslung his bow, which was the only weapon he had brought, and carried it ready in his hand. Yet if Odd had hinted of danger he would have paid no attention to the warning. Danger was miles away on the other side of Dieskau and his men. It would come no nearer and he would never have a chance to meet it. In Toinette's eyes he would always remain a renegade and a coward.

Night thickened. The stars came out. Deepening shadows lay about them as they climbed the tallest of the hills, from which they could look over the ridges and woods between them and Forbidden Valley.

From this hill, which was four miles from the Bulain clearing, they had gazed many times upon an amazing world. In all directions but one their eyes could reach over endless miles of unpeopled domain until the sky seemed to touch the timber. But on the point from which they might have viewed the Tonteur seigneurie, trees had grown tall and thick, shutting out their vision.

Because from this hill it was possible to see over the Big Forest which sheltered their farm from the north winds, Jeems and his father called it Home Mountain.

Odd whined as he climbed it to-night. He went ahead of Jeems, and when he gained the crest his whining changed to a howl, so low that one would scarcely have heard it at the foot of the hill.

Jeems came to him and stopped.

For a space, there was no beating of a heart in his breast—nothing but a stillness that was like death, a shock that was like death, a horror that could come only at the sight and the feeling of death.

Rising from the far side of the forest into which Hepsibah had gone that morning was a distant glow of fire. Nearer, over the rim of Forbidden Valley, the sky was a red illumination of flame. And this illumination was not of a burning forest. It was not a torch of burning stumps. It was not a conflagration of dry swamp grass reflecting itself against a moonless heaven. It was a tower of blazing light, mushrooming as it rose, flattening itself in a sinister scarlet radiance under the clouds, dripping at its edges into colours of silver and gold and blood.

His home was burning!

With the cry that came from his lips, there leapt madly into his mind the words that Hepsibah had spoken to him a last time that morning: "*If ever I'm off there and you see a fire lighting up the sky by night, or smoke darkening it by day, hurry to the seigneurie with your father and mother as fast as you can go, for it will mean my hand has set the heavens talking to you and that the peril o' death is near.*"

CHAPTER IX

FOR a space Jeems could not move as he gazed at the crimson sky. Doubt might have eased the thoughts that crowded on his senses, but during the time in which he stood numbed and voiceless there was no doubt. His home was in flames. This alone would not have deadened him with horror. His father was there to care for his mother, a new home could be built, the world did not end because a house burned. But there were two fires—and the other, farther on, reflecting itself dimly and yet more sombrely, was the one that terrified him. It was Hepsibah's fire talking to him through the night!

Then the choking thing in him gave way, and as the power to act returned, he saw Odd facing the lighted heavens—and in every muscle and line of the dog's rigid frame the Indian sign was clearly written. Until now this admonition had never sent through him a thrill of dread or fear.

He set off at a run down the hill, and as he ran bushes whipped at his face and shadows gathered under his feet and long arms of gloom reached out from among the trees to hold him back. When he came to the bottom he ran faster, and so thick and dark were the walls of the forest about him that they hid the radiance in the sky. Silvery threads of starlight illumined his way, and he darted through splashes and pools of it and crossed opens where it swallowed him in cobwebby seas. He could not come up with Odd. Like two shadows in a playful night, one closely pursuing the other, they ran until Jeems's breath began to break from his lips in gasps, and at the end of a mile he fell back to a walk. Odd lessened his pace to his master's. They climbed a lower hill, and once more Jeems could see the glow of fire. In the upper vault of the sky it was fading to a ghostly pallor against the sweeping arc of the Milky Way.

They ran on, and the spirit of hope began to fight for a place in Jeems's brain. He seized on this ray of light shining out of the darkness of shock and panic and hugged it to him eagerly. It gave life and force to the arguments with which he now made an effort to hold back the grimmer thing. His home was burning. But it must be an accident, nothing that should fill him with fright. The other fire—off in Forbidden Valley—was no more than a coincidence, probably a conflagration started by a careless Indian or a white man's pipe. The woods were dry. Windrows of fallen leaves carpeted the earth ready to catch the spark from a bit of steel, a crumb of tobacco, or a smouldering wad from a gun. He had never been afraid of forest fires!

He paused again to get his breath, and Odd stopped with him. They stood in one of the pools of starlight, their ears straining, their eyes staring, and it was the dog who held back a greater triumph of optimism. His shaggy body was trembling with the pent-up emotions of suspense and passion which possessed him when he caught in the air the deadly poison to his nostrils—the

Indian smell. The crest along his spine had stiffened. His eyes shot flame. His powerful jaws were drooling as if hunger instead of hatred were moving him. Jeems struggled not to believe the evidence which he saw, and told himself that if by any chance there were Indians at his home they were friends helping to save what they could from the tragedy of the fire.

A faint wind whispered in the treetops as he listened. Dry oak leaves rustled on their branches as if fleshless hands were shaking them. Then the rustling and the whispering passed, and shadows lay like solid substance on the earth. Out of the silence Jeems heard a sound which rose above the pounding of his heart. It was so far away, so indistinct, that the stirring of the leaves had kept it from his ears. The wind began to play softly among the oaks again, as if that were its intent.

But Jeems had heard.

He had heard the firing of guns.

Over the hills and forests the sound had come to him from the direction of the Tonteur seigneurie. He did not wait for the oaks to drowse again. Odd led him in their last heartbreaking race into the Big Forest. Leaden weights seemed to be dragging at his feet before they were through it. He had run too hard. He stopped and sagged against a tree, with Odd growling in a low and terrible way close to his knees. He was not trying to prove or disprove matters now. A catastrophe had happened to his thoughts with the firing of the guns. Taking the place of hope, even of his fears, was the one great desire to reach his father and mother as quickly as he could.

His exertions had beaten him when they came to the

edge of the forest and he could have run no farther without falling. Before them was the slope, a silvery carpet of the starlight. At the foot of it was what had been his home.

That it was a red-hot mass without form or stability, a pile out of which flame rose lazily, its fierceness gone, added nothing more to his shock. He had unconsciously looked for this. The barn was also a heap of blazing embers, and what remained of the smaller buildings near it glowed like the stub ends of huge candles against the earth. Everything was gone. Even this fact was not the one which began to break down his reason, which he had struggled so hard to keep. It was the stillness, the lifelessness, the lack of movement and sound that appalled him at first and then closed in about him, a crushing, deadening force. The fires lit up the bottom land. He could see the big rock at the spring. The paths between the gardens. The bird houses in the nearest oaks. The mill. A patch of sunflowers like slim-bodied nymphs. Details were there, clearly illumined, down to the little heap of cider apples which his mother and he had gathered a day or two before. But he could see nothing that had been saved from the burning house. He could not see his father or his mother or Hepsibah Adams.

Even Odd's heart seemed to break in these moments, A sound came from him that was like a sob. He was half crouching, no longer savage or vengeful. But Jeems did not see. He was trying to find some force in him that could cry out his mother's name. His lips were as dry as sticks, his throat failed to respond. The silence was terrific. In it he heard the snapping of an exploding ember, like a pistol going off. He could hear the water in the creek where it splashed over the stones near the mill. In the woods behind him an owl hooted, half subdued by the starlight. He could hear no one talking, no voices calling.

Fear, the repulsion of flesh and nerves to danger, was utterly gone from him. He was impelled only by thought of his father and mother, the mystery of their silence, his desire to call out to them and to hear their voices in answer. If there was a spiritual self alive in him, that alone kept him from shouting at last. It was not because he was afraid. He did not fit an arrow to his bow as he walked down through the starlight, his feet travelling a little unsteadily. What was there or was not there could not be changed by an arrow. He did not screen himself in the shadows. He was looking for nothing and wanting nothing but his father and mother.

Unexpectedly, he came upon his father. Henri was on the ground near one of Catherine's rose bushes, as if asleep. But he was dead. He lay with his face turned to the sky. Firelight played upon him gently, now increasing, now fading, as the embers flared or died, like fitful notes in a strain of soundless music.

As softly as the light, without a sob or cry, Jeems knelt beside him.

It was strange that in this moment he could speak, while a little before that power had been choked in him by things less terrible than death. There was no hysteria in his voice. His own ears caught it as one which did not seem to come from himself. He spoke his father's name, yet knew that no answer would rise from the lifeless lips. He repeated it in an unexcitable way as his hands clutched at the silent form. As death draws near, numbing the senses and drawing a golden veil of relief over pain, it brings with it a great calm, and it was this —the mental inertness of death without its physical change—that came over Jeems. For the starlight left nothing unrevealed; his father dead, his white lips twisted, his hands clenched at his side, the top of his head naked and bleeding from the scalping knife. Jeems slumped down. He may have spoken again. He may have sobbed. But the thing like death that was creeping over him, its darkness and vastness, hid him from himself. He remained beside his father, as motionless and as still. Odd crouched near. After a little, an inch at a time, he crept to the dead man. He muzzled the hands that were growing cold. He licked Jeems's face where it had fallen against his father's shoulder. Then he was motionless again, his eyes seeking about him like balls of living flame. Death was in the air. He was breathing it. He was hearing it. It was in the mournful rustling of the oak leaves. The softly dancing shadows of the fire flung it at him. A nighthawk swooping near the glow bore it with his wings. The stillness was weighted with it. At last, irresistibly impelled to answer the spirit of death, he sat back on his haunches and howled. It was not Odd's howl any more than it had been Jeems's voice speaking to his father a few moments before. It was a ghostly sound that seemed to quiet even the whispering of the leaves, an unearthly and shivering cry that sent echoes over the clearing, with grief for company.

It was this which brought Jeems out of the depths into which he had fallen. He raised his head and saw his father again, and swayed to his feet. He began seeking. Close by, near the pile of apples which she had helped him gather from under their trees on the slope, he found his mother. She, too, lay with her face to the sky. The little that was left of her unbound hair lay scattered on the earth. Her glorious beauty was gone. Starlight, caressing her gently, revealed to her boy the hideousness of her end. There, over her body, Jeems's heart broke. Odd guarded faithfully, listening to a grief that twisted at his brute soul. Then fell a greater silence. Through long hours the burning logs settled down into flattened masses of dying embers. A wind came dismally over the Big Forest. The Milky Way began to fade. Clouds gathered to shut out the stars. The darkness came which precedes the day, and after that, dawn.

Jeems rose to face his blasted world. He was no longer a youth but a living thing aged by an eternity that had passed. It was Odd who led him in the quest for Hepsibah Adams. He sought like one half blind and yet sensed everything. He saw the trampled grass, the moccasin-beaten earth at the spring, a hatchet lost in the night, and on the hatchet *an English name*. But he did not find his uncle.

In the same gray dawn, stirring with the wings of birds and the play of squirrels among the trees, he set out for Tonteur Manor.

He carried the hatchet, clutching it as if the wood his fingers gripped held life which might escape him. Because of this hatchet there grew in him a slow and terrible thought that had the strength of a chain. The weapon, with its short hickory handle, its worn iron blade, its battered head, might have been flesh and blood capable of receiving pain or of giving up a secret, so tenacious was the hold of his hand about it. But he did not see the iron or wood. He saw only the name which told him that the English had come with their Indians, or had sent them, as his uncle had so often said they would. The English. Not the French. *The English.*

And he held the hatchet as if it were an English throat.

But he was not thinking that. The part of him conscious of the act was working unknown to the faculties which made him move and see. His thoughts were imprisoned within stone walls, and around these walls they beat and trampled themselves, always alike, telling him the same things, until their repetition became a droning in his brain. His mother was dead—back there. His father was dead. Indians with English hatchets had killed them, and he must carry the word to Tonteur.

The whole thing was like a twilight of unreality through which he was passing, a grotesque nightmare of some kind. The rising sun did not dispel this illusion, which came and went like waves of light and darkness in his brain. Day with its warmth and beauty, the hundreds of birds gathering for their southward flights, the cheerful calling of turkeys under the chestnut trees, the soft blue in the skies all added to it. At times he almost cried out the impossibility of what had happened, and only a little less than believed that his eyes had lied to him.

After a time, the effect of these things began to give way before the steady progress of other forces in him, the saviours that rise or fall between madness and reason, between hysteria and calmness. He paused when he came to Squirrel Rock and looked over Forbidden Valley. With its autumn colourings it was more than ever like an Oriental tapestry laid out under his eyes, its lakes gleaming with friendliness. He could see no smoke and no sign of invasion or enmity. The song of the squirrels floated up to him. The wings of two eagles he had known since childhood flashed against the sky. His mind cleared, and he was conscious of regaining strength which he had lost. He spoke to Odd, and the dog pressed close to his knee and looked up at him with the language which he, too, had allowed to grow numb and dead for a space. Courage grew between them. When they turned away from the valley, Jeems's eyes were filled with a different light.

Thought which had been wrecked and beaten until now possessed him with a flame behind it that began to burn fiercely but which seemed to give no heat or excitement to his flesh. Only his eyes changed, until they were those of a savage, flinty in their hardness and without depth in which one might read his emotions. His face was white and passionless, with lines caught and etched upon it as if in bloodless stone. He looked at the hatchet again, and Odd heard the gasp which came from his lips. The hatchet was a voice telling him things and gloating in the story it had to tell. It made him think more clearly and pressed on him an urge for caution. He did not follow this immediately, for what lay behind made the matter of personal danger a trivial thing, not because of his courage, but because he was deadened to fear. As he drew nearer to Tonteur Manor, the instincts of self-preservation awoke in him. They did not make him leave the open trail or travel less swiftly, but his senses became keener, and unconsciously he began to prepare himself for the physical act of vengeance.

To reach Tonteur was the first obligation in the performance of this act. Tonteur still had a few men who had not gone with Dieskau, and as Jeems recalled the firing of guns, a picture painted itself before his eyes. The murderers of his father and mother had swung eastward from Forbidden Valley, and the seigneur, warned by Hepsibah's fire, had met them with loaded muskets. He had faith in Tonteur and did not question what had happened in the bottom lands. Before this no doubt had crossed his mind as to Hepsibah's fate. The English hatchets had caught him, somewhere, or he would have come during the long night when he and Odd had watched alone with death. But now a forlorn and scarcely living hope began to rise in his breast as he came to Tonteur's Hill—an unreasoning thought that something might have driven his Uncle Hepsibah to the Richelieu, a hope that, after lighting his signal fire, he had hurried to the Manor with the expectation of finding his people there. His father must have seen Hepsibah's warning across Forbidden Valley, and had waited, disbelieving, while death travelled with the shades of night through the lowlands.

He might see Hepsibah, in a moment, coming over the hill. . . .

Hepsibah, and the baron, and men with guns. . . .

Even Odd seemed to be expecting this as they sped through the last oak open and climbed the chestnut ridge. There were partridges here from dawn until half the morning was gone, and a covey rose before them with a roar of wings. Maples grew on the side toward the Richelieu, and the leaves were knee-deep. Beyond these were the thick edging of crimson sumac, a path breaking through it, and the knob of the hill where they had always paused to gaze over the wonderland which had been given by the King of France to the stalwart vassal Tonteur.

Jeems emerged at this point, and the spark which had grown in his breast was engulfed by sudden blackness.

There was no longer a Tonteur Manor.

A thin, earth-embracing fog covered the bottom lands. It was a veil drawn lightly to cover the ugliness of a thing that had happened, something that was not entirely unbeautiful, a cobwebby, multi-coloured curtain of pungent smoke drifting in the sunlight, a fabric strangely and lazily woven by whitish spirals that rose softly from wherever a building had stood in the Tonteur seigneurie.

Now there were no buildings but one. The great manor house was gone. The loopholed church was gone. The farmers' cottages beyond the meadows and fields were gone. All that remained was the stone gristmill, with the big wind wheel turning slowly at the top of it and making a whining sound that came to him faintly through the distance. That was the only break in the stillness.

Jeems, looking down, saw in the drifting veil of smoke a shroud that covered death. For the first time he forgot his father and mother. He thought of someone he had known and loved a long time ago. Toinette.

CHAPTER X

HIDDEN against the scarlet-topped sumac Jeems stood for many minutes gazing upon the scene of ruin in the valley, too heavily scarred by his own tragedy to be conscious of great shock again. The thing was an enormity which stunned him, but it did not lock his reason and his power to act as the other had. Here his hopes were set at an end, and his mind, seizing upon facts as the death shroud in the valley told them to him, cut away with the keenness of a knife the mental umbra which had obscured his visions. The last of his world which might have remained was destroyed, and with it, Toinette.

Below the thin veil of smoke through which he surveyed the bottom land there was no sign of life, and no movement except the turning of the wheel at the top of the mill. The wide pasture which extended to the river was empty. Cattle and horses and sheep were gone. This emptiness lay over the earth as far as he could see. Death had gone its way as swiftly as it had come, and no enemy remained to exult over what had happened.

As he had stood at the edge of the Big Forest seeking for a figure that might have been his mother's, he now quested for one that might be Toinette's. But the same hope was not in his breast, nor the same fear. Certainty had taken their place. Toinette was dead, despoiled of her beauty and her life as his mother had been. A fury triumphed over him that was as possessive in its effect as the colour which blazed about him in the crimson bush. It had been growing in him since the moment he knelt at his father's side; it had strained at the bounds of his grief when he found his mother; it had filled him with madness, still unformed in his brain, when he covered their faces in the early dawn. Now he knew why he gripped the English hatchet so tightly. He wanted to kill. It was a terrible and totally unexcitable feeling in him. It did not give him the desire to cry out defiance or to hurl himself headlong at something. The passion which consumed him, searing his veins while it left his flesh calm, was a thing whose object of vengeance was not an individual or a group of individuals. He did not analyze the philosophy or the absurdity of this fact, but his eyes turned from the smoke-filled valley of the Richelieu to the south where Champlain lay gleaming in the sun miles away, and the hand which held the hatchet trembled in its new-born yearning for the life blood of a people whom he hated from this day and hour.

He was vaguely conscious of the whine of the mill wheel as he went down into the valley. He did not feel fear or the necessity for concealing his movement, for death would not trouble itself to return to a desolation so complete. But the wheel, as he drew nearer, touched the stillness with a note which seemed to ride with strange insistence over the solitude, as if calling to someone. It became less a thing of iron and wood that was crying in its hunger for oil, and more a voice which demanded his attention. It seemed to him that suddenly he caught what it was saying: "*the little English beast—the little English beast*"—repeating those words until they became a rhythm without a break in their monotony except when a capful of wind set the wheel going faster. It was as if a thought in his brain had been stolen from him. And what it expressed was true. He was the English beast, coming as Madame Tonteur had predicted. Toinette had been right. Fiends with white skins, who were of his blood, had sent their hatchet killers to prove it. And like a lone ghost he was left to see it all. The mill wheel knew and, even in moments of quiet, seemed to possess the power to tell him so.

With stubborn fortitude he faced the gehenna through which he knew he must pass before he could turn south to find his vengeance with Dieskau. Toinette belonged to him now as much as his mother, and it was for her he began to search.

In a ditch which had run almost under the eaves of the loopholed church, he stumbled on a body. It had fallen among tall grass and weeds and had remained hidden there. It wore a Mohawk war tuft, and in one of its stiffened hands was another English hatchet like the one Jeems had. A scalp was at the warrior's belt, and for a moment Jeems turned sick. It was a young girl's scalp, days old.

As he advanced, he could see there had been an alarm and a little fighting. There was old Jean de Lauzon, the *curé*, doubled up like a jackknife, half dressed and with a battered old flintlock under him. He was bald, without a hair that an enemy might take, so he had been left unmutilated. He had fired the gun and was running for the fortressed church when a bullet had caught him between his thin shoulder blades. Jeems stood over him long enough to make note of these things. He saw several more dark blotches on the ground quite near to where the thick oaken door to the church had been. There were Juchereau and Louis Hebert, both well along in years, and not far from them were their wives. Raudot was a fifth. He had been a slow-witted lad, and now he looked like a clown who had died with a grin on his face. These people had lived nearest to the church. The others had been too far away to answer the alarm quickly, but the result had been the same. Some had come to meet their death. Others had waited for it.

Between this group and the smouldering pile that had been the Manor, a lone figure lay on the ground. Jeems went to it slowly. The smoke-scented air suffocated him as if it were a fragile weave which lacked the gift of life. This oppression was heaviest when he saw that the sprawled-out form was Tonteur. Unlike the others, the baron was fully dressed. He undoubtedly had been armed when he rushed forth from the house, but nothing was left in his hands but the clods of earth which he had seized in a final agony. A cry broke from Jeems. He had loved Tonteur. The seigneur had been the one connecting link between his older years and the dreams of his childhood, and it was because of him that he had never quite seemed to lose Toinette. Until now he had not realized how deeply Tonteur had found a place in his affections or how necessary he had been. He crossed his hands upon his breast and loosened the earth from his fingers. He could feel Toinette at his side, and for a brief interval the sickness in his head and body overcame him so that he could not see Tonteur at all. But he could hear Toinette sobbing.

Against this clouding of his senses he felt himself struggling as if swimming in an empty space. Then he could see Tonteur again, dimly at first, and for an instant he had the impression that a long time had passed. He picked up his hatchet and his bow and rose to his feet. He had not lost sound of the mill wheel even when Toinette's sobbing had seemed to be at his side. It was crying at him now, but before he turned toward it his eyes rested on Tonteur's wooden peg. It was half cut off, a mark of grim humour on the part of a butcher. The mill wheel was forcing his attention to that fact. "*Look—look—look*"—it said, and then repeated the old song, calling him an English beast.

He faced it in a flash of resentment, not because of the wheel alone but on account of what lay at his feet and what he knew he would find nearer to the walls of the manor. Between him and the mill was a low current of air with which the smoke drifted in a sun-filled fog which gave to this remaining building an unreal and grotesque appearance. Through the smoke he could scarcely see the wheel as it turned at the top of the tall, pyramid-shaped structure of stone. He was silent, listening for other sound in the sleeping stillness. But his mind was hurling anathema at the wheel. He wanted to tell it that it lied. In this hush of death he wanted to cry out that he was not of the murderous breed who had sent the killers. Proof was over there, in the valley which at last was well named. His mother. His father. His Uncle Hepsibah. Not one of them had been of this breed in their hearts, and all of them were dead by its hand. He had been left alive—by chance. That was proof. The wheel was wrong. It lied.

He looked at Tonteur again, strengthening himself to go a little farther and find Toinette. He knew how it would be. Toinette's young body, even more pitiful than his mother's. He forced himself to turn toward the smouldering walls. *Toinette—dead!* His father might die, and Tonteur, and all the rest of the world—but these two, his mother and Toinette, inseparable in his soul forever, the vital sparks which had kept his own heart beating—how could they die while he lived? He advanced, pausing over one of the slaves, a woman almost unclothed, inky black except the top of her head, which was red where her scalp was gone. In the crook of her arm was her scalpless infant. White, black, women, babies—the loveliness of girlhood—it made no difference.

Jeems scanned the earth beyond her, and where the smoke lay in a white shroud he saw a small, slim figure which he knew was Toinette. Another young body might have lain in the same way, its slenderness crumpled in the same manner, a naked arm revealed dimly under its winding sheet of smoke. But he knew this was Toinette. The dizzying haze wavered before his eyes again, and he put out his hand to hold it back. Toinette. Only a few steps from him. Dead, like his mother.

Odd went ahead of him halfway to the still form and stopped. He sensed something Jeems could not see **or** feel through the smoke mist which undulated before their eyes. Warning of impending danger confronted the dog, and he tried to pass it to his master. In that moment, a shot came from the mill, and a flash of pain darted through Jeems's arm. He was flung backward and caught himself to hear echoes of the explosion beating against the forested hills and the wheel at the top of the mill screaming at him.

He answered the shot by dropping his bow and dashing toward the mill. Odd was a leap ahead of him when they reached its broken-down door, and the dog stopped as he faced the shadows that lay within the stone walls. Jeems went on. Death might easily have met him at the threshold, but nothing moved in the vaultlike chamber he had entered, and there was no sound in it except that of his own breath and his racing heart. Odd came in and sniffed the grain-scented, musty air. Then he went to the flight of narrow steps which led to the tower room and told Jeems that what they sought was there. Jeems ran up, his hatchet raised to strike.

He must have been an unforgettable and terrifying object as he appeared above the floor into the light which forced its way through the dusty glass of three round windows over his head. There must even have been a little of the monster about him. He had left some of his garments with his mother and father, and his arms and shoulders were bare. Char and smoke and the stain of earth had disfigured him. His face appeared to be painted for slaughter and a greenish fire glittered in the eyes that were seeking for an enemy. Blood dripped to the oaken planks from his wounded arm. He was a Frankenstein ready to kill, dishevelment and fury concealing his youth, his stature made appalling by his eagerness to leap at something with the upraised hatchet.

If the hatchet had found a brain, it would have been Toinette's. She faced him as he came, holding the musket which she had fired through a slit in the wall as if she still possessed faith in its power to defend her. Her pallor was heightened by the silken darkness of the long hair which streamed about her. Her eyes had in them a touch of madness. Yet she was so straight and tense, waiting for death, that she did not seem to be wholly possessed by fear or terror. Something unconquerable was with her, the soul of Tonteur himself struggling in her fragile breast to make her unafraid to die and giving to her an aspect of defiance. This courage could not hide the marks of her torture. Death had miraculously left her flesh untouched in passing, yet she stood crucified in the mill room.

Expecting a savage, she recognized Jeems. The musket fell from her hands to the floor with a dull crash, and she drew back as if retreating from one whose presence she dreaded more than that of a Mohawk, until her form pressed against the piled-up bags of grain, and she was like one at bay. The cry for vengeance which was on Jeems's lips broke in a sobbing breath when he saw her. He spoke her name, and Toinette made no response except that she drew herself more closely to the sacks. Odd's toenails clicked on the wooden floor as he went to her. This did not take her eyes from Jeems. They were twin fires flaming at him through a twilight gloom,

The dog touched her hand with his warm tongue, and she snatched it away.

She seemed to grow taller against the gray dusk of the wall of grain.

"*You—English—beast!*"

It was not the mill wheel this time, but Toinette's voice, filled with the madness and passion which blazed from her eyes.

With a sudden movement she picked up the musket and struck at him. If it had been loaded, she would have killed him. She continued to strike, but Jeems was conscious only of the words which came from her brokenly as she spent her strength on him. *He* had come with the English Indians to destroy her people! *He* and his mother had plotted it, and they were alive while everyone who belonged to her was dead! The barrel of the gun struck him across the eyes. It fell against his wounded arm. It bruised his body. Sobbingly, she kept repeating that she wanted to kill him, and cried out wildly for the power with which to accomplish the act as he stood before her like a man of stone. An English beast—her people's murderer—a fiend more terrible than the painted savages . . .

She struck until the weight of the musket exhausted her and she dropped it. Then she snatched weakly at the hatchet in Jeems's hands, and his fingers relaxed about the helve. With a cry of triumph, she raised it, but before the blow could descend she sank in a crumpled heap upon the floor. Even then her almost unconscious lips were whispering their denunciation.

He knelt beside her and supported her head in his

unwounded arm. For a moment it lay against his breast. Her eyes were closed, her lips were still. And Jeems, sick from her blows, remembered his mother's God and breathed a prayer of gratitude because of her deliverance.

Then he bent and kissed the mouth that had cursed him.

CHAPTER XI

TOINETTE was alone when she awoke from the unconsciousness which had come to ease the anguish of her mind and body. It seemed to her she was coming out of sleep and that the walls which dimly met her eyes were those of her bedroom in the Manor. That a truth whose evidence lay so horribly about her could be reality and not a dream broke on her senses dully at first and then with a swift understanding. She sat up expecting to see Jeems. But he was gone. She was no longer where she had fallen at her enemy's feet. But Jeems had made a resting place for her of empty bags and must have carried her to it. She shivered when she looked at the musket and the stain of blood on the floor. She had tried to kill him. And he had gone away, leaving her alive!

As had happened to Jeems, something was burned out of her now. It had gone in the sea of darkness which had swept over her, and she rose with an unemotional calmness, as if the tower room with its dust and cobwebs and store of ripened grain had become her cloister. Passion had worn itself away. If a thought could have slain, she would still have wreaked her vengeance on Jeems, but she would not have touched the musket again that lay on the floor.

She went to the head of the stair and looked down.

The son of the Englishwoman had left no sign except the drip of blood that made a trail on the steps and out of the door. Exultation possessed her as she thought how nearly she had brought to the Bulains the same shadow of death which they and their kind had brought to her. The thrill was gone in a moment. The red drops fascinated her, painted brightly by the sun. Jeems Bulain— out there with her dead! The boy her mother had tried to make her regard with bitterness and dislike from childhood—a man grown into an English monster! She struggled to bring back her power to hate and her desire to kill, but the effort she made was futile. She followed the crimson stains, hearing nothing but the mill wheel over her head. Emptiness was below, a loneliness wherein the sun itself seemed to lose its warmth.

She stood in the doorway, and all about her was the haze of smoke, soft and still in the air. In the distance, obscured by the fog which ran from the smouldering ruins, she saw a form bent grotesquely under a burden. It was a shapeless thing, distorted by the sun and the smoky spindrifts dancing before her eyes, but living because it was moving away from her. Behind it was a smaller object, and she knew the two were Jeems and his dog.

She watched until they were blotted from her vision, and minutes passed before she followed where they had gone.

Jeems must have seen her, for he reappeared with the dog like a werewolf at his heels. He had found a coat somewhere and did not look so savage, though his face was disfigured and bleeding where she had struck him, with the barrel of the musket. He was breathing deeply, but his face was as dispassionate as it had been in the tower room—an Indian's face, with flesh tempered by the impassiveness which she had assaulted so bitterly. She tried to speak when he stopped before her. Accusation and a bit of ferocity remained in her soul, but they were impotent in the silence between them. His eyes meeting hers steadily from under the lurid brand of her blow, seemed less like a murderer's and held more the gaze of one who regarded her with a cold and terrible pity. He did not put out a helping hand though she felt herself swaying. He was no longer youth. He was not the boy her mother had trained her to hate. He was not even Jeems Bulain.

But his voice was the same.

"I am sorry, Toinette."

Jeems scarcely knew he spoke the words. They rang back through the years as if a ghost had come to life whose memory they had flayed out of their hearts *?* long time ago.

"What are you doing here?" she demanded.

She might have asked that same question in those unimportant years when he had dared to visit Tonteur Manor with his foolish gifts. *Why was he here?* He turned in the direction from which he had come and held out his hand, not for her to take, but as a voice. She understood what his burden had been. Tears? Such trivial things could not exist in the after-heat of the holocaust that had consumed them. A stray undercurrent of wind flung back her hair in a lacy mantle of jet silk. Pride, defying grief, raised her chin a little as she obeyed Jeems. It shone in her widening eyes and in her parted lips as she looked ahead. She knew to what she was going. And when she came to the place which Jeems had prepared, she was like a white angel who had appeared to gaze for a moment or two upon the dead.

With a tool he had found, Jeems had made a grave. It was shallow and made less unbeautiful with a bed of golden grass. Tonteur did not seem unhappy as he lay upon it. The top of his head was covered so Toinette could not see. She knelt and prayed, and Jeems drew back, feeling that to kneel with her, with the marks of her hatred on his face and body, would be sacrilege.

Even now, when it should have known better, the mill wheel continued to whine and scream, and suddenly it occurred to Jeems that it could not have been that way yesterday when Tonteur was alive. A devil must have come to abide at the top of the mill!

He waited, scanning the horizons that were thinning of their smoke. Death had passed and death might return over its own blackened trail. Toinette, beside her father, made him think of that. It seemed a long time before she rose to face him. She was not crying. Her eyes were blue stars in a countenance as pale as marble. The sun shone on her and gave an unearthly radiance to her hair. Her beauty held him stricken just as his own terribleness forced from her a gasp of protest when he drew off the coat borrowed from one of the dead men and spread it over Tonteur. But she did not speak. Only the mill wheel continued its virulent plaint as the loose earth fell on the baron. Toinette looked steadily toward the sky, and when Jeems was done she accompanied him back to the mill. She watched him go for his bow, where he saw that the form he had thought was Toinette was the wife of Peter the Younger.

He came back and spoke to her a second time. The lips she had broken with the musket barrel were swollen, and the brand across his forehead was turning a dark and angry colour. The cloth he had twisted about his wounded arm was red. Sickness and pain were forcing their way into his eyes.

"I must take you away," he said. "There is not time to care for the others. If they come back——"

"They will not harm *you*," she said.

Jeems made no answer but looked away over the Richelieu toward Champlain and Dieskau.

"And they will not harm your father or your mother or anything that belongs to the Bulains, but will reward them for their loyalty to murder and outrage. Is not that true?"

Still Jeems did not answer, but stood listening for sound to come out of the distance.

Her voice was quiet and mercilessly unmoved by the marks of the punishment which her hands had inflicted. He had received less than her own people, and it was only an accident of her weakness and want of skill that he had not suffered equally with them. She saw the sickness gathering in his face and eyes, but pity for him was as dead in her breast as her desire to live. She knew where he would take her. To his home—a place left unscathed by the killers. To his mother, the soft and pretty woman in whom her father had believed so faithfully. To Henri Bulain, the traitor, who had bartered his honour for an Englishwoman. Over her father's hill, in Forbidden Valley, were safety and mercy at the hands of her country's enemies.

Her lips found a way to cut him deeper.

"Your father and mother are waiting for you," she said. "Go, and leave me here. I prefer to wait for the return of your Indian friends. And I am not sorry because I tried to kill you!"

He moved away from her to where Hebert and Juchereau and the simple-minded Raudot lay on the ground. This time it was the idiot's coat he took, a fine coat made by the idiot's mother. The boy had loved birds and flowers, and on the lapel of the coat was a faded geranium bloom. Jeems took it off and tucked it between the dead lad's fingers.

Then he went back to Toinette and said, "We had better go." After that he added, "I am sorry, but I must go to my mother and father first."

He staggered as he set out, and Tonteur Hill dipped and wobbled before his eyes. There was an ache like a splinter twisting in his head, and as she followed him, Toinette could see the effect of her unresisted blows with the iron gun barrel. For she did follow, out of the smoke fumes into the clearer air of the meadows and across them to the worn path that led to the Indian trail and the home of Catherine Bulain. She followed as if drawn by chains, but after a little the weight of these chains seemed to leave her, and when Jeems stumbled and caught himself from falling, she almost breathed a cry. The hardwoods swallowed them, and about them now even more than in the earlier morning were the warmth and golden riot of the Algonquin Indian summer which precedes the killing frosts and the opening of the chestnut burrs. In this autumnal peace and quiet, gentle with the subdued notes of birds and with the fragrance of a ripened earth between her and the blue of the sky, the bitterness she was fighting to hold against the one ahead of her became almost dispelled at times. In these moments the spirit of her father was with her again. This was the path he had loved best, over the hill and through the forest to the clearing in Forbidden Valley. His horse's feet had worn it smooth, and in the earth were hoofprints so clear and fresh he might have ridden it an hour ago. Close to Squirrel Rock he had always loitered to look over the grandeur of the valley, and there Toinette paused with Jeems, standing in the worn spot her father had made.

"They're down there," said Jeems, and pointed, speaking to Odd more than to her.

He took the hatchet from his belt and carried it in his hand. They crossed the open where he had killed Paul Tache, the turkey cock, and passed through the screen of brush which the fairies had built. They entered the greater stillness of the Big Forest, and Odd, who had travelled between them, dropped back to Toinette's side and thrust his muzzle against her hand.

She did not snatch it away from him now.

They came to the slope, and Jeems forgot that Toinette was behind him. He walked straight down like a tall, thin ghost—and the girl stopped and stood alone, staring at the place where his home should have been, a cry wringing itself at last from her lips.

Jeems did not hear. He saw nothing but the clump of rose bushes and the place where his mother lay. He went to her first, oblivious of other presence, unconscious of the sun, of the ruins still smouldering, his soul stirring once more with the faint mad spark of incredulity. But she was dead. He saw her with clearer eyes, though he was sick with hurt. He knelt beside her calmly for a little while. He touched her face gently with his hand, and then went to his father. Odd trailed at his heels. In the stump field was a shovel, and they found it and bore it back with them together. Under his mother's big tree he planned to dig.

When he returned, his mother was not alone. Toinette was there, on the ground, with the English woman's head in her lap. Her eyes blazed up at Jeems, and something like defiance was in them, something that was possessive and challenging and which hid whatever pity she might have had for him, or pleading for his forgiveness. Her hands were pressing the cold face of the woman she had wanted to hate, and she continued to look at Jeems, so hard, so terribly, so understandingly that she seemed almost to be waiting for him to punish her with a blow.

Then she bowed her head over his mother, and the shining veil of her hair covered death.

Under the big tree he began to dig.

CHAPTER XII

IT WAS late afternoon when they left the valley, a still, slumbering hour when the sun was about to go to its early rest, leaving glows and sunset paintings behind that might have been made of swimming metals.

Toinette's hand lay in Jeems's as they went.

They were like a young god and goddess ready to face the hazards of a savage world with a strength wrought out of fire. The sickness had left Jeems. His wounded arm was cared for by fingers as gentle as his mother's had been. Hot tears caressing his flesh from Toinette's dark lashes had cured his physical pain. Words spoken in a voice he had never heard from her lips entreating his forgiveness for years of misunderstanding were like the peace of the day itself about his heart. Out of ruin she had raised his soul to splendid heights of courage and resolution. Seared by grief, but a grief no greater than her own, he saw once more the ghosts of dreams.

Toinette, at his side, had gone back to the days when those dreams were in the making. He might have imagined her the Toinette of Lussan's place except that she was less than magnificent now, with her dress soiled and torn and her hair in a braid of straight tresses instead of lustrous curls. Under the big tree, with his mother, things had broken away from her—a great deal of her strength, a little of her courage, but chiefly years of pride built out of hollow teachings. There, just as the fires had changed Jeems in another way, they had made of her the child whom Catherine had prayed would come to her some day.

She was not so tall at Jeems's side. She was not so dispassionately cold and white, ready to hold out her arms to death if it should come her way. The glow in her eyes was a different glow. It was dark with desolation and held imperishable depths of torture. But in it were other things. She was seeing the endless walls of the forest again, the coming of night, the loneliness of the world, her helplessness, and the strength of the one at her side. Her cup filled with horrors had turned her, like Niobe, to stone, but now warm flesh was returning with its frailties and weaknesses, giving her once more a recognition of life and a hunger for it. She looked at Jeems. As a child, years ago, she might have let him lead her in this way deep into a forest where he was unafraid and sure but where shadows and mysteries set her heart quaking. Her fingers clung to his.

They passed his mother's gardens of flowers where choice blooms were nodding, filled to overflowing with ripening seeds; they skirted the turnip field where a purple-breasted crop lay waiting for spicy frosts to give crispness and flavour to its flesh; they cut through the heart of a new clearing where many shag-toothed stumps were piled ready for winter use in the cabin fireplace. In a place where fresh dirt was scattered about were tools used yesterday—axes and shovels and hickory prying poles and the big double-bladed grub hoe which Hepsibah had made at Tonteur's forge. On a stump partly dug from the earth was one of Hepsibah's pipes made of half a corncob with a hollow reed for a stem. Near this stump, looking at them shyly, was the gopher who had once lived under it.

Jeems stopped and looked about, his throat almost tensing for the old familiar call to Hepsibah. Many times he had made the woods and the lower lands echo with that cry and had heard his uncle answer it. But now the stillness warned him. Like a friend it was whispering the sacredness of another trust. His eyes turned to the lovely head near his shoulder. In a moment Toinette raised her eyes to meet his, and even with his mother they had not been so deep and gentle.

"They must have caught my uncle out there," he said, keeping his voice steady and gazing over the forest tops of Forbidden Valley. "He set the signal fire for us and then was killed. I would go and find him, if it were not for you."

"I will go with you," answered Toinette.

But Jeems turned west and did not look back at his home or betray the choking in his breast. In the maple wood, where the sap spigots and poplar troughs were still under the trees, fallen leaves made a frolicsome sound as they went through them. Their loudness did not alarm Jeems and he found himself talking to Toinette as if she were the child of the old days, and he, changed into a man, were explaining things. He described for the first time how the savages had come while he was on his way home from Lussan's place, and gave his reasons for believing they had departed in haste, leaving many things, like the gathered crops, of fruit and grain, which they would surely have taken had they not been pressed by circumstance. He thought their number must have been as great as Toinette supposed—and she had seen them by scores from her bedroom window at the Manor. He was sure they had not gone farther down the Richelieu but had turned back through Forbidden Valley to the Mohawk country. Their own hope was to swing westward out of the path of stragglers, then eastward again toward Lussan's. He told her not to be frightened at the noise the leaves made. They would soon be out of them and would come to hidden trails which he knew and to the shelter of woods and swamps where were fastnesses so thick and untrodden that it was dark in them now, with the sun still glowing in the west. To-morrow or the day following, he would have her safely at the next seigneurie, and there she would find means to be taken to her friends in Quebec. He would then join Dieskau to fight the English. He made this statement without passion or boastfulness, as if to fight were the one thing to do, a fact settled in her mind as well as in his own. The important thing was to reach Lussan's to-night. The Indians would not go near there, for they believed all abandoned places to be inhabited by ghosts and evil spirits. If they stumbled upon it by accident they would get away as quickly as possible. While he talked of these matters, he wanted to ask her questions. How had she got into the mill-tower room—unhurt? Where was her mother? But he set his lips tightly, knowing that he must heal her wounds a little if he could.

In the deeper woods where the Big Forest began were

greater stillness, more gloom, endless and mysterious aisles of twilight all about them. The sun went out. Under their feet was no beaten trail but only the rough and uneven mould, a pad of spongy softness incapable of giving sound. He still held her hand as darkness gathered closer.

In this gloom she whispered:

"Does your arm hurt, Jeems?"

"No. I had forgotten it."

"And your face—where I struck you?"

"I had forgotten that, too."

Something touched his shoulder lightly. He could not tell what it was, for they were in a pool of darkness. But whatever it might have been, a falling leaf, a twig, even shadow itself—it filled him with a strange exaltation.

He would have felt the same if his mother had been at his side, as helpless as Toinette and as dependent upon him. Out of the wreck of a world obliterated in a scourge of horror he had a soul besides his own to fight for.

Twice in the next hour Odd halted and gave a growl which warned of danger in the air. Jeems strained his eyes to see and his ears to hear—and once more, when they stopped to listen, he felt the gentle touch against his shoulder.

They struck a deer run and followed it into a plain between two lines of hills where a devastating fire had passed some years before. Here they travelled through a young growth of bushes and trees reaching scarcely above their heads, with the light of the stars falling on, them. It stirred a soft radiance in Toinette's smooth hair and illumined Jeems's face until the wounds made by her hands were plainly revealed. They climbed the northernmost hill after a time, and at the top of it stopped again to rest.

Jeems, like Odd, stood tense and listening, searching the slumbrous distance of the wilderness which lay about them. He caught all movement and all sound, the direction of the wind, the shifting play of the shadows, the almost noiseless flutter of an owl's wings over their heads.

And then he knew what had touched his shoulder in the darkness—Toinette's cheek pressing against it for a moment as lightly as a feather.

He felt her trembling. When she looked at him, her eyes rested on the brand of the musket barrel which lay in a red stripe across his forehead. The stars seemed bigger and clearer when at last they came to the half mile of abandoned road which ended in Lussan's clearing. It was the road down which Jeems had watched Tonteur and Paul Tache and a proud little princess ride to the sale years before. Now the princess walked unsteadily at his side. She was white and fragile in the starlight, and her strength was gone. Her dress was torn by brush and briars, and the thin soles of her shoes were almost worn from her feet. They came to the old tree where he had concealed himself while they passed, and something made him tell her about it. He was sorry, for, in a moment, a sob answered him. She caught herself and struggled bravely as they entered the clearing, with the ruin of the house ahead of them. Both were so tired in soul and body that their minds seized upon this end of their journey as a relief from longer supporting the burdens of the flesh. In a way, it was like coming to a home which they had forgotten. For this was Lussan's, a place filled with memories of hope and triumph and bitterness out of which it built a welcome for them even in its loneliness. Toinette's lips almost smiled, as if she saw Madame Lussan at the threshold of the door calling to her above the laughing voices of men and women, above her father's cheery greetings to friends and neighbours, above the restless stamping of her horse's hoofs and the crying of the auctioneer. She might have seen and heard these things but yesterday; now there was sleep—a dark and lifeless ghost of a house, crickets rasping their wings in the tangled grass, a jungle growing where before there had been a broad and level green.

Both were children now, seeing the ghosts as only children could see them, wide-eyed and a little afraid at first, and yet comforted by the nearness of that yesterday in their lives. The stars and the crickets and the rustling grass and the wind in the trees seemed to listen and move to the cautious tread of their feet. A rabbit ran ahead of them. An owl flew off the roof of the house. A bat dipped in spirals and curves before their eyes, and thorns caught playfully at their shoes and clothes. And they felt safe. A warmth crept through their blood, and with it a relaxation of nerves and eyes and brain. Here was sanctuary. Rest. Peace. They sensed these things without speaking as they approached the building. The door was open. Starlight splashed like the golden glow of candles on the floor. They entered and stood silent as if listening anxiously for the voices of sleeping ones whom their entrance might arouse. A cricket singing in a starbeam greeted them cheerily. Emptiness was here, a spectral vacancy, but with it were neither death nor fear.

They were a little apart, and Toinette looked like a broken flower ready to fall.

"Wait for me here," said Jeems. "I am going for an armful of grass."

One of Tonteur's farmers had cut the hay in Lussan's abandoned meadow where Jeems had seen a stack the previous day, and he hurried to this, returning with all he could carry. He made a bed in a corner of the room, and Toinette sank upon it. He covered her with his father's coat which he had brought from the valley and went outside to watch and guard with Odd.

He could hear her sobbing as tears came at last to give her comfort. He fought back a thickening in his throat and a hot flame in his eyes as the boy in him called out for his mother. He, too, wanted this easement for his grief. But he stood—a man. Odd watched tirelessly and sleeplessly with his master.

After a long time, there was silence in the old house, and Jeems knew that Toinette was asleep. He went in quietly and replaced the coat about her. Her face was white and lovely, and wet lashes glistened on her cheeks. Timidly his fingers pressed the silken braid of her hair. He brushed a wisp of hay from her forehead. Unconsciously his lips moved. Hope and faith and prayer seemed to stir in the room as he dared to raise the soft braid to his lips, and then he returned to his place outside with something like a glory enshrined with his sorrow.

He sat on the ground with the house at his back and his bow and sheaf of arrows and the English hatchet within reach of his hands. The stillness seemed a live thing that had barred all sound from solemn hours of meditation, and he soon began to feel its influence. Slowly and irresistibly it brought the desire to close his eyes and sleep, and he rose to his feet in a struggle to keep awake. Odd's teeth clicked and his eyes gleamed with undimmed vigilance.

For hours they watched together and marked every changing shadow. They skirted the edges of the open, advancing a step at a time and with as little noise as the owl wings that now and then floated about them. They scanned Lussan's meadow, and Jeems climbed a tall tree to see if he could discover a glow of fire. At intervals he returned to the house and looked in at Toinette. It was after midnight when he sat down again, and soon the stars seemed to be laughing at him and to be drawing nearer as if they had beaten him in a game. They closed his eyes. Odd rested his heavy jaws between his forepaws and gave a deep sigh. Exhaustion—then sleep. Even the bat, grown tired, went to its retreat in the barn. The stars receded and the world began to take on a deeper gloom. Out of this came an animal scream as a late-hunting owl swooped down and killed the rabbit in the clearing. Odd heard it and whined, but it did not awaken Jeems.

He was at home, in the valley. The apple trees were about him and the sun was shining and he was with his mother. They were seated under a tree, resting from their labour of picking up cider apples while his father drove a cartload of fruit down the slope. He could hear the creaking of the wheels. Close to the cabin his Uncle Hepsibah was working the cider press. His mother's head touched his shoulder, and he could feel the softness of her hair against his face. Then they were laughing at a chipmunk who came to stare at them with his cheek pouches so full of corn that he looked as if he had the mumps. Quite unexpectedly, a black cloud shut out the sun and everything was obliterated in darkness. When this happened he seemed to be holding his mother from some force which was trying to drag her from him. This darkness came and went, and the odd part of it was that his father and Uncle Hepsibah did not move from their original positions—one was always halfway down the slope with the ox cart and the other was working at the capstan of the cider press. The chipmunk continued to stare at them with his mouth full of corn.

With an effort, Jeems roused himself from his dream. He saw Odd at his feet and beyond him a clump of briars, a tangle of long grass, an overgrown clearing in which there were no apple trees, no home, no Hepsibah at a cider press. It was Lussan's place. Day had come, and the sun was rising. He sensed these things first, in a flash of wakefulness, and then felt a weight against him and the softness of his mother's hair on his cheek. Only it was Toinette and not his mother. She must have come to him before the dawn broke. Her head was resting on his shoulder and his arms were about her as they had been about his mother. His movement had not awakened her, but now a slow tightening of his arms brought a tremor to her lashes and a deeper breath to her lips. He kissed her pale face, and her eyes opened. He kissed her again, and the act did not seem to disturb her any more than it amazed or shocked him. There was a responsive greeting in her eyes.

Then she sat up straight beside him and faced the rising sun.

The air was so cold that she shivered. Every shrub and briar and blade of grass in the clearing glistened with frost. The coat she had brought from the house slipped from her shoulders, and Jeems drew it about her again. They stood up, and strength returned into their cramped limbs. For a little while they did not speak. They heard a boastful blue jay screaming half a mile away, and in Lussan's meadow crows were gathering. A woodpecker drumming at a hollow stub made the sound of a man with a hammer. Sounds carried far in the silvery sun-streaked mist which lay between the earth and the sky.

That they belonged to each other was a truth which pressed itself on them without effort or confusion. Toinette was not ashamed that she had come to him nor that her act had proclaimed what pride and false prejudice had so long hidden from him in her heart. Her eyes glowed with a light which shone softly out of fathomless depths of pain and grief. She wanted him to know how completely the folly of her pride was gone and how glad she was that it was he who stood beside her now. They might have been years older, so calmly did the sense of surrender and of possession hold them. Except for the new tenderness in her eyes, Toinette was unchanged. But Jeems felt himself taller at her side and something had entered him which was like the spirit of a conqueror. It was another world now. A vast mystery ahead of him. Something to fight through, to win from, to live for. Mysterious, it was still very real. It set his heart throbbing with an unappalled and challenging force. Yesterday, black with tragedy and grievous with its pain, was a long time ago, but, with Toinette, to-day had become a tremendous living present. Gently her fingertips touched his shoulder. Then she looked with him toward the east and the Richelieu— and what lay beyond.

From the moment they had risen to their feet, Odd had stood as rigid as carven wood in the white-coated grass with his muzzle levelled toward Lussan's meadow. Something definite had come within his reach, which made it unnecessary for him to measure the wind, and suddenly there rose above other sound the wild and raucous crying of a blue jay, and a cawing of alarm among the crows. Black wings flashed over the treetops, and Odd's gaunt body quivered as he watched them disappear. A second and a third blue jay joined the first, and their tumult came to an end when a piercing bird call terminated sharply in a single screeching note.

"That was an arrow," said Jeems, beginning to string his bow. "More than once I have had to kill a noisy blue jay when creeping up on game."

He drew Toinette into the shelter of the house and called Odd. A few minutes later—swiftly moving, sombre horrors in a world of shimmering white—they saw the Mohawks come out of the edge of Lussan's meadow.

CHAPTER XIII

THE spectacle of death marching back over its trail brought no terror to Jeems. He had watched for it, had half expected it, and in a way it was like the answer to an unvoiced prayer which had followed his awakening when he had found Toinette in his arms. To fight for her now, to rush forth from the house with a battle cry on his lips, and to be cut to pieces in her defence was not a prospect which dismayed him, but which, instead, inspired in him a fearless exaltation. It was Toinette who saved him from whatever folly was brewing itself in his brain as he stood with a long hunting arrow fitted to his bow. With a breathless cry, she drew him away from the broken door, and there, safe for a moment from the savages who were entering the clearing, she flung her arms about his shoulders. For in these tragic seconds a look had come into Jeems's face like that which had frightened her in the tower room of the mill, a look hard and vengeful with the desire to kill.

"Jeems, dear, we must hide," she pleaded. "*We must hide!*"

The futility of trying to conceal themselves when their footprints were clearly left upon the frosty ground did not occur to him at once. It was her voice and the name it claimed for him that broke down the resolution which soon would have betrayed them.

"I know of a place," she was saying. "We must hurry to it!"

She ran ahead of him and he followed her into another room where a stair was falling into ruin. A bit of sun splashed on the floor, and through the paneless window which admitted it they caught a glimpse of the Mohawks. The red killers had paused at the edge of the open. They stood motionless, like stone men, listening and watchful, the upper parts of their bodies still unclothed until colder days and glistening with grease and paint. Toinette did not allow Jeems to pause, and the steps made complaint as they trod upon them. Jeems looked down from the top and saw the marks of their feet in the dust below. Their fate was certain if the Mohawks came this far, but with only the narrow stair for their enemies to ascend he was determined, in this event, that each of his twenty arrows should find a home.

Toinette preceded him into the room above. She went directly to a panel-like board which held a wooden peg and in a moment they were peering into the musty gloom of a huge black hole under the roof, which the Lussans had used as a garret. Mice scampered about as the first light of years impaled the darkness.

"Madame Lussan brought me to this room after your fight with Paul," she whispered. "I flung my spoiled clothes far back in there!"

Even with the savages so near, pathos and memory were in the tremble of her voice.

Jeems faced the narrow aperture in the wall which

Lussan had left as a window and a gun-hole for defence. Yesterday—Paul Tache—Toinette, the little princess with her riding habit and lustrous curls—and now just they two alone in the room where she had hated him so desperately! He went to the window, and Toinette came close to his side. No eyes could see them as they looked through the rectangular slit shadowed under the eaves. The sun had not risen high enough to direct its warmth effectively upon a whitened earth. The clearing was a paradise made by sprites and nixies out of jewelled frost, with trees about it in gold and white, and thick hazel clumps transformed into glowing polychromes of fringy petalled yellow. Deeper into this scene of purity and beauty the Mohawks had not moved, and from the steadiness of their attitude Jeems knew they had come upon the open unexpectedly. A dozen warriors stood revealed outside the bordering thicket, and twelve pairs of eyes were fixed upon the abandoned house in a tense and suspicious scrutiny. Yet not a hand among the silent savages had moved to hatchet, bow, or gun.

This fact drew a hopeful whisper from Jeems.

"They see the place is deserted, and unless they find some sign of us, they won't come nearer," he said. "Look, Toinette! There is a white man among them with a prisoner's collar around his neck——"

His words were cut short by a sudden movement among the watchers, as if a command had stirred them to life again. The man in the lead, with three eagle feathers in his tuft, stalked alone into the clearing, a tall and sinister figure burdened only with his weapons and a warrior's diminutive travelling pack—a giant who was red and black and ochrish yellow in his war paint, and at whose belt hung a bundle of scalps in which the sun played and danced with changing lights as he moved. These horrid objects, one of which was a woman's with hair so long that it could not escape the eyes of those who were in the house, wrenched a shuddering cry from Toinette, yet even then she thanked God it was as fair in colour as the day itself and not the gleamy cloud of darkness which might have been Catherine's. Faintness swept over her, and she closed her eyes that she might shut from her vision the grisly trophies of a warrior's success. When she opened them again, twoscore warriors in single file were following in the footsteps of the leader and passed within a hundred feet of what once had been Lussan's home, casting furtive sidewise glances as they went. In more than one belt, fresh scalps shone in the sunshine, and two white men and a boy with their hands tied and prisoner thongs about their throats walked in the line. A little more to the right, and the presence of other things than emptiness and ghosts must surely have been discovered by the Indians, for from their window Toinette and Jeems could see the telltale imprints of their shoes in the white frost dangerously close to the thin straight line of their enemies.

Not until the trees on the other side of the clearing had swallowed the last of the Mohawks did Toinette's straining eyes turn to Jeems. There had been no sound in the passing of the red scourge, no cautious voice, no clatter of wood on steel, no crackle of brittle grass or weeds under fourscore moccasined feet. Where their tracks lay in the grass, one might have thought that three men had travelled instead of forty. And the world was dead behind them. Crows did not return to the meadow, and the blue jays had flown into safer distance. The woodpecker had gone to a farther stub. Even in the old house there was no longer the scurrying and squeaking of mice—no sound but the tumultuous throbbing of three hearts, two of them human and one a beast's.

It was then Jeems spoke.

"I swear there was a white man—a free white man—in that painted crowd, and long hair was hanging from his belt," he said.

"I saw his blond head and lighter skin, but thought my eyes were lying to me," replied Toinette.

"An Englishman," said Jeems. "A murderer for money such as my Uncle Hepsibah told me about."

"And yet—he might be French."

They stood looking into each other's eyes, she of the aristocracy of Old France and he of the New World's freedom, and her hands rose slowly to his face as his bow and arrow fell to the floor. For the first time she raised her mouth to his.

"Kiss me, Jeems—and pray a little with me in gratitude for the mercy God has shown us!"

The thrill of her lips lay for a moment against his.

"I am sorry for everything in the world," she said.

Some of the softness and beauty of boyhood returned into his face as she drew herself from his arms and he descended the creaking stair ahead of her.

They did not go out at once, but stood near the lower door, listening for sound and watching for something to move, while Odd kept his eyes on the forested walls of the clearing. The sun rose higher, and before its devastating warmth the fragile structures of the frost builders crumbled away, fairy cities and kingdoms giving place to the more colourless blankets of autumn. Not until then did the earth seem to live again. A cheery group of chickadees settled among the bushes, and a red-squirrel's feet pattered across the roof of the house. The woodpecker was back at his old tree, hammering and digging to get at a grub. Odd moved and heaved a sigh as if he had begun to breathe freely once more, and when the throaty, chuckling song of the red-squirrel sounded over their heads, Jeems drew his gaze from the open.

"They are gone," he said. "But there may be stragglers behind, and it is safer not to show ourselves too soon."

It was easier for them to talk after this, speaking of death and ruin as though they had been made less terrible by the passing of time. So swiftly had events come into their lives that they seemed to have been living them through days and weeks instead of hours, and quite calmly, as if looking back on a distant thing, Toinette told Jeems of the tragedy of Tonteur Manor. Her mother, he learned, had left for Quebec two days preceding the coming of the Indians. Toinette expressed her thankfulness because of this, but no great gladness was in her voice. She could not remember in vivid details all that had happened it had been so sudden and overwhelming, like a stream of fire engulfing a black night. Peter Lubeck was with Dieskau, and Héloïse, his young wife, had come to stay with her. Both were asleep when the savages attacked in the early morning, and she was of the opinion that most of the killing was over before they were fairly awake—and before any guns were fired. Then came shots and her father's voice roaring through the big house. They were out of their bed when the seigneur came in and told them to dress and keep to their room. She did not know what had happened until she looked out of her window, and then she saw what seemed to be hundreds of naked savages running about. She rushed after her father, but he was gone. When she returned to her room, Héloïse had disappeared and she did not see her again. She could hear screaming and terrible cries, and dressing hurriedly, as her father had commanded, she disobeyed him by going downstairs, calling for him and for Héloïse. The front part of the house was filled with flame and smoke, and when she turned to the servants' quarters she was cut off by fire and there was no response to her cries. It was then she thought of the mill which she had often heard her father say was impregnable against both fire and guns. She descended into the cellar and went from it through a short underground passage to an outdoor *caveau* made of sod and stones, in which they kept fruit and vegetables during the winter. She hid herself in this earthy place, and then dared to raise the surface door a little. The worst must have been over, for she could see only a few Indians about, and everything was on fire. There was yelling in the distance where the savages were attacking the farmers' homes. When she ascended from the *caveau*, she stumbled over the body of old Babin, the miller, who had fallen with a musket in his hands. She took the musket and went to the mill, and after that she did not see an Indian about the seigneurie. Sickness overcame her, and she was half unconscious in the tower room. Later, looking through one of the narrow windows, she saw four men come from the south. She was sure they were white men, but was afraid to reveal herself because their appearance was so terrible. They were like monsters, remaining only a little while to look at the dead. Now, since she had seen the white warrior among the Mohawks, she was even more positive that they belonged to the war band and that she was fortunate to have kept herself concealed.[1] When she found that Babin's musket was loaded, she regretted that she had not used it to kill one of the murderers. That was why, mistaking him for another straggler, she had fired at Jeems.

One might have expected excitement in her narrative, but it was told quietly as she looked from Jeems across the clearing. It was a recital of fact without the embellishment of pathos or drama, and Jeems remained silent for a time when it was ended. Then he told of his visit to Lussan's and of his race home and what he found there. He spoke of Hepsibah.

"He must have discovered the Mohawks on the far

---

[1]Toinette must have been mistaken. These four men were undoubtedly the Black Hunter, David Rock, Peter Gagnon, and Carbanac, in their epic race against death to Grondin Manor, where their loved ones were. See *The Black Hunter*, published 1926.

side of the valley and started the fire which he had always told me to expect. After that, he tried to reach us and they killed him."

"He may have escaped," suggested Toinette hopefully.

Jeems shook his head.

"He would have come to us. He is dead."

His voice possessed the unemotional certainty with which she had referred to her father and Héloïse. There was no possibility of his uncle being alive. He repeated that belief, and added that their salvation was little short of a miracle. But now, he thought, their way would be clear to friends farther down the river. The Indians could not have gone many miles in that direction, for evidently they were hurrying back before Baron Dieskau learned of their presence in the French country and sent out forces to cut them off. It did not occur to Jeems that the baron and his men might have been defeated, as was true in that very hour.

He produced apples and a pair of purple-topped turnips from the provision pouch which he wore at his belt, and they ate these as they waited. Until the juice of the fruit was in his mouth, Jeems did not realize how long he had gone without food. He urged Toinette to eat, and without apparent desire she made a breakfast of her apple.

Meanwhile, he told her what they must do. Their trail led first through the old garden and past the barn, and then a few miles westward before they could safely turn to the north and east again. They would be forced to spend a night in the woods, but he was sure he could make a comfortable place for her. He was anxious about her light shoes, which were beginning to fall apart, and sometime during the day would reinforce them with moccasin hoods made from his leggings. Toinette was not disturbed by thought of physical discomfort. With a new light in her eyes, she listened to Jeems. It was pleasant to have him planning for her in this confident and masterful way.

He walked ahead instead of at her side when they began their journey. At the end of the tangled path they came to the thicket of briars and bushes which had grown up about the barn during the last six years, and Jeems wondered if Toinette were thinking of another day in that same place. He carried an arrow fixed to the string of his bow, and suddenly a twig caught it and it slipped from his fingers and fell to the ground. He was stooping to recover it when a terrified scream from Toinette brought him erect.

Not more than eight or ten paces from them stood a painted and half-naked savage whose intention had been to make his way toward the abandoned house. He was an appalling figure, and during the few seconds in which they faced each other Jeems recognized in him the white-skinned scalp hunter he and Toinette had seen with the Mohawks. At this discovery there shot through him a flash of relief, but a second glance showed him a fiend more dangerous than an Indian, one of the merciless butchers who hunted human hair for the price his own people had set upon it. *A blue-eyed Indian!* How often had he heard his uncle curse their breed! Beasts more cruel than tigers, demons set loose and paid by English money until their sport as well as their livelihood became an orgy of ambush, murder, rape, and fire! Here was one of them. The man was greased and painted, but he was white. His war-lock was light and his eyes were small and blue. He carried a gun, a knife, and a hatchet, and at his belt was a woman's hair, and with it another scalp that must have been taken from the head of a child.

So quickly did Jeems see these things that the echoes of Toinette's scream had scarcely died away before their meaning pressed itself upon him. The savage possessed a moment of advantage, and as Jeems made a movement to whip an arrow from his quiver, the scalp hunter swung his gun to fire. Seeing the hopelessness of his position, Jeems sprang forward and hurled his useless bow at his enemy. This and the impact of his body came at an instant when the other let the hammer of his flintlock fall, and with the explosion of the gun the lead from its barrel flew wild. The scalp hunter had seen only a boy and a girl, and a vision of easy victims had leapt to his mind. Now he found upon him an antago-nist of unexpected strength and ferocity. In the first few seconds of the fray, neither had a chance to draw knife or tomahawk, and with all the pent-up madness of his body and brain Jeems struck at his enemy and clutched his slippery throat as they crashed to earth together. In the struggle which ensued, the bushes broke under their bodies, and so swiftly did they change positions, choking and gouging as each endeavoured to keep his adversary from gaining a deadly weapon, that for a space Toinette's horror-filled eyes could scarcely tell which was one and which the other; and Odd, snarling white-fanged at their heels, was unable to become a partner in the conflict. Then, with a powerful effort, the scalp hunter freed himself and sprang to his feet, drawing his tomahawk in the act. As he prepared to use his weapon, Odd vaulted for his throat, and the blunt head of the hatchet met him in midair, striking with such force upon his head that he fell a limp and inert mass to the ground.

A cry of triumph came from the bleeding lips of the Frankenstein, who saw victory within his reach, for he now regarded the youth, who was on his feet with a hatchet in his hand, as an insignificant obstacle between himself and the pallid-faced loveliness of the girl whom chance had so fortunately placed in his way. This cry, disguised by guile and habit, betrayed only a trace of the white man. It was a guttural exultation of one lost to all the obligations of blood and race, a cry loosed not so much by heat and passion as by the promise of what he saw as his eyes appraised Toinette.

Toinette had possessed herself of the empty gun and stood at Jeems's side, prepared to fight.

Jeems was so near that his arm pressed against her and he gave a sidewise thrust which sent her headlong among the bushes. In this same movement he hurled his hatchet at the scalp hunter, who was slowly advancing. As the other dodged to avoid the hurtling missile Jeems snatched one of his scattered arrows from the ground and ran to his bow. Toinette saw what happened then. She saw the slim, beautiful figure of Jeems drawn as tensely as his weapon in the pathway. She saw the painted monster descending upon him. She heard the musical twang of the bowstring and saw a silvery flash —a flash which passed in at one side of the blue-eyed Indian and went out at the other, a flash which fell to earth a score of paces beyond, a bloody and broken arrow that had done its righteous work.

CHAPTER XIV

THAT the explosion of the gun would reach the ears of the Mohawks was in Jeems's mind as he comforted his shocked companion. For a few moments it was difficult for her to believe the combat was over and that the fiend who lay like a great spider on his back was no longer a menace to them. To her relief and her faith in Jeems was added an emotion of joy when she saw that Odd was alive. The dog had dragged himself to his feet and stood watching the slain man grimly.

Jeems picked up a number of arrows that had escaped injury in the fight. Then he hesitated, looking at the gun on the ground.

"My bow is better than that," he decided, answering the question in Toinette's eyes as he flung the rifle aside. "An arrow makes no sound and I have more confidence in it."

The dead man stared up at them as they passed. In their path lay the arrow which had gone cleanly through him. Toinette could not keep back the hysterical sob which came in her throat, but she looked at Jeems with such wonder and love in her face that he heard only the throbbing tumult in his heart and brain. He had fought for her and won! And he had fought on that same ground where almost six years before he had failed to whip Paul Tache!

"The Indians have heard the shot and will return," he said. "This white man must have discovered some sign of us and came to do murder and have his spoils alone. Dear God, when I think——"

He was looking at Toinette's tresses, which had burst free from their plaited bonds.

"We must run," he said.

They passed the barn and went through the deserted field behind it, Odd following them.

"There is a stony ridge less than a mile from here," he encouraged. "If we can reach it, I know of twenty places where bare rock will let us throw them off our trail."

"We will reach it," breathed Toinette.

He pointed the way and let her go ahead of him, turning his head every dozen steps to look behind.

Along the hardwood knoll where the Lussans had gathered their fuel, Toinette sped like a graceful nymph, her long hair streaming about her in the sun until at times Jeems saw nothing but its beauty; and in the contemplation of its loveliness a shuddering horror ran through him. In the stump field at home Hepsibah had told him how both the English and the French had begun to make use of women's hair, and that many a gentleman and courtly dandy wore shining curls taken by the scalping knife in wilderness orgies of rapine and murder. In the narrowness of Toinette's escape, the thought oppressed him with sickening force.

Soon her lack of endurance compelled them to slacken

their pace, and when they reached the rocky ascent which led to the crest of the ridge, Toinette's breath was breaking sobbingly from her lips and for a while she could go no farther. Her face did not betray the weakness of her body. Her cheeks were flushed. Her eyes were filled with a liquid flame, and her slender form seemed defiant of its frailty. She gazed in the direction from which they had come, unterrified, and almost with challenge in her look, her breast wildly throbbing, her hand reaching out to Jeems.

Each of the few minutes that passed seemed an hour to him.

Then they climbed to the crest of the ridge.

It was more than a ridge. It was a broken and flat-topped mountain of rock upheavals with bushes and scrub trees growing where pits of earth had gathered, a place so wild and twisted that to advance at more than a snail-like pace was a physically impossible thing to do. Here Jeems picked his way, choosing the places where their feet would not touch scattered stones or grass or soil, until half an hour of slow and tedious progress lay between them and the point where they had come from the valley. The ridge had widened, and on one side it extended in a plateau of rocky terrain which apparently had no end. Here was smoother and more facile travel, while, reaching southward, like a long and slender mammilla leaving the parent breast, was another ridge, narrower than the first and even more rugged and forbidding in its aspect. Jeems chose this least attractive way of flight.

"If they come this far, they will think we have taken

the wider and easier country," he explained. "Can you hold out a little longer?"

"It was the running that turned me faint," said Toinette. "I am as strong as you are now, Jeems. But may I stop to braid my hair? It is cumbrous and warm, and I wish you would cut it off!"

"I would cut off my arm first," declared Jeems. "We will be safe farther on, and if you will wait until we have put ourselves beyond that mass of rocks off there——"

His words remained unfinished. From behind them came a cry. It was neither loud nor very near, yet the still air bore it to them so clearly that the throat which made it might have been no more than the distance of a rifle shot away. The cry was not fierce nor one that seemed to carry menace, and bore with it a strange and almost musical softness. Jeems had heard White Eyes and Big Cat give this cry when they were hunting together, rolling the sound in the hollows of their hands until it carried for half a mile. And he knew its meaning now. The Mohawks were on the ridge. One of them was calling his scattered companions to evidence of their passing which he had discovered.

Jeems hastened Toinette over the rocks.

"They have found some sign of us," he explained. "It may be one of Odd's claw marks on a stone, or the scratch from a nail in your shoe. Whatever it is, they only know we have come this way and will still believe we have taken to the plain."

Toinette saw how desperately he was trying to keep from her the real nearness of their peril.

"I have seen Indians climb over rocks and windfalls. They are like cats—and I am so slow and clumsy," she said. "You can move faster than any Indian, Jeems. Hide me somewhere among these rocks—and go on alone. I am sure they will not harm me if they should happen to discover where I am."

Jeems did not answer. They had come to the rocks which he had observed a few moments before. It was a cairnlike pile tossed up in the play of neolithic giants, battered and worn by the ages until its sides were pitted with crypts and fissures, and about it lay the crumbling ruin of timeless disintegration. Here, if anywhere, was a place for concealment. It was filled with dark and cavernous refuges, and where the boulders met and crushed together were hidden pockets where their bodies might lie unseen. Toinette perceived these things with a heart that lightened with relief and hope. She looked into Jeems's face as he paused for a moment to study the ground about them.

A dozen steps from where they stood were three boulders apart from the others. They were small and unimportant and seemed to shrink like outcasts before the scowl of their mightier neighbours. One of the three had split itself so that one half of it was a slab that formed a roof for the crevice between the other two. An animal would not have sought refuge there. Instinct and experience would have directed it to the larger pile.

Jeems's eyes revealed a deeper excitement as he pointed it out to Toinette.

"We will hide—and in there!" he cried. "Make haste,

Toinette! It is smooth rock and will leave no sign behind us. Go in and keep Odd with you!"

He began to throw loose stones about the huge boulder heap. Some he flung over the top of it so that they fell on the opposite side, and at last he sent a few into the edge of the valley, each farther than the other. He finished by shooting an arrow which descended in an open space at the foot of the ridge.

Toinette watched him in amazement and alarm until he commanded her in a sterner voice to crawl quickly under the stones. She waited no longer but pulled herself a few inches at a time beneath the boulders. Jeems, thrusting Odd ahead of him, had greater difficulty in performing this same feat, and for a little while they squirmed and twisted until they found a dark recess in which they could crowd themselves and even sit upright. This was a good fortune which Jeems had not expected, and jubilantly he explained to Toinette the meaning of his strange behaviour outside.

"First they will find the loose stones and the marks I made and search for us in every hole and cranny of the pile," he said. "When they discover the arrow I hope they will believe we have fled into the forest. If they come this far, I doubt they will look under these stones, and if that should happen, they cannot see us unless one of them takes a notion to crawl in."

They waited in a silence wherein the beating of their hearts was like the sound of tiny drums in the gloom of their hiding place. A shaft of light came through a narrow crevice between the rocks, but this fell short of the pocket which concealed them. Odd heaved a deep sigh to relieve the tension of his body. After this, his eyes stared at the gleam of light, but he lay as still as death.

A shudder ran through Toinette, but she whispered: "I am not afraid."

She felt Jeems fumbling for his hatchet and heard him place it quietly on the naked rock at his side.

Then the rock itself seemed to give forth a faint sound as if someone had tapped it gently with a stick.

This sound grew into others that were soft and swift, and Jeems knew that moccasined feet were all about them. Low voices added themselves to the pattering tread. Then came a louder voice, and there followed a sudden movement of unseen bodies and a storm of guttural, low-toned exclamations giving vent to freshly stirred excitement. Toinette understood what was happening a few yards away. The Indians had found the signs Jeems had made and were searching in and about the upheaval of rock. She fixed her eyes on the crack through which came the shaft of light, and occasionally it was darkened as a body passed it. The tread of feet came and went, and they heard the clatter of rocks. But for a time all voices died away, and it was this silence which became almost unbearable for Toinette. Shouts and yells were human and implied fleshly limitations, while the movement near her, unearthly in its repression of noise, was that of tongueless beings whom she could imagine were *smelling* them out like hungry wolves. This clutch of a danger which they could not see or cope with seized upon her until each moment she expected to hear a ghostly creature stealing into their hiding place or to see a pair of flaming eyes on a level with her own. It was a feeling of horror instead of fear, and with it came a strong desire to cry out and ease her suspense in a scream. She heard Jeems whispering to her, but did not sense his words as she fought with what she believed to be her cowardice.

He, too, had almost found himself in the grip of something which he could not control. Not more than a quarter of an hour passed in this suspense, but it seemed to be a lifetime. Then there were voices again which increased in number and excitement until, above them all, a yell rose from the valley as one of the searchers discovered the arrow.

When Toinette raised her head, she heard no evidence of life other than their own on the ridge. Odd breathed deeply, as if his lungs had been on the point of bursting.

"Thank God, they think we have gone into the valley!" said Jeems.

Toinette touched him with a cautioning hand, and in the same moment he was aware of the sound her ears had caught! Someone was near the rock! More than one—there were two! Their voices were distinct though low, and they stood so close that their forms shut out the light from the crevice. To his astonishment Jeems heard a language which Hepsibah Adams had taught him, and it was not Mohawk. Surely none but a Mohawk had left a track in Lussan's clearing except the white-skinned prisoners and the dead scalp hunter, yet these were Senecas. The discovery thrilled him. He hated the Mohawk hatchet wielders who were the scourge of the southern frontier, but the Senecas, also brethren of the Six Great Nations, he doubly feared, for while the Mohawk killers were the wolves of the wilderness, the Senecas were its foxes and panthers combined. One was a creature of darkness and surprise, the other a lightning flash that came and went with deadly swiftness. He might trick a Mohawk, but a Seneca was the cleverest of his kind.

He felt his blood turn cold as he listened to the two. One was arguing that the arrow was a ruse and that the fugitives were somewhere not far away; the other, whose mind was still on the huge pile of stones, discredited the thought that it had been thoroughly searched and set off to find some proof of his suspicions. The first of the two speakers remained, and neither Toinette nor Jeems could hear him move. For a space the thought possessed Toinette that the savage had placed his ear against the rock and was listening to the beating of their hearts, or that he was looking in through the narrow crack, piercing the gloom of their concealment with gloating eyes. It seemed an infinity of time before movement came again outside the rock. Metal scraped it as the Seneca made a resting place of it for his gun; footsteps went away, returned, and halted close to the narrow aperture through which they had squeezed their bodies under the stones. Jeems held his breath that he might catch the slightest break in the stillness.

The savage was looking at the entrance to their hiding place! He pictured the warrior, his doubt and hesitation, and was as sure in his visioning as though no barrier lay between them. He heard a grunt. The Seneca was on his stomach, peering in, and the grunt was an expression of the foolishness which had made him grovel like this. In a moment, he would rise and go away. But the moment passed. One—two—three—a dozen. Toinette was like one dead—unbreathing. Odd, sensing a mighty danger, knowing that it was coming, crouched like a sphinx. The hush held substance, a physical thing that pressed against their flesh. It possessed the weight of death.

At last it was broken so softly that the disturbance might have been that of a tress of Toinette's hair falling from her shoulder across Jeems's arm. The Indian had thrust in his head. He was listening—*smelling*—then advancing slyly and cautiously like a ferret on the trail of prey. There could no longer be a doubt. He knew there was something under the rocks and, with true Seneca courage, foreseeing glory for himself even if death paid for it, he was coming alone. With the same philosophy he had reasoned that if it were only an animal he had smelled, a fox, a young bear, a fat badger, there would be none to laugh at him for the trouble he had taken.

He must have been larger than Jeems, for he began to advance with difficulty. His body scraped the sides of the little tunnel. His hatchet made a clinking sound on the stone as he thrust it ahead of him a few inches at a time. His breathing became unrestrained. Evidently the handicaps of his procedure were convincing him that nothing more dangerous than a creature of hair and claws had lured him in.

Every instinct reached its highest tension in Jeems as a danger approached which he would be able to touch with his hands in another moment or two. He removed himself gently from Toinette's embrace and prepared his arms and body for action. Their eyes had grown more accustomed to the gloom, and Toinette could see him as he crouched forward and gathered himself for the struggle which would mean life or death for them. Suddenly she understood that it would not be a struggle. When the Seneca's head appeared Jeems's hatchet would smash it in. She could see the hatchet. It was poised to strike. There would be no cry—no moan— only that terrible, hidden sound. She listened to the doomed man slowly coming.

His progress was easier now. The cavity grew larger and he grunted his approval. There was something of humour in the guttural chuckling with which he continued his invasion. A dog and a badger smell alike. A warrior, painted, with three feathers in his tuft, crawling for a badger! That must have been his thought.

The feathers appeared first, then the long black scalp lock, the hair-plucked head, a pair of shoulders. Jeems put all his strength behind the upraised hatchet. He knew there must be but one blow—well-placed in the middle of the skull. That would end it. He almost closed his eyes and the hatchet descended a little, an overwhelming sense of the horror of the thing holding back his stroke. It was not simply killing: it was murder. The Seneca turned his head and looked up. His eyes were trained for use at night, and he saw more clearly than Jeems. He saw the white face, the hatchet, the death behind it, and he waited, transformed to stone. No voice came to his lips and no movement to his cramped body in this moment of shock and stupefaction when he must have realized that all the power of his forest gods could not help him. The pupils of his eyes glowed darkly. He did not breathe. Conscious of his impending end, he was amazed but not terrified. His fine countenance did not shrink from the steel about to sink into his brain. He gave a gasp of wonderment as he realized how surely he was caught.

For a second more the blade did not fall, and in that second Jeems's eyes and those of the savage met steadily. Then the hatchet clattered to the rock floor, and with a protest of revulsion at what he had almost done, Jeems clutched at the Seneca's throat. The Indian was at a disadvantage, and though his powerful body strained and fought to loosen the choking grip, his position was so hopeless that in a short time he was limp and unconscious.

The Seneca's adventure, and the combat—if it could be distinguished by that name—had not terminated a moment too soon for those concealed under the rocks. The trail hunters were now aware that the placing of the arrow had been a ruse to delay them and began swarming back to the ridge. Half a dozen warriors gathered in a fierce and animated debate close about the rocks.

Back in his corner, Odd had struggled to understand and obey the discipline of his master. Years of comradeship and training had given to him a knowledge of silence and its value, and though he had yearned to confront the invading savage and afterward to join in the struggle with Jeems, he had not moved from the watchful position he had occupied at the beginning. If Toinette's nerves were on the point of breaking, then Odd's were in no better condition when the Senecas returned to the ridge. A hundred generations of carnivorous fighting blood were at work in the dog's body. His eyes had grown green and red in the gloom until they were pools of living flame; his teeth were bare; his jaws clicked at times like castanets, his heart was breaking in its subjection to inactivity and stillness. Now he looked again on victory. His master was triumphant as the Indians returned and crowded about the rocks. Defiance rose in his soul in an overwhelming flood. He hated the smell outside. He hated the creatures who made it. Without warning, his passion broke loose in the howling rage of a beast gone mad. Toinette's arms and Jeems's hands were futile in their efforts to stop it.

The Seneca on the stone floor moved a little.

Outside there fell an awful stillness.

Then Odd realized what he had done and grew quiet. They could feel rather than hear a velvet-footed, voiceless cordon gathering about them in a ring of death.

The warrior on the floor opened his eyes. His ear was close to the rock, and he could hear the footfalls which were scarcely louder than the sound of leaves falling to earth from a tall tree. So near to him that he could have touched them he saw the woman with the long hair and the man who had throttled him, white-faced, in each other's arms. He closed his eyes, feigning unconsciousness. But his fingers crept over the stone floor with the stealth of a serpent until they found the hatchet which the white-faced man had dropped.

CHAPTER XV

TWENTY minutes after Odd had revealed their hiding place Jeems and Toinette were standing in the sun. Mysterious things had happened in this time. Unseen hands had dragged the warrior from under the rocks. An interval had followed in which excitement gave way to solemn and low-voiced talk outside. Then someone had called in guttural, broken French commanding them to come out. They had obeyed, Jeems first, Toinette after him, and Odd last with the downcast air of a beast who knew he was in disgrace.

It was an astounding and unexpected reception by enemies at whose belts scalps were hanging. There were between twenty and thirty of the Senecas, splendidly built, keen-eyed, lean-faced, most of them young men. Even in the shock of the moment, Toinette surveyed them in startled admiration. They were like runners ready for a race. They were not painted as the Mohawks had been, and were less naked. Staring at the youth with his bow and at the girl with her tangled, shining hair, the Indians returned their gaze with a look of amazement not unmixed with approval. They seemed scarcely able to believe these two had fooled them so completely, capturing one of their number in the bargain, yet conceded the fact with glances in which passion was held subdued.

A young savage who stood before them seemed largely responsible for this attitude. Purplish lines were around his throat as if a rope had choked him. Two of the eagle feathers in his tuft were broken, and his shoulder was bleeding where the skin had been torn by a jagged tooth of rock. His eyes were as piercing as those of the bird he had robbed for his plume, and evidently he held considerable influence in the war party of which he was a member. Beside him was a much older man of even more powerful figure with a face scarred and cut until it bore an unalterable expression of ferocity.

It was he who spoke in Seneca to the younger.

"So this is the boy who made my brave nephew a captive to be saved by the voice of a dog!"

The other scowled at the taunt in his voice.

"He could have killed me. He spared my life."

"This is the young he-fawn to whom you owe a feather from your tuft!"

"I owe him two—one for himself and one for the maiden whose presence must have stayed his hand."

The older man grunted.

"He looks strong and may stand to travel with us. But the girl is like a broken flower ready to fall in our path. She will cumber our feet and make our way more difficult, and great haste must be our choice. Use your hatchet on one and we will take the other."

At this command Jeems gave a sudden cry, and the faces of the savages again relaxed in astonishment when he began to speak in their language. Hepsibah Adams's schooling and the comradeship of White Eyes and Big

Cat had prepared him for this hour. His tongue stumbled, some of his words were twisted, there were gaps which only the imagination could fill, but he told his story. The Indians listened with an interest which assured Jeems they had not been a part of the force that had massacred his and Toinette's people. He pointed to the girl. He related how the Mohawks had destroyed his father and mother and all who had belonged to Toinette; how they had fled together, how they had hidden in the old house, and that with an arrow he had killed the white man who had fired the gun. He was pleading for Toinette as he had once heard Big Cat plead with his father for the life of a dog that had gone lame. He bared his breast, even as the Indian boy had offered his own with the demand that his father strike there before robbing him of the comradeship of his four-footed friend. Bronzed and dishevelled, the long bow in his hand, Jeems made a vivid picture of courage and eloquence that would remain with Toinette as long as she lived. She drew herself up a little proudly, sensing that he was fighting for her. She stood straight, her chin high, gazing with unafraid eyes at the leader of the war party.

With the courtesy which Tiaoga had already established for himself in borderland history, the chieftain listened attentively, piecing the story together where Jeems's verbal powers were at fault, and when the youth had finished, he spoke words which sent two of his men running down the ridge in the direction of Lussan's place. Then he asked questions which let Jeems know the Senecas had not gone as far as Lussan's, but that they had heard the gun, and in seeking for the one who had fired it, had stumbled upon their trail in the hard-wood slope half a mile from the abandoned house. When he spoke of the Mohawks, Tiaoga's ugly face grew darker, and behind this look Jeems saw the blaze of an age-old Seneca hatred and jealousy of the Mohawk, though both were of the same powerful confederacy. That Jeems and Toinette had been sufferers at the hands of these eastern rivals seemed to be a small point in their favour.

When his brief questioning was over, Tiaoga turned his attention once more to the young man beside him.

"I think the boy is a great liar, and I have sent back for proof of it," he said. "If he has not sped an arrow through this friend of the Mohawks, as he claims, he shall die. If he has spoken the truth in the matter, which will be proof that he has spoken it in others, he may travel with us, and his companion also, until her feet tire so that death is necessary to bring her rest." Then he spoke to Toinette in the broken French with which he had called under the rocks. "If you cannot keep up with us we shall kill you," he said.

Toinette began to prepare herself for the ordeal, braiding her hair swiftly. Jeems came to her, and she saw the torture of doubt in his eyes.

"I can do it, Jeems," she cried softly. "I know what you were saying and what they were thinking, and I can do it. I *will* do it! I am going to live—with you. I love you so much that nothing can kill me, Jeems—not even their tomahawks!"

The tall young warrior approached. He at least was one friend among the many who stood about them.

"I am Shindas," he said. "We are going to a far town—a long way. It is Chenufsio. There are many leagues of forests, of hills, of swamps between us and it. I am your friend because you have been a brother and allowed me to live, and I owe you two feathers from my tuft. I brought your hatchet from under the rocks because I did not want you to strike and be killed in turn. You love the white maiden. I, too, love a maiden."

The Seneca's words brought to Jeems not only hope but shock. These savages were from Chenufsio, *the Hidden Town*—a place which even the adventurous Hepsibah Adams had looked upon as in another world, a goal which he had dreamed of reaching in some day of reckless daring. Hidden Town! The heart and soul and mysterious Secret Place of the Seneca nation! It was a vast distance away, first beyond the country of the Oneidas, then the Onondagas, and then the Cayugas. A land which touched Lake Ontario on one side and Lake Erie on the other, with the Great Falls of which he had heard roaring between the two. His uncle had once said, "You must be a strong man before you can travel to it. That is why the Senecas, who range far, are the finest of all two-legged beasts."

Shindas spoke again.

"Tiaoga, my uncle, who is a great captain, is not as bad as he looks. A Mohawk cut him like that in a quarrel over a game of ball when he was a boy. But he will keep his word. He will kill the little fawn who is with you if her limbs fail her."

Jeems looked from his friend to Toinette. She had approached the fierce old warrior and was smiling into his face, her eyes aglow with confidence as she pointed to her ragged shoes. For a moment Tiaoga repulsed her advance with stoical indifference. Then his eyes shifted to her feet. But he revealed no evidence of an intention to better their condition as he turned his back on her and gave a command which quickly put a prisoner's thong of buckskin around Jeems's neck and relieved him of his bow.

Down into the valley and through the forest the long, grim march began.

Something had been said to Shindas as they gathered for the trail, and when the two runners overtook them from Lussan's place and Tiaoga paused with his band to hear their story, the young Seneca gave to Jeems a pair of moccasins which he had taken from the bundle at his side. Jeems knelt at Toinette's feet with these clumsily large but more dependable travelling gear.

The two braves had returned with the white man's scalp and the broken arrow that had killed him. They talked excitedly, and Toinette could understand by their actions the story they were telling. It was the portrayal of a desperate struggle between their prisoner and the white-skinned Mohawk. They measured the difference in their weight and size. One of them seized Toinette's discarded shoe and pointed to its heel as another evidence of the truth of Jeems's words, and as a final argument the broken arrow was compared with its fellows in the quiver. Tiaoga's rocklike countenance changed slightly, and he regarded Jeems's bow with new interest. It was not an unusual bow, and again he expressed his doubt that a white vouth could send a shaft through the thickness of a man with it. He strung the weapon and fitted it, then turned to Shindas.

"Let him show us what he can do, Broken Feather," he said, still taunting his nephew for the disgrace which had befallen his war tuft. "You, who are so proud of your skill, shoot with him!"

Jeems had risen from his task of binding the oversized moccasins about Toinette's small feet and took the bow which Shindas proffered him. Then he swung his quiver over his shoulder so that other arrows would be ready and looked about him for a mark. Toinette saw the colour creeping into his cheeks, and she cried out to him with pride and encouragement. He was not afraid of this test, for even Captain Pipe, who could vanquish his sons, had been slower than he in flashing arrows from quiver to bow and sending them to their mark like a flight of swift birds. He pointed to a fire-blackened stub six feet high not less than a hundred and fifty yards away and fired a shaft which fell twenty paces short. Thus measuring the distance and finding his point of aim, he sent four other arrows, one after another, so swiftly that the first gray streak had scarcely thrown a cloud of black char from the top of the stub before his final shaft had left the bowstring. Two of the arrows struck the stub, a third shattered itself against a rock at its base, and the fourth whistled past it waist-high and a foot to the right, in which direction the wind was blowing.

It was Toinette who gave a glad cry as she looked at the unperturbed face of the Seneca chief. When he turned, he gazed at her and not at the one who had done the shooting, and found her smiling at him again in such a fearless and amiable way, as if she already counted him her friend, that he turned to Shindas with a leer, which, under other conditions, would have covered nothing short of murder.

"You need not shoot, Broken Feather," he exclaimed. "You are beaten before you start, and I would not see you more deeply disgraced. This youth will make a Seneca who will more than equal you. He shall go with us, and in turn for his brotherhood, we will take the maiden to fill the place of Silver Heels in my tepee. See that he is given the scalp which is his that he may have a feather in his tuft when we arrive." Then he spoke to Jeems: "You hear! Gather your arrows and keep them for an enemy of the Senecas!" Then to Toinette: "You are Silver Heels. She was my daughter. She is dead."

No flash of emotion, no softening of his features, no sign of friendship crossed the chieftain's countenance. He turned and put himself at the head of his band, huge among his men, a monster to look at because of the ferocity of his mutilated face, yet with the dignity of a king in his bearing. Without a sound of voice the warriors leapt to their positions. Two ran ahead like hounds to make the trail safe, two fell behind to watch the rear, and on each side an outrunner disappeared. Shindas sped aside to recover the arrows while one of the braves who had gone to Lussan's fastened the white man's scalp at Jeems's belt in spite of his protest and abhorrence.

Once more the westward march resumed its way—

a single file of soft-footed, noiseless men with a girl midway in their line—a girl whose long dark braid gleamed in the shafts of the sun, whose cheeks were flushed, and whose eyes held something more than the depths of tragedy and grief as she looked ahead to the great adventure, and heard behind her the tread of a dog and the steps of the man she loved.

CHAPTER XVI

TOINETTE was not astonished that her fear was gone or that her anguish because of the loss of her father was relieved. Her emotion was that of one upon whom events had pressed themselves as necessary and predestined in a struggle which had been intended for Jeems and her. It was a fight put on her shoulders in place of a burden of grief, and she was not afraid. The savages no longer frightened her, though at least half of them carried in their belts the little hoops of hickory or alder on which were stretched the still undried trophies of their success on the warpath. Something in their appearance began to give her confidence: the lithe grace of their bodies, the sinewy strength of their shoulders, the proud and listening poise of their heads, the animal-like smoothness with which they sped over the earth. *And Jeems was like these forest men!* It was this wild beauty and freedom in him that she had loved from the beginning, and which, because of its effect upon her, she had tried to force herself to hate. That she had made this effort seemed impossible now, for she realized that she had loved him since the day his face had gone so silently white at Paul Tache's insult in the bottom land.

She travelled easily in her moccasins. She was not as fragile as Jeems had thought when she had tried to keep up with him in her high-heeled shoes. Her slim body was strong and supple, her eyes quick, her feet sure. Shindas dropped back from man to man to see that all was well, and his eyes gleamed with satisfaction when he measured how lightly Toinette was following those ahead of her. He fell in close to Jeems, and the two talked in low tones. Even Odd seemed to have changed now that he was a part of those whom he had mistrusted and feared all his life. Shindas liked the limping beast, and twice he laid a brown hand on the dog's head. A bit at a time Jeems heard strange things from Shindas's lips and was anxious for an opportunity to tell Toinette of the young warrior's confidences.

To an observer, the passing of the Senecas would have revealed no sign of peace or mercy. Even the quietness of their dress added to the deadliness of their appearance. They were not painted in black and red and blue like most savages on the warpath, but had unadorned skins coloured only by the sun and the weather. They were not naked and did not wear rings of brass wire in their ears. Each had two bundles at his side, in the smaller of which was food and in the larger a beaverskin blanket. Some carried hickory bows, and all had guns and hatchets. That it was a force chosen with care for a long and dangerous mission, there could be no doubt, and that it had met with success was equally certain. There were twenty-six scalps among its warriors, which was triumph in ample measure. Eighteen of these had been taken from men, five from women, and three from children.

At the head of the sinister line, Tiaoga stalked like a panther, and wherever the trail turned sharply, Toinette caught a glimpse of his face, in which unhappiness and cruelty seemed to have settled permanently. But the sight of his countenance did not chill her. Twice Tiaoga's eyes rested on her during the first few miles of travel, and twice she smiled at him and once waved her hand in cheery greeting.

She was not afraid, though she could not account for her feeling of security. She was not only unafraid of Tiaoga, but there was something she liked about the man whom others would have regarded as a monster. She was sure he would not kill her. She spoke this conviction to Jeems when he was at her side. But Shindas had said to him, "I have greater hope, for she travels lightly and well. She must keep up. If she fails, Tiaoga will kill her even though he has chosen her to take the place of Silver Heels."

The Indians had been travelling since dawn, and at noon they stopped for their first meal of the day. It was the simple repast of a strong breed of men who were never heavy eaters except at occasional feast times, and who ascribed their endurance to this fact. "Those of my braves who eat much will fight little," was the warning of Cornplanter to his powerful nation, and for centuries nature had been fitting the Indian stomach to the exacting necessities of a life where food sobriety was the great law of existence.[1] From his

---

[1] Indians were not gourmands as so many fictionists and careless historians have led us to believe. Careful research proves them to have been, until degenerated by the white man, a race from whose abstemiousness modern civilization might gain many good lessons. It is interesting to note that they were largely vegetarians whose subsistence was made up exclusively for long periods of time of fruits, nuts, roots, and the products of their own fields.

provision pouch each warrior filled the hollow of one hand with coarsely crushed whole-corn meal mixed with pea meal and a flavour of dried berry, which he ate slowly until the last crumb was gone. Toinette, whose border home had known the luxuries of civilization since she could remember, was moved by this scant fare of the warriors to offer Shindas one of the two apples which Jeems had placed in her lap. Shindas said something to Jeems, who translated his words by saying, "Shindas thanks you, Toinette, but he says that if he eats more he will not be able to travel comfortably."

Toinette kept from Jeems the fact that she was growing tired and that sharp pains had begun to shoot like needles through the overtaxed muscles of her limbs. She ate an apple and half of a turnip, and Jeems brought her water in a birchbark cup from the cold stream beside which they had stopped.

After Shindas had gone, he told her of the amazing adventure ahead of them. They were going to Chenufsio, which Shindas had said was three hundred miles westward as the crow would fly. He concealed his fear for her as he talked. Chenufsio, he explained, was the mystery place of the wilderness, the Hidden Town to which the Senecas had been taking white prisoners for generations. One of his Uncle Hepsibah's dreams had been to reach it, and twice he had failed. But his uncle knew what the place was like and they had talked about it for hours. Many white children must have grown up there with the savages, becoming savages themselves. Some day the governors of the Colonies would send an army of soldiers to free them. One of his own hopes had been to

visit this barbaric town, and now it seemed inconceivable that the thing was actually happening. He
then spoke of the fortunate circumstance which had
saved them. A white woman had come to Chenufsio as a
prisoner when Shindas was a boy. She had carried her
baby all the way through the forests, and it was this
baby, now a beautiful maiden, whom Shindas loved.
Inspired by this love, Shindas had spoken in their
favour outside the rocks and had asked that their lives
be spared by his uncle, whose daughter, a girl of
Toinette's age, had drowned while swimming in a deep
pool only six months before. Tiaoga, whose wife was
dead and who had no other children, had worshipped
Silver Heels and had spared Toinette's life with the
intention of giving her his daughter's place in his tepee.

Jeems assured her this meant safety for them both.

He did not tell her the darker news he had learned—
that there had been a great slaughter of the French
under Baron Dieskau and that the southern frontier
lay at the mercy of Sir William Johnson and his hordes
of savages.

Nor did he tell her that because of trouble with a
band of Mohawks, three of whose number had been
left dead in a personal quarrel, Tiaoga planned to reach
the Seneca stronghold in six days and nights.

He was heavy with doubt when the march was resumed, for he saw the bitter souls hidden in the breasts
of the warriors. Hepsibah Adams had made him see the
truth, and he knew these men owed nothing to the
people of his race except loss and shame. Many times

he had thought that, if fate had placed his fortunes among them, he would have hated with the grimness of their hatred. The freedom and pride which were once the heritage of their wide domains were no longer the controlling factors in their existence. Their wars had ceased to be wars which gave birth to forest gods and epics of unforgettable heroism. Their star was setting, and with its decline the white man had transformed them into common killers, and in this new calling it made small difference to them whether they slew enemies or those who posed as friends, as long as the skins were white. So the nobility which Toinette saw in their captors was poisoned for Jeems by what was concealed within their hearts. The greatest of all hates was not the hate of a man for a man, but the hate of a race for a race, and he knew that at a word from Tiaoga the men about him would be turned into fiends. Most of all he feared Tiaoga, for Shindas had told him that Tiaoga's father had been killed by a white man and his son by an English Mohawk.

Whatever their fate was to be, this day would bring it. He was sure Toinette could not keep up the pace much longer, and he strengthened himself for the moment when the Seneca chief would find himself compelled to give a decision. That Tiaoga had claimed her for his daughter gave him hope, but if in her frailty Toinette was condemned to die, he was determined that she should not die alone.

Shindas, whose place in the line was close behind his uncle, had more than one evidence that Tiaoga was pondering over the dilemma in which the presence of the girl had placed him, and his mind was not more clearly settled in the matter than Jeems's. When it was possible for him to speak to Tiaoga without being overheard, he referred subtly to the prisoner's gentleness and beauty and to her resemblance to Silver Heels. With sly artfulness he drew a picture of his uncle's lonely tepee again bright with laughter and happiness, and persisted until Tiaoga commanded him to hold his tongue. It was not long afterward that the warriors observed Tiaoga limping slightly. This sign of physical difficulty increased in his walk until, furious because of his weakness, he drove his hatchet head-deep into a tree and paused to bind a piece of buckskin tightly about the ankle he had wrenched. Shindas felt something lacking in this rage of a man who had suffered every hurt that flesh could bear, yet he was not certain and helped Tiaoga with the offending joint. Progress was slower after this. It continued to slacken as the afternoon waned, until the hand of a spiritual guidance seemed to be working for Toinette. It was useless to attempt a concealment of her condition. Her strength was gone. Her body was racked as if it had been beaten. Another mile and she would have sunk to the ground, glad to have an end to her torture. But fate, and Tiaoga's hurt, intervened to save her. They came at last to a hardwood plain in which was a pigeon roost. It was this roost, where thousands of birds would come at sunset, that brought the Seneca to another pause. His warriors did not doubt he was in pain but were puzzled that he should reveal it.

He spoke to Shindas.

"We have been a long time without meat, Broken Feather. In a few hours there will be plenty here. We will feast and then sleep and will not travel again until morning."

Then Shindas knew the truth, but his countenance did not change.

He soon had a chance to speak to Jeems.

"For the first time I have discovered my uncle to be a great liar," he said. "His ankle is as sound as mine. It is for the little fawn he has pretended a hurt and stops here for meat. She is safe. He will not kill her."

When Jeems translated this Toinette bowed her head and cried softly. Tiaoga saw her. Crumpled on the ground with Jeems's arm around her, she looked like Silver Heels whose beautiful body had been brought from the pool with her long black braid falling over her shoulder. No one was conscious of the strain at his heart as he came toward her. Warriors, wide-eyed, saw that he did not limp, and in his attitude was a tigrish defiance of what they might think. He paused before the girl and dropped his beaverskin blanket at her feet. Toinette looked up through tears and smiled again as a strange softness stole over the savage face. She held up a hand as though it had been Jeems or her father who stood there. But Tiaoga did not seem to notice it. He gazed at her steadily, as if he were seeing a spirit, and said:

"Shindas is right. The soul of Soi Yan Makwun has come to abide in you!"

Soi Yan Makwun was Silver Heels.

Tiaoga turned away, and his warriors knew that his decision had been made. There would be no haste after this in the direction of Hidden Town.

On a couch made of the beaverskin and armsful of balsam boughs which Jeems had carried from the creek-bottom, Toinette rested while the Indians prepared for the evening feast. She smoothed and rebraided her hair as she watched them, and although every bone in her body seemed to have an ache of its own, she felt a sensation of complete relaxation stealing over her for the first time since the tragedy at Tonteur Manor. She had no desire to sleep, but only to rest without moving, realizing in this way the full reaction from the strain which had been imposed upon her. There was something in the movements of the young warriors which added to her peculiar serenity of mind. They were like housewives at work, making ready to light half a dozen small fires of dry, smokeless wood; cutting and peeling the bark from innumerable sticks about the size of arrows on which pigeons would be spitted and roasted; making receptacles of bark; bringing stones to be heated for the boiling and baking of wild artichokes and yellow pond-lily roots, laughing and talking in low voices until the thought faded from her mind that they were killers whose hands were red from recent slaughter. This mental ease which came to soften her environment embraced her in such a stealthy way that she was unconscious of the moment when her eyes closed in complete surrender to the exhaustion which was claiming her.

The Seneca camp was some distance from the pigeon

roost because of the unpleasant odour which rose from it, but it was within easy vision, and Jeems could see the birds arriving before the sun was down. At first they came in small flocks which increased in size as evening approached until the swarming of wings above the roost formed an undulating cloud half a mile square. Not until it was totally dark did a dozen of the Indians leave for the kill, some with pitchwood torches still unlighted and others with long poles to be employed in knocking the birds from the lower branches of the trees. Jeems was not commanded to accompany the hunters, and with a feeling of relief he saw the last of their number depart. Later he caught the flash of moving tongues of flame in the forest, and it seemed less than half an hour afterward that the savages returned with their feathered meat. The bodies of the pigeons which had been swept from their sleeping places were piled within the circle of the six small fires.

Odd had attached himself in no uncertain way to Toinette since their capture, his loyalty to Jeems being not only divided but strongly in her favour. It would be unwise to assume that her greater frailty and her dependence upon the enemies who so completely encompassed them were in any way responsible for this change in his attitude, but that the change had occurred and was marked by an extreme devotion was apparent to them both. He lay at her side while she slept, watching with tireless eyes the activities of the savages about the fires. He did not move when the aroma of roasting flesh came to his nostrils, though he had fasted long and his stomach was empty. Not until

Jeems returned from one of the fires bearing a stick on which a dozen of the cooked pigeons were spitted could the dog be induced to move a little from his position so that he might eat.

Jeems did not awaken Toinette, but after he had finished his meal, he broiled another dozen of the pigeons until they were as brown as chestnuts and stored them away with a roasted lily root and a few artichokes.

For two hours the cooking continued, and when it was finished, with the night's kill ready for future use, Tiaoga's warriors wrapped themselves in their blankets and lay down to sleep. Jeems was amazed that men who indulged in the extreme of every physical act should practise such temperateness in the employment of their food. It seemed to him Tiaoga had scarcely eaten, while he—with his stomach trained by the gormandizing habits of culture and education—had disposed of six of the tender birds.

The camp was soon in silence, and for a long time Jeems sat meditating upon the changes which had come into his life within the space of two days and nights. No spark of the fires was left burning by the cautious Indians, but he could see his companion's face pillowed on her arm. He rejoiced that she slept, for these were hours in which time seemed to shorten itself, and anguish pressed upon him. That everything was gone and that they were the only ones left of those who had so recently made up their world seemed a monstrous exaggeration of fact. Toinette, sleeping quietly, forced the truth upon him, and from the racking visions of his thoughts he turned to her with a yearning to hold her closely in his arms. Her face was of childlike loveliness in the glow of the stars. Her hair lay upon her pale forehead and against her throat in a frame of jet which accentuated the exquisite fairness of her skin. So complete was her fatigue that dark dreams did not mar the solace of her unconsciousness. The spirit of the peace which had come to her crept into Jeems, and as the stillness grew deeper a sense of great possession filled him. When the night was half gone, he made a pillow of balsams, and before he fell asleep he drew Toinette's hand to him gently and pressed his lips against it. After that Odd watched the shadows and the burning out of the stars.

Dawn, another day, then night again. One after another they came and went in Tiaoga's march through the western wilderness. There was no haste now. In her first dawn in a Seneca camp Toinette had opened her eyes to see a tall dark form standing over her. It was Tiaoga. He saw her hand against the lips of the sleeping youth. She looked up at him starry-eyed. Tiaoga grunted and turned away. After this his guardianship was that of a hawk over its young, yet he did not display it, and seldom voiced his wishes or his thoughts except in low, terse words to Shindas. The journey was no longer impossible for Toinette. When she neared exhaustion, camp was made, and when she awoke the march was resumed. Tiaoga called her Soi Yan Makwun, and the warriors regarded her with kindlier eyes. As the days continued and they witnessed her courage, their hearts grew warm toward her, and at times their glances revealed an admiration and friendliness which were never in Tiaoga's.

These days served also as the bridge across which Jeems and Toinette were passing into a future that was all their own, and the poignancy of the loss they had suffered was mellowed by these newer aspects so vital to themselves. The world they had known was a fabric which had crashed in ruin about them—a desolation out of which another existence was building itself. As the deeper solitudes of the wilderness claimed them, this feeling became a bond which nothing could break. Wherever they went and whatever happened, they would belong to each other, for death might separate but it could not destroy.

On the fourteenth day, Tiaoga sent a messenger ahead. That evening he sat on the ground near Toinette, and Jeems translated what he said. He smoked dry sumach leaves in a long pipe, interrupting himself to speak in tones that were sometimes like the growls of an animal. To-morrow they would reach Hidden Town, and his people would be expecting them. There would be great rejoicing because they had taken many scalps and had not lost a man. They would honour her—and Jeems, accepting them as flesh of their flesh and bone of their bone. Toinette would live as his daughter. Silver Heels' heart would live in her song. She would be of the forests—forever. That was the word he had sent ahead to Chenufsio. *Tiaoga was coming with his daughter.*

He stalked into darkness, and for a time Jeems and

Toinette were afraid to speak the thought which was choking at their hearts.

"Your children and your children's children . . ."

That night Toinette lay staring at the sky with sleepless eyes.

CHAPTER XVII

CHENUFSIO, the Hidden Town of the Senecas, was on the Little Seneca River seventy miles from Lake Ontario. By means of this stream its inhabitants could drift in their canoes to the shore of the lake or work southward almost to the Ohio River which was called the Allegany above the location of Fort Pitt. Four trails led from it through dense wilderness. These were foot-wide paths which the Indians had used many generations, and in places were worn so deep that traces of them were destined to be left a century after the people whose moccasined feet had made them had ceased to exist. One path led to the River of the Great Falls, or Niagara, another to the country of the Ohio and the lead mines of Pennsylvania, a third northward to Lake Ontario, and a fourth hundreds of miles eastward to the scalp-hunting grounds of the white men beyond the Cayugas, the Onondagas, and the Oneidas, over which trail Tiaoga and his war party were returning. Oddly enough, there was no trail in the direction of Lake Erie, whose eastern shore was scarcely farther away than the sandy beaches of Lake Ontario. Hunters and warriors adventured through the swamps and forests to Misow Kichekume, or the Big Sea, but for some reason they blazed no common way.

Guarded like a precious jewel on all sides, a hidden

town literally as well as in name, Chenufsio was one of the greatest of the strange social centres of the Indians to which prisoners with white skins were brought to be adopted by their captors. That such places existed was a fact which had but recently gained credence in both the English and French colonies. Not until 1764 was Colonel Boquet to free the "white" population in the first of these mystery villages, and then the deliverance which he brought about resulted in less of happiness than of tragedy, for the life and associations which he disrupted in the name and claim of the Colonies had their roots as far back as the third and fourth generations. Hearts and homes were broken as well as prisoners' shackles.

Chenufsio was the Rome of a wide domain in that period of its history when Jeems and Toinette came with Tiaoga and his warriors. In it were three hundred people, and at full strength it numbered sixty fighting men. It nestled at the edge of a large meadow which the river embraced in a horseshoe curve and its centre was a stockaded stronghold with long-houses, storage buildings, cabins, and tepees sufficient for the entire population in times of stress. An arrow-shot away from the gates of the stockade was the border of a forest of magnificent oaks, and under these ancient trees rather than in the fortified place the people made their homes in spring and summer and autumn, the gnarled limbs of the wood forming a cathedral-like roof over their habitations. Half a mile from the forest was an encircling hill, the inner rim of the horseshoe made by the river, and between this hill and the stream were the fields and orchards cultivated by the savages. The Senecas had vineyards and fine orchards of apples, cherries, and plums, and they also grew tobacco and potatoes on a considerable scale. The fields were laid out neatly about Chenufsio, including about two hundred acres in all. Half of this space was devoted to the production of corn of several varieties, sweet or puckered corn, Calica, Redpop, Whitepop, Sacred or "original" corn, and Red and Purple Soft. In the cornfields and growing from the same hills were pumpkins and beans, Crook-neck and Scalloped and Winter squash, and everywhere were sunflowers of a dwarfish kind grown for the oil which was extracted from their seeds.

When the season was good, Chenufsio lived in comfort during the long winter months. The granaries were full, large quantities of dried fruits were in the storehouses, and underground cellars were stocked with apples, pumpkins, potatoes, and squashes. When the season was bad, Chenufsio drew a belt tightly about its stomach for five months of the year. For three of these months it starved.

This was a bad season. Spring frosts had killed the early vegetation and had blackened the buds of apples and plums. The corn was so poor that, after roasting time, only enough was left for the next year's planting, and beans and potatoes had suffered until there was less than a third of a crop. In the forests and marshes and on the plains as well as in the fields it had been a "dark year." Most of the nut trees were barren, the wild rice had headed poorly, from strawberry time until the ripening of the small purple plums there had been little fruit to gather. Because of these things the people of Chenufsio were preparing themselves for the "break-up" as the first chill nights of autumn came.

The "break-up" was a tragic event in the life of an Indian town. It meant a shortening of rations, and then, as in the case of Chenufsio, a scattering of three hundred men, women, and children over a vast stretch of wilderness in parties seldom larger than a single family, every unit dependent upon itself in its struggle to hold body and soul together until another spring. Each family sought a separate hunting ground, but this did not mean that all its members would be together. If a certain family possessed the strength of two or more hunters, one of the men would be detailed by the chief of the town to accompany a less fortunate group made up of old people or a widow and her children, and he was held as accountable for their welfare as though they were his own flesh and blood. It was a campaign against hunger. When the fight was over and spring came again, the town would reassemble and its village life be continued.

Ordinarily, an atmosphere of gloom preceded the break-up. When it came, friends and relatives were parted for months. Deaths always occurred during the period of separation. Lovers were disunited. A father gave up his son. A mother saw her daughter taken as a member of a family better able to care for her than her own. The sick and the infirm were left in the village with food sufficient to carry them through.

But the people of Chenufsio wore no appearance of gloom on the day when Tiaoga and his triumphant warriors were to arrive from the east. They awakened at dawn with hearts in which gladness dispelled whatever unhappiness may have oppressed them before. Half of their men folk were returning, and they were coming in triumph. Tiaoga's messenger had brought the news that not a man had been lost in their invasion of the territory of their enemies. This was unusual, and it put fresh courage into the hearts of those who had seen the year go against them. Tiaoga's homecoming with the spoils of war was an augury which more than discounted empty cellars and granaries.

As a part of these spoils, they knew Tiaoga was bringing a daughter to take the place of Silver Heels.

This convinced them that fortune was bound to smile on them again. They had loved Soi Yan Makwun. With her death had come bad times. Now the spirits would give them an easy winter, and next year would see the earth flowering with good things.

Chenufsio made ready for the feast. There were still plenty of earthy things and a supply of late green corn packed away in husks and kept for this occasion. The skin of every drum in the village was tightened on the morning of the day Tiaoga was expected, and no one thought of work or of a duty outside the celebration. Fires were built under the huge oaks and part of the fun for girls and boys was the gathering of fuel. Children had toy tom-toms and beat them incessantly, there were games and races, laughter and good-natured banter and wild hallooing, the grown-ups themselves turning children. The quieter ones among the adults as well as the children had white skins. There were twenty, of these in Chenufsio. One would scarcely have accepted them as alien to the tribe except in their colour and a slight difference in manner of dress. They did not bear the appearance of captives, and while their demeanour was one of anticipation, their emotions were more repressed than those of the brown-skinned people about them. Among them were women in whose arms were children born of Indian husbands. There were white maidens who had lived in Chenufsio since baby-hood and whose eyes glowed softly as they watched for the young warriors who held their hearts. There were some whose darker skins were the heritage of a second or a third generation, and a few with eyes that still held the shadows of grief and yearning—those whose visions of homes and loved ones would never die.

These were the people and this the town that waited through a sun-filled autumn day for the coming of Tiaoga and his captives.

The last day was long for Toinette. It had begun at dawn, and though Tiaoga halted his men at intervals to let her rest, it had not ended with dusk. Darkness came before they reached a plain on the far side of which was a hill. Beyond this hill was Chenufsio. They could see the glow of a great fire lighting the sky.

Toinette forgot her exhaustion at this sign of the end of their journey. She observed that someone took from Jeems the scalp of the man he had killed which he had tried to conceal from her eyes under a flap of buckskin. Then she saw all of the scalps taken by the Senecas fastened like dangling fish to a slender pole which was carried on the shoulders of two men, the hair of one of these scalps reaching almost to the ground. With the scalp carriers in the lead, they came to the hill at the edge of the plain and looked down on the valley of Chenufsio.

A mile away in the great oak forest near the river a score of red fires were burning, but everywhere, in spite of the fires, was an engulfing silence. Toinette stood close to Jeems, and it was not the exertion of hill-climbing that made her heart pound as it did. A spirit seemed breathing to her out of the strange and awesome stillness. A spirit of life, yet also of death. It was a still-ness filled with the beating of hearts, the repression of living things, the staring scrutiny of eyes she could not see. Only the fires gave evidence of life that was un-leashed. As unseen hands added fuel, they were like notes in a piece of flaming music, pitchwood sending up crescendos of sparks and light, hardwood and river logs giving forth steadier pools of illumination. She could not see those who waited tensely about the rims of the fires. It was the end of the world for Jeems and her; she had expected that, but not the threatening quiet which was like death thrusting its head out of a pit.

Suddenly it was broken. A tall figure had mounted a rock from which he sent forth a cry which began almost in a murmur but which increased in volume until it filled the valley. Toinette had never heard such a cry come from a human throat, so far-reaching, so free of raucous effort, a long note whose depth and steadiness sent it into farther and farther distance. The voice had in it the soul of a god. She tried to make out the identity of the figure in the darkness. Then she drew her breath sharply. The man on the rock was Tiaoga.

When the cry ended, a bedlam of sound burst from Chenufsio. Those who had been chained to silence as they listened for Tiaoga's voice from the hilltop sprang to a life that was almost madness. Men hallooed and yelled, children screamed, women cried out in their joy. Pitchwood torches were lighted, and as the population streamed out into the night in a wave of fire, the beating of tom-toms and skin drums and wooden gongs mingled with human voices and the barking of dogs. At the beginning of Tiaoga's cry the men bearing the scalp-laden pole had gone ahead, and now Tiaoga followed with his men in single file. Toinette and Jeems were midway in the line. Wide slave collars of buckskin had been placed about their necks, and Jeems was stripped of his weapons. The warriors did not hurry. Their step was slow and steady, and not a man broke the silence with a whisper or a word. The sea of torches advanced. It rolled in and out of hollows like a flood, then came to a level place and formed two streaming lines of fire. The scalp bearers reached these a hundred yards ahead of Tiaoga and his men. Toinette could see them enter the light of the torches, and in these moments the voices of the savages rose to the heavens. Tiaoga paused, and not until the scalp bearers had paraded their grisly burden the entire length of the gauntlet of flame did he proceed again.

Toinette felt stealing over her a strange faintness of body and limb. Stories which she had forgotten, stories she had heard of the Indians from childhood, stories that had sent shivers through the hearts of a thousand homes along the frontiers all crowded upon her at once. Wild tales of appalling torture and vengeance, of stake and fire and human suffering. She had listened to them from her father's lips, from passing voyageurs, had heard them in the gossip of the seigneurie. And she remembered by name this ordeal which awaited them. It was *Le Chemin de Feu*—the Road of Fire—through which they must pass. Others had died in it. Roasted by pitchfilled torches. Blinded. Killed by inches. So she had been told.

She looked at Jeems in the first outreaching glow of the torches. It was for him she was afraid. Tiaoga would not kill her, he would not let the torches burn her—she knew that as surely as she knew the torches were waiting for them. Jeems turned to meet her look with a smile of encouragement.

Tiaoga and his warriors moved slowly. They were like bronze men without flesh or emotions. Their heads were high, their bodies straight, their jaws set hard as they stalked at a death-march pace between the columns of their people. Jeems fell into this rhythmic movement as the mouth of the torch monster began to swallow them. And then with eyes that became flame-lit pools of fear and exhaustion Toinette saw that not a hand gave a sign of rising against them. Silence had fallen again on the people of Chenufsio, a silence broken only by the tread of feet, the sputter and crackle of burning pitchwood, the breathing of a multitude. Not a word or a cry, no sudden reaching out of a mother's arms, no flutter of a sweetheart's hand, no name trembling on a wife's lips broke the tenseness of Tiaoga's triumph. The whole was a living picture which burned itself in Toinette's brain detail by detail. She saw the faces staring at her, men, women, boys, girls, little children—without hatred, without desire to harm, but with a great curiosity which was almost friendship in their eyes. And then her heart stood still for a moment as she saw a white face looking at her—a face framed in a mass of hair that gleamed with gold in the torchlight and with lips that smiled a half-sad, gentle welcome. There were other pale-faced people in both lines, and one of them, who was a young girl like herself, greeted her with gladness, then flushed a deeper colour as Shindas passed. Shindas allowed his eyes to steal for a single instant to hers.

"*Opitchi!*" cried Toinette softly, and the girl seemed about to fly to her side. "*Opitchi—the Thrush!*"— and Toinette spoke the full name of Shindas's white-skinned sweetheart.

The threat of death could not have kept her from giving that greeting to the other, for it was her heart that leapt to her lips, hope, confidence at last, the knowledge that love was here, even happiness, where she had expected only gloom and tragedy.

The torches coughed and flared, but not a spark touched their skins in passing. No eyes gleamed hatred at them. No fingers clenched, no hand was raised. The things she had heard in the land of her people were lies. The Indians killed in war but they did not torture. They did not pull out eyes and thrust sticks through quivering flesh. They were men and women and children like all other men and women and children. These truths she thought she had discovered for herself.

But one thing she did not fully know. She might have learned it had she caught the low-voiced whisperings which followed the passing of the warrior: "*She is Tiaoga's daughter—she is the spirit of Soi Yan Makwun returned to us in the flesh—now our good fortune will return—the sun will shine—light and laughter will come—for Soi Yan Makwun is here, out of the pool, out of death to live with us again!*"

The wild outburst of voices after the parade, the fierce beating of drums, the mad tossing of burning torches high into the air, the pæans which rose from dusky throats, did not tell her how deeply Chenufsio had loved Silver Heels.

They crossed a field of darkness toward the fires, and when they came among them Tiaoga was marching in Jeems's place and Jeems had disappeared. She had not sensed his going or Tiaoga's presence, and before she knew that Jeems was no longer among the warriors, she found herself standing alone with the Seneca chief, the people gathering in a circle around them. It was like the setting of a stage with flame on all sides of it, and for the first time she realized that something was about to happen in which she was more important than the scalps which had preceded Tiaoga. But where was Jeems? Why was he not among those about her whom she scanned so closely? Fear trickled through her veins. It turned her flesh cold, so that with the darkness of her eyes and the pallor of her face she was like a white spirit in the illumination. In a moment, Tiaoga began to speak. His voice renewed her confidence as she searched for Jeems. It went on quietly for a space. In it was the deep timbre of the voice that had reached out over the valley from the rock. It began to stir with emotion. He was describing the pool where Soi Yan Makwun had died, the wickedness of the evil spirits there and the success of their gods in restoring Silver Heels to her people. It did not take long for Tiaoga to tell his story. His voice rose. His scarred and bitter face assumed a strange gentleness, and Toinette knew that Jeems was safe though she could not see him. She waited, trembling, and at last Tiaoga was finished and stood for a moment with upraised hand amid a great hush—then spoke a single name, *Opitchi*. The Thrush sprang forward, and as she came Tiaoga took the slave collar from Toinette's throat and crushed it into the earth with his moccasined foot. A murmur ran through the circle. Tiaoga stood with his arms folded across his breast, and Toinette felt the hands of the Thrush drawing her away.

They paused at the edge of the circle, and for a little while no one moved or spoke. Then there was a break in the ring behind the Seneca chief, and through it came Jeems, escorted between Shindas and another warrior. Toinette gasped and almost cried out. There was an amazing change in Jeems. He was stripped to the waist and painted in stripes of red and yellow and black. His face appeared to be cut in crimson gashes. His thick blond hair was tied in a warlock from which streamed a feather showing he had killed a man. At Tiaoga's command there advanced from the circle an old man with a wizened face and white hair and a younger man whose form was bent almost double because of a deformity. Behind these two came a little girl. The old man was Wuskoo, the Cloud. The younger was his son, Tokana, or Gray Fox, a name of which he had been proud in the days before a tree fell on his tepee and crooked his back, when he was the fastest runner in the tribe. Tiaoga spoke again. He told of the days when the aged Wuskoo had been a great warrior and had slain many enemies; he described the increasing of years and the coming of adversity, the valiancy of his son, the stroke of evil that had made him what he was, and then exulted in the fortune which had sent another son to Wuskoo, a son with a white skin and a strong body who would care for him and who would be a brother to Gray Fox. With his thin and quivering hands, Wuskoo took the slave collar from Jeems's neck and stamped it joyously into the ground while the broken Gray Fox raised a hand in brotherhood and friendship. There was something so wistfully sweet in the big dark eyes of the little Indian maiden that Jeems drew her to him and put an arm protectingly about her. It was then Toinette left the Thrush and ran to him, so that all saw her held in his painted arms, with Wanonat, the Wood Pigeon, a happy partner in the moment when Toinette proudly and a bit defiantly told Chenufsio and through it the whole Seneca nation that this was the man to whom she belonged.

Like a flood burst loose from a dam, the night of feasting and rejoicing began. It was preceded by a combat among the dogs in which Odd established his right to a place among the four-footed citizens of Chenufsio. After a time he found a scent on the beaten ground that led him to the tepee which had been prepared for Toinette. It was a small tepee near Tiaoga's, furnished with freshly gathered cedar and garlands of bittersweet, and with the soft skins and pretty raiment which had belonged to Silver Heels. Here he found Toinette and the Thrush, whose name—a long time ago—had been Mary Daghlen.

It seemed to Jeems that from the beginning his freedom among the Senecas was as great as if he had been born of their blood. Gray Fox took him to the tepee of his father, which was to be his home, and food and drink were brought to him. Then he was left alone, for even the delighted old man whom Tiaoga had honoured by the gift of a son could not be kept away from the celebration which was in progress. The thought came to Jeems that no impediment had been placed in his way if he chose to steal off into the night and disappear. The ease with which he might have set out on this adventure was proof of his helplessness. Like the others, he was a captive forever. There was no escape from Chenufsio unless one accepted death as the route. A false move, an hour of desperation and attempt, and Seneca trailers would be like hounds at his heels.

He did not think of escape because its desire possessed him. He was measuring his world and adjusting himself to its limitations with emotions which were far from unhappy. With Toinette, he could find here all that he wanted in life. Tiaoga and Shindas knew that she belonged to him, and the people of Chenufsio were now aware of it. His heart exulted and his spirit rose with the chanting of the savages. What difference did it make that they were buried in the heart of the forests for all time? He had Toinette. She loved him. Chenufsio would not be a sepulchre. Their love would transform it into a paradise.

He was eager to see Toinette again, and began to seek for a place where he could clean himself of the coloured clay plastered on his face and body. With his clothes, he went to the river, and after a thorough scrubbing returned fully dressed with the eagle feather still in his hair. His weapons had been given to him, and these he carried boldly when he joined the Indians. The triumphal fire was blazing, and as soon as the hungry town had fed itself, the scalp dances would begin. The scalps were already suspended on the victory pole in its light. Children were playing about them. The fine dark hair of one was so long that they could reach the tresses with their fingers, and when they did this they shrieked with ecstasy. Among them was a white-skinned boy of seven or eight who laughed and shouted with the others.

Jeems found an opportunity to have a word with Shindas and learned that Toinette and Opitchi were together. Shindas could not tear himself from the martial dignity which was expected of him until the warriors had told of their exploits in the scalp dance, so Jeems went alone and found Tiaoga's tepee and the smaller one near it in which were Toinette and the Thrush. It was lighted by a torch, and he drew back among the dark boles of the trees and waited. The night was clear and the full moon had begun to rise so that, outside the circle of fires, the gloom gave way to a soft and silvery radiance among the oaks. At the end of half an hour, Toinette and Opitchi came out into the illumined forest. For a little while they stood under the gnarled limbs of the trees which cast shadows from over their heads. He did not reveal himself until Opitchi's form disappeared among the pools of light and darkness as she went toward the fires. Then he advanced, calling Toinette's name softly.

Her appearance surprised him. His first thought was that he had made a mistake and that she was not Toinette but some princess of the tribe. She was not the ragged and dishevelled young woman who had arrived with Tiaoga's men. Mary, the Thrush, had dressed her in the prettiest raiment left by Silver Heels. Her awnskin jacket and short skirt of doeskin had the glow of golden velvet in the moonlight. Her parted hair was brushed smooth as a bird's wing and fell in two gleamy braids over her shoulders. A filet of scarlet cloth was around her forehead, and in it was a single feather of vivid yellow. There was something about the long yellow feather, the filet of scarlet cloth, and the boyish closeness of her dress which made Jeems give a wondering cry. It was as if they had come to her from an obscure and distant past and had always belonged to her. He had dreamed of this lovely wilderness princess; through years of boyhood hopes and plannings he had built up worlds about her, and in those worlds he had fought for her and had adventured with her where he alone was her champion and her hero. He had carried gifts of feathers to her—feathers and fawnskin *and a piece of cloth like that which she now wore in a crimson band about her forehead!*

To him it was the precious red velvet, there in the glow of the moon.

He opened his arms, and Toinette came into them.

CHAPTER XVIII

FOR half an hour Jeems was alone with Toinette. Then Mary Daghlen returned, and with her came a messenger who took him back to the dances which were beginning about the scalp-fire.[1] He was not embarrassed by the critical eyes upon him. The wildness of the night entered his blood, a heat set blazing by the joy of his possession, and as he chanted the Seneca victory songs with the others, Toinette was in his heart, and words she had whispered to him under the oaks repeated themselves until they dulled his senses and blinded his eyes to everything but their import. As soon as God would let them bring it about *she would be his wife*. She had said that! So he danced. He shouted at Tiaoga's side. The curious and the suspicious became his friends. Eyes that had followed him sombrely grew warm with approval. He vindicated Tiaoga for allowing him to live, and Wuskoo swelled with pride and boasted that he had another son as great as Gray Fox had been. Toinette, horrified at first, saw him in his madness. Then she began to understand. But not until he took his turn among the warriors and danced alone

[1]Mary Daghlen's people moved westward from the valley of the Juniata in 1738. A year later William Daghlen was slain by the Senecas and his wife and infant daughter were taken prisoners. The mother died in Chenufsio when Mary was ten years old. When the Seneca villages were made to surrender their white prisoners, Mary Daghlen refused to give up the life of her Indian husband and his people.

in the light of the fire, chanting his story in the language of his adopted people, did Opitchi—translating what he said—let her know fully the daring of her lover. Jeems's story began with his earliest thoughts and memories of her. He told of their homes in the country of the Richelieu, of his dreams and hopes, of his yearnings and prayers, and of Paul Tache. He told how he had fought and lost, described the passing of moons and the growing of his love and how death had come with the Mohawks from the south. Then he came to the finding of Toinette, their flight, the triumph of his love, his fight with the scalp hunter at Lussan's place, and their capture by Tiaoga and his warriors. He praised these warriors. They were not like the Mohawks, who were sneaks in the night. The Senecas were clean and swift and brave. He was proud to be a brother and a son among them. His dog, who hated the Mohawks, had accepted them as friends. He wanted this people to respect him, and he wanted them to love Toinette whom Tiaoga had honoured by taking as his daughter. *For Toinette belonged to him. She wanted to be his wife. She wanted to bear his children among the Senecas.*

He stopped at last and thanked God that Hepsibah Adams had made it possible for him to do this thing in the light of the fire at Chenufsio. A murmur of approbation stirred the people. It rippled and died out as another warrior took his place.

Jeems had seen Toinette's white face and her eyes radiant in their message to him, but she was gone when he sought for her, and later the torch was burning in her tepee again. Wuskoo and Gray Fox and Wood

Pigeon remained near him. They were proud of him, but there was something besides pride in the way Wood Pigeon slipped her small brown hand in his. He observed more closely her too fragile loveliness. She was like a flower hungry for something which meant life to it, and when he made inquiry, Tokana said the child was eight years old and that with each winter her frailty had become more noticeable. The tree which had broken him had killed her mother. Others had been good to her, but Wood Pigeon missed something which seemed to be eating her life away. He told Jeems he thought it was the spirit of the mother calling to her, and that Wood Pigeon was trying to free herself from the flesh to go to her. Of course, the child did not know, but it was happening in spite of them all. Jeems felt the little Indian maid creeping into his heart. Whenever she looked at him, she revealed the beginning of a timid worship, and when at last she grew tired and went to her lonely bed, he knelt at her side for a few moments and talked to her, then kissed her. It was startlingly new and strange for Wood Pigeon. Something sent her arms up through the darkness around his neck. That, too, was a new thing for Jeems. Almost baby arms claiming him.

Long after midnight the revels ended, and Chenufsio grew quiet. For a time, he looked at the stars and the changing shadows of the moon through the open door of Wuskoo's tepee. He entered sleep as if going into a long avenue of golden colours. Only happiness rising like a flower from the ashes of a torture that was gone could have made it like that. His mother seemed a part of it, her voice a glad melody somewhere in the radiance which embraced him. In the avenue of gold, he saw Wood Pigeon smiling happily between his mother and Toinette. Then he sank into deeper sleep.

This was the beginning of the strange life of Jeems and Toinette in Chenufsio which Colonel Boquet, afterward Major General and Commander in Chief of His Majesty's forces in the Southern Department of America, described as "an episode of fact which is difficult of belief and astounding in the new viewpoint which it and others of a similar kind give us of savage life."

To Jeems and Toinette there was nothing spectacular in their first day or in the many that followed. After the triumphal night, the Indian town fell once more into the routine of its existence. Men hunted, women worked, children played. Warriors met in solemn councils and smoked incessantly as they discussed the affairs of their commonwealth and planned for the future. The "Dark Year" was upon them. Winter threatened. But there were other matters to be settled. Tiaoga had brought unusual news. The English, under a general named Braddock, had been defeated and massacred. The French had been destroyed on Lake George. Sir William Johnson, the White Father of the Sioux Nations, was victorious, and the Mohawks were profiting greatly. This brought sombre looks into the faces of the Senecas. The eastern wilderness was bound to run red with war. Tiaoga was sure. His warriors were sure. The long-expected struggle between the English and the French was at hand, and there would be no rest for the tomahawk until the land was free of one or the other. During the latter part of October, many runners visited Chenufsio from distant villages and towns; from Karaqhiyadirha at the headwaters of the Little Seneca; from Tyanagarante down on the Allegany; from Kanestio in the direction of Pennsylvania; from Canadaragey and Canadasegy at the western gates of the Cayuga country—from all over the broad domain of the Senecas came the accumulating evidence of fierce and bloody war impending. It brought a problem for Tiaoga and his councillors in Chenufsio. They faced war—and famine. If their fighting men went into the east, who would keep the people from starvation? It was decided that Tiaoga should take the warpath again with thirty men chosen by lot, while thirty of his braves should remain to fight hunger and death during the winter months. The drawing came, but Jeems was not included. Shindas was doomed to leave his sweetheart again.

These were days when misgivings assailed Jeems and Toinette in spite of their hopes and plans, yet no cloud more than temporarily darkened their visions. In the heart of each was the prayer that a wandering priest might come their way, so that the ceremony could be performed which would make them husband and wife. In the town were a number of white women who had accepted Indian husbands in the Indian way, but against this practice Toinette revolted. She prayed and Mary Daghlen prayed with her, for through the years since her mother had died the Thrush had kept her faith unbroken. The Seneca, worshipping her, honoured it.

Two years before three Jesuits had come to Chenufsio, one after another, since then there had been none.

Jeems was sure Tiaoga would permit Toinette to go

with him when the break-up came. Wood Pigeon had found a sister and a mother in Toinette, and her love was divided between her two white friends. Tiaoga no longer assumed an attitude of indifference when Toinette was in his presence, and his affection for her came also to tolerate, if not actually to include, little Wood Pigeon. This fact gave Jeems his greatest confidence when, as the day for the town's dissolution grew near, he approached Tiaoga on the subject of making Toinette a fifth member of Wuskoo's family. Neither had anticipated an objection, and his unrelenting disapproval filled them with despair. Shindas was not surprised, and it was he who explained Tiaoga's attitude. Toinette was not only Tiaoga's daughter by adoption; the chief had accepted her wholly, blood and spirit, and it was inconceivable in the moral and social ethics of the Senecas that a maiden, and particularly a chieftain's daughter, should abide with the family of the man to whom she was betrothed. That Tiaoga conceded their betrothal was the one consolation they had in their disappointment; that his objection might be overcome by an acceptance of the Indian custom of marriage was a thought which Toinette rejected when Shindas suggested it to her and to Jeems. In the young Seneca's mind was the hope that Toinette would accept this easy way to the possession of a husband and that she might also persuade the Thrush to do the same. But the companionship of Toinette and Mary Daghlen served to strengthen them in their resolution to wait for one who could bless their unions with the holy bonds of the Church.

Early in November groups began to leave, each with the small amount of food which remained as its share. Mary was to accompany two families of eight people under the protection of Thunder Shield, a valiant warrior and a splendid hunter. They were going toward Lake Ontario. Toinette was given to Ah De Bah, the Tall Man, a relative of Tiaoga's. He was a thin and sinister-eyed man who might have been named the Serpent, for he moved with the sinuous stealth of that creature and possessed other characteristics which made him almost as unpleasant. But like the snake he was an unexcelled hunter, the best in Chenufsio, and for this reason Tiaoga entrusted to him the one he treasured most. Ah De Bah's family was a large one. In it were eleven, including his old mother and father and two boys who were large enough to be of assistance. Chenufsio knew that no matter how long the winter might be, hunger would have to fight to reach the Tall Man's camp. He was going into the country near Lake Erie.

Hiding their disappointment, Jeems and Toinette encouraged themselves with visions of a future which they tried to paint in bright colours. The months would pass quickly. With the earliest days of spring, they would return to Chenufsio. Every hour they would live in each other's thoughts, and at night their prayers would cross in the wilderness. Next year there would surely be a way. Fate would not separate them again. In their final moments together, Toinette's eyes glowed with a depth of faith and love which it was impossible for Jeems to measure fully.

In this way they parted.

He went north and west with Wuskoo toward the Tyanagarunte River which emptied into Lake Ontario. Odd struggled between his devotion for Jeems and for Toinette. He followed his master a distance, then hesitated and turned back. A lump rose in Jeems's throat, and he could not see clearly as his comrade sat in the trail and watched until he disappeared.

This was on the fifth of November. By the twentieth, they had reached the headwaters of the Little Selus eighty miles from Chenufsio. Jeems now realized the seriousness of the task which had been imposed upon him by Tiaoga. Wuskoo, infirm as he was, could travel farther and faster than his broken son. Five or six miles a day was all that Tokana could stand, and in this distance he was sometimes put to great extremity. The courage with which he faced his unhappy life won Jeems. He was distressed that he could carry no burden and that Jeems was often compelled to help him over rough and uneven places. Sometimes he laughed as if it were a joke, yet Jeems knew that his heart was aching and that he was filled with shame. It was not difficult to see what a magnificent savage he had been, though now he walked with his head almost on a level with his waist. Jeems wondered at the fidelity which kept him with his aged father and little girl when he might have lived in comparative comfort at Chenufsio. Until Wuskoo told him, he did not know that all of them would have remained in the town that winter had Tiaoga not made him their son and brother. "And now Chenufsio will have three less mouths to feed," chuckled Wuskoo.

The old man's faith and the younger man's spirit

were an inspiration to Jeems, but it was Wood Pigeon who became his real strength. The child worshipped him, and her presence eased the burden of his separation from Toinette. He began to teach her French, and they exchanged confidences which were all their own. He explained to her that Toinette, who was Soi Yan Makwun, belonged to him, and tried to make her understand why she was not with them. Next year she would be. One day Wood Pigeon asked if she might go with him and Toinette—wherever they went. After this the bond between them seemed to hold her closer than ever to Jeems.

Wuskoo had led the way to a hardwood country in which he was sure there would be hunting that would last through the winter. There were plenty of raccoons, and the mergansers, or fish ducks, would come to the swift-running headwaters to feed as soon as ice closed the lakes and the mouths of the streams. Here they made their lodge of saplings. It was a new kind of home for Wood Pigeon. Jeems built it with a cooking hearth and a chimney and a tiny room set apart for Wood Pigeon herself. The child's eyes glowed with delight at this possession. Each day Jeems told her more about Toinette—how Soi Yan Makwun cared for her beautiful hair, how it was part of her religion to keep herself clean, how and why she did this thing and that, until thoughts and desires grew in Wanonat's head, and she employed the comb and the brush which Jeems made for her until her sleek black hair was never untidy.

Heavy snow and extreme cold came early in the season. By the middle of December, Jeems was compelled to hunt on snowshoes, and so bitter were the nights that the first of January found even the headwaters freezing out the mergansers.

This was the memorable winter of 1755 and 1756, the story of which the Senecas handed down from father to son for many generations—a winter in which all game seemed to have gone from the face of the earth, and when hardship and starvation killed a tenth of the three westernmost of the Six Great Nations, the Senecas, the Cayugas, and the Onondagas.

The deer seemed to have migrated east and south. Bears went into their winter sleep in November. Raccoons, the staff of Indian life when crops were a failure, hid themselves away in long and unbroken slumber. The fish ducks disappeared in a flight for open waters. It was the "seventh year" for rabbits, when extinction seemed to have overtaken them. Elk and buffalo remained below the Alleghany. The flesh of beaver and otter became more precious than their fur. Wildcats and foxes and other carnivorous creatures were driven to faraway hunting fields by the scarcity of small game. Hunger rode stark and merciless over the land of the three nations.

At first Jeems was partly prepared, because he had killed a buck, and with Wuskoo's shrewd assistance had marked a number of trees in which raccoons were sure to hibernate. But late in January famine drew closer about the cabin on the Little Selus, and Jeems travelled farther in his hunts, until he was gone two days at a time. In February, he made four of these hunts and found no game. The cold was terrific. Trees cracked like rifles in the woods. Bitter winds continued night and day. Wood Pigeon's eyes grew larger and her body more fragile as the weeks passed. Each time Jeems came in from his hunts she blazed up like a fire in her happiness, but he could mark the steady fading of her strength. He hunted with almost insane energy. Everything was for her when famine clutched at them hardest—a pair of snowbirds which he shot with arrows, a red-squirrel's flesh, acorns which he found in a stub, the fleshy root of a pond lily secured by hacking through two feet of ice. Then—a hollow tree— a raccoon asleep—and for a few hours food enough for all. Thus one week dragged at the heels of another with death held off by the length of an arm.

Torturing fears assailed Jeems. Toinette was never out of his mind, for even in his sleep he dreamed of her. She, too, was a part of this fight to hold life together. *And Ah De Bah had eleven mouths to feed instead of four.*

At night, when the wind howled and trees wailed in their distress, he sweated in fear, and more than once the thought came to him to abandon his family and go in search of Toinette. His visions of the fate which might be overtaking her became almost unbearable. Wuskoo added to his burden, for the old man's courage broke under slow starvation, and his dismal forebodings drove Jeems nearly mad. Gray Fox kept his cheer, though he became so emaciated that his cheekbones were ready to break through the skin. Wood Pigeon's eyes stabbed Jeems deepest. They grew so big and dark in her little thin face and were filled with such hungry depths that he expected the gentle spirit to leave her body at any time. Yet she made no complaint, and the pathos of her smile always greeted him. His hunts were not long now, and seldom took him more than three or four miles from the cabin, for his own strength was ebbing. His only hope was to kill an occasional bird, and it was in the darkest hour that an answer came to his prayers. In a blizzard against which he was working his way in half-blindness, he stumbled upon a doe as weak as himself and killed her. Without this stroke of fortune, Wood Pigeon and Wuskoo must have died. When the thaws came, they were alive. Raccoons began to appear and fleshy roots could be gathered out of the opening streams. Early March brought a warm break in which Jeems and his companions started for Chenufsio. Food was plentiful on the way, and each night they gathered strengthening sap from the maples.

They arrived at Chenufsio. The people there had lived frugally on their supplies, and from the first running of the maple sap had been making sugar. Only four families had preceded Jeems to the village, and of their number, which was twenty-eight, five had died. No word had been received from Tiaoga and his warriors.

The maple sap ran steadily. A few iron kettles and many birchbark cauldrons steamed night and day in the making of the biggest run of sugar that had been known in years. In spite of this opening grace of spring, there hung over Chenufsio a grim spectre whose shadow grew darker with each day that passed.

This spectre was death. Scarcely a family returned which did not bring grief with it. And Ah De Bah, the mightiest hunter of them all, did not come. No one had heard of him. No one knew where he was. Fifty—seventy—a hundred—and then a hundred and fifty of those who had gone in the break-up were accounted for by the end of March. Among them was Mary Daghlen. Of their number, thirty had died. Still Ah De Bah, the Tall Man, did not come.

Then he appeared one day. He was a grotesque rack of fleshless bones whom Tiaoga would not have recognized. Behind him trailed his people. Jeems counted them before he could tell one from another. Eleven! He ran toward them, and Toinette swayed from the line at the head of which the Tall Man marched. He might not have known her at first if she had not met him in this way, for those who were behind Ah De Bah walked with bowed heads and dragging steps like death figures in a weird parade. Her eyes stared at him from a face so strange and thin that it choked his joy. Her body was not heavier than a child's when he clasped her. Then she began to cry softly with her face against his breast.

He carried her to the tepee. Her clothes were in tatters, her moccasins worn to shreds. She was so small a burden that her lightness sent horror through him and his eyes were blinded by a hot fire when she raised a cold hand to touch his face. He placed her on the soft skins in the tepee, then he was conscious of Wood Pigeon near him, and in a moment Mary Daghlen came in. Jeems made way for them. He went outside, and in his path was a creature who leapt weakly against him. It was Odd, a skeleton with red and watery eyes and jaws falling apart. Jeems waited until the Thrush came out and told him she was going for warm water and food and that Wood Pigeon was undressing Toinette. Then he sought the others. All but Ah De Bah had disappeared and were being cared for. The Tall Man could scarcely stand as he told his story. He had brought his eleven people back alive—*the dog and he*. Like the truly great, he gave credit to his inferior. Without the dog, he would have failed in his struggle to feed eleven mouths—and Jeems knew why Odd had not been eaten.

After a time, Mary Daghlen let him see Toinette again. She was in her bed of skins. The look which had frightened him was gone from her eyes, and they were bright with the joy of his presence. Her hair was brushed and replaited in two gleamy braids. She held out her arms to him, and he knelt beside her. Wood Pigeon looked at the two with shining eyes, and a soft mist gathered in Mary Daghlen's. After this, Jeems did not see Toinette again for an afternoon and a night. During this time she slept, and the Thrush and Wood Pigeon were never far from her side. The next day she walked with him about the town.

What was in Toinette's heart was also in Mary Daghlen's. The young girl who had known no other life than that of her adopted people since babyhood, but whose mother had kept God and Church alive in her soul, watched with increasing anxiety for the return of Shindas, and she told Toinette that at last she was prepared to yield to her environment, and if no priest came that spring or summer she would marry Shindas in the Indian way. This thought now held less of horror for Toinette. She had seen the fidelity and courage of

an Indian family in its struggle against death; she had
seen the Tall Man gnaw at bitter bark that his women
and children might have scraps of skin and flesh; she
had seen a mother hide her portion of food day after
day that she might save it for her children; she had
witnessed a faith and devotion which could have been
inspired by nothing less than the strength of God in
their souls. Her prejudices melted away in spite of their
background of unforgettable tragedy, and she began
to experience emotions which had not come to her
before. She loved Wood Pigeon with the passion of a
mother, and no sister could have found a warmer place
in her breast than Mary Daghlen. Friendships grew up
quickly about her, children were happy when she was
with them, men and women accepted her with quiet
devotion. And though she said nothing of it to Jeems, the
conviction was growing in her heart that she would not
allow another winter to separate them, even if a priest
did not come to Chenufsio.

But he came, following closely the months of starvation. He was a gaunt, death-faced man, on his way to
take the place of a brother who had died among the
Indians of the Ohio. That was what he said. History was
to relate otherwise, for a year later he was the force
behind the Abenakis in their slaughter of the English
at Fort William Henry. His name was Father Pierre
Roubaud. He was a cold, terrible man of God. He did
not smile in Chenufsio, he did not bring solace, he was
like a sombre cloud that drove on with the *threat* of
God and not with Divine promise and cheer. Yet he
was the Church. He would have died a thousand deaths

for the Cause of which he was the spiritual if not the moral representative. He would have eaten human flesh in defence of it. He did see such flesh eaten by his savage disciples at Fort William Henry. He remained in Chenufsio two days. On the second of these days he married Jeems and Toinette according to the ritual of the Catholic Church.[1]

The gloom he brought with him was dissipated by this event. Chenufsio gave itself up to a few hours of rejoicing in honour of Tiaoga's daughter and the son of Wuskoo.

But this happier spirit could not endure long with the people. Death had settled on them heavily. No word had come from Tiaoga and his warriors. There were whisperings that they had been annihilated in battle and would never return. Anxiety grew into fear, fear into certainty. The grimness of a tragedy darker than the sable robes of the priest hovered over Chenufsio.

In their happiness, Jeems and Toinette did not feel the undercurrent of change about them. Their abiding place became a home whose roots spread so securely that death could not have torn them up. Where there had been the restlessness of doubt and uncertainty was now the mental absoluteness of two lives transformed into one. The cloud of the tragedy through which they had passed was a curtain vaguely soft and distant be-

---

[1]Daniel James Bulain and Marie Antoinette Tonteur were married by Father Pierre Roubaud on the twenty-seventh day of April, 1756, as recorded later by Father Roubaud, after the massacre at Fort William Henry.

hind them; they thought of it, they talked of it, and dreams sometimes awakened Toinette to find comfort in Jeems's arms. But its memories did not wound so deeply. The spirits of Tonteur and of Jeems's mother drew nearer to them each day, strengthening with invisible chains the love which bound them. Like all the pure loves of youth, theirs was widely encompassing. It embraced the whole world and made a paradise of their small and savage part of it. It was the Thrush who first made them see what was happening about them. At heart Mary was Indian. Her babyhood, her childhood, her budding womanhood had been spent among her adopted people, and love had come to make more complete the allegiance which had grown through the years. As days and weeks passed without word from Tiaoga, the fear that Shindas was dead clutched her with an evil hand. She began to avoid Toinette and kept to herself. Toinette had never seen an Indian woman cry; she had comforted a mother who held a dead child in her arms, yet a grief as old as the world had failed to bring tears into that mother's eyes. The Thrush did not weep in her sorrow. The hardness which had settled in the faces about her came into her own. She was a changed Mary Daghlen. She was Opitchi the Seneca.

It was this change in the one she had come to regard as a sister which startled Toinette into a realization of the situation which was gathering about her and Jeems, and she was now destined to witness in all of its savagery that streak in Indian character which arouses hate and the desire for vengeance in the face of adversity at the hands of human enemies. Jeems marked its rising symptoms. He was no longer greeted with friendliness. Men were sullen and aloof, and women toiled without their usual chatter. Hunters went into the forests without enthusiasm and returned in stoical gloom. The old men met in endless councils, while the younger ones sharpened their hatchets and waited with increasing restlessness. Death and misfortune had ridden too hard, and human nerves were at the breaking point. Chenufsio was like a handful of powder ready for the touch of fire.

Then came the lightning flash.

It was an afternoon late in May when Shindas appeared in Chenufsio, and with a white woman's abandon Mary Dahglen ran into his arms. Shindas held her for a moment before warrior ethics made him thrust her away. He was alone. His arms and shoulders were hacked and cut and some of the wounds were scarcely healed. A scar lay across his cheek. His moccasins were in tatters, and his eyes held the ferocious light of a wolf that had been hunted. He made no effort to soften the news of which he was the bearer. He had come from the border of the Cayuga country as a messenger from Tiaoga and was many hours ahead of his comrades. *Tiaoga was returning with nine of his thirty warriors. The others were dead.*

This tragedy was a cataclysmic one even for a tribe of the most warlike of the Six Nations. Nothing had equalled it in Seneca history for generations. Twenty were dead out of thirty—the flower of Chenufsio—the very sinew of Tiaoga's people!

Shindas waited until his words had sunk like barbs of iron into the hearts of the men and women about him. He waited until there seemed no relief from the despair which settled over them, and then slowly gave the names of those who had been slain by their enemies. He was like an inquisitor revelling in the torture he inflicted, and at the end his voice rose until it carried far back among the oaks. A white man had killed three of the twenty warriors. He was a prisoner now—with Tiaoga. They had put out his eyes so that he could not see. They had built a fire around him in which it had been their intention to see him die. But in the last moment when the flames were scorching him Tiaoga had pulled the blazing fuel away with his own hands in order that the people of Chenufsio could witness his writhings at the fire stake.

After this one might have thought that mad men and women and not a grief-stricken people filled Chenufsio. For hours the lament of the women did not die out. Still Toinette saw no tears. Her horror increased as she observed the preparations for vengeance; the digging of a hole and the setting in it of a tall stake, all by women's hands; the gathering of pitchy fuel by little children and their mothers; the transformation of friends she had known into fiends whose eyes filled with hatred when they looked at her. She tried to hide from these things in their home and to keep Jeems with her. Shindas came to them. He had a command from Tiaoga for Jeems. It was that Jeems should go to the village of Kanestio seventy miles distant and bear news of a war party from that town. Shindas gave him this message and saw that he departed with it. He was no longer a brother. He disclosed no sign of pleasure when he learned that Toinette was Jeems's wife. Mary Daghlen found him so grimly changed that he frightened her.

Toinette remained alone. No one came to see her except Wood Pigeon, and the afternoon following the day of Shindas's arrival the child ran in with wide eyes to tell her that Tiaoga was approaching. Toinette knew she must see this white man and be one of the first to greet Tiaoga. She bound the red filet of cloth around her forehead and fastened the long yellow feather in it. She wore the most treasured of the things which had belonged to Silver Heels. The populace had gathered in the edge of the plain, and when she joined it a murmur of disapproval swept about her. Women's voices made this sound while men looked away from her sullenly. Wherever she moved, people drew back as if her touch held the blight of plague. Wood Pigeon innocently repeated words which brought the truth to her. Chenufsio no longer believed in her. She was not the spirit of Silver Heels. Tiaoga had made a mistake, and bad fortune instead of good had come with her—famine, death, this defeat at the hands of their enemies. Wood Pigeon heard a woman hiss between thin lips that the interloper who had taken Silver Heels's place should die at the stake with the white man. The child did not repeat this. Her hand trembled in Toinette's.

They were standing at the head of the waiting lines when Tiaoga and the remnant of his band came over the hill and across the fields. Shindas had said there was to be no physical demonstration against the prisoner, who was to be kept strong for torture at the stake. Toinette shivered. It was a different homecoming this time. The people were like tigers holding their passions in leash. There was something demoniac in the faces of the children. Even the eyes of those whose loved ones had escaped death held only the deep-seated fire of hatred. Tiaoga came. His face was like a mask of rock as he passed so near that Toinette might have touched him. The prisoner followed. His clothes were torn from the upper part of his body. He was a powerfully built man with great hands and wide shoulders. On each side of him walked a warrior, for he was blind and needed guidance. His empty eye sockets, hidden by drooping lids, gave to his round red face the appearance of one walking in a ghastly sleep. Yet he was not overcome by the enormity of the catastrophe which had befallen him, nor did he betray fear of what lay ahead. He sensed the presence of the people and held his head high as if trying to see them. It was a bald head.

Toinette swayed backward and struggled in a moment of darkness to keep herself from falling.

The prisoner was Hepsibah Adams.

CHAPTER XIX

NO ONE but Wood Pigeon observed the faintness which came over Toinette. Some force had drawn a smothering curtain about her making it difficult to see or breathe. When the shock passed, they were standing alone with the mob closing in behind Tiaoga and his single captive. Its pent-up emotion burst loose in a pandemonium, and amid the excitement Toinette went back to the cabin which Jeems had built near Tiaoga's tepee.

She sent Wood Pigeon in quest of Shindas, and when the young Seneca appeared, she pleaded with him to save the prisoner from death, urging him with all her strength to put aside his bitterness and help her in this hour. She told him the white man was Jeems's uncle and her father's old friend, a man who had always been a brother to the Indians until the Mohawks murdered the sister whom he had loved with an even greater love than that which Shindas had for Mary Daghlen. But Shindas was unmoved. Her words fell upon a heart of flint, and no sign of sympathy crossed his countenance as he listened. He left without betraying a gesture of hope.

Her failure to interest Tiaoga's nephew added to the difficulty of the situation. At first she had regretted the absence of Jeems, but now she was glad he was gone, for the increasing tumult in the village, the chanting of death songs by the women, the screaming of children, and the yelling of savages who were working themselves into a frenzy of rage about the fire pole which would soon receive its victim terrified her with the growing conviction that nothing could save his uncle. If Jeems had been there, she knew he would not have seen Hepsibah Adams put to death without a struggle fatal to himself. This thought, together with the reflection that it was a fortunate chance which had sent him away, strengthened her determination to help Hepsibah, and she watched with Wood Pigeon until she saw the chief enter his tepee. Then she hurried to him with Wood Pigeon and Odd following her.

Tiaoga's greeting held no promise. She fancied he made a movement to extend his hands and that he relaxed in his harshness. The impression was dispelled as the Seneca folded his arms across his breast and regarded her calmly, revealing no gentle aspect as he spoke a few words in acknowledgment of her visit. The tragedy which had befallen his people seemed to have given him a nobler bearing. A defeated chief returning to a home racked and torn by death, he retained the majesty of a king, but this character of the man seemed to project itself from a thing of stone rather than a substance of flesh and blood. That his prisoner bore the same relationship to Jeems which he bore to Shindas and that the man about to die was loved by Silver Heels brought no surprise or hesitation to his face. He waited patiently for her to finish, then shook his head and pointed through the door to the shadows gathering in the path of the setting sun. He stated coldly that the prisoner must die. His people demanded that the spirit of the white man who had slain three of his warriors be destroyed in flames. They would wait until it was dark, which was the tribal custom. Then the prisoner would be brought from the tepee in which he was lying bound, and the fire would be lighted.

If it were her desire, she might talk with Jeems's uncle, Tiaoga said. He was looking into the twilight when he made this concession. The Indian women at the farther end of the village were chanting more loudly as darkness came on.

Tiaoga spoke again.

She must hurry. It was growing late. The captive was in Ah De Bah's tepee, near the river, and the Tall Man and Shindas were guarding him.

He watched her depart with Wood Pigeon and Odd. Then she might have seen a change in him, a change which came when he knew he was alone.

Women and children were wailing behind her— women who had lost their husbands, others who grieved for their sons, children who were fatherless. A ring of fires were burning with the torture stake in the centre. When the stage was ready for its victim, it would be an amphitheatre of flame.

Toinette caught a glimpse of the preparation and trembled at its clamour. She was breathless when she came to Ah De Bah's home, which the hunter had set apart from the others. The Tall Man stood motionless before the door with a rifle held in the crook of his arm, and Shindas sat on the ground near him. Both saw her coming. She paused a few paces from them with her mind struggling against a chaos of uncertainty and dread. What could she say to Hepsibah Adams? How could she help him when Tiaoga and Shindas and Ah De Bah were eager for his death? A moment of cowardice assailed her, a moment in which she knew it would be easier to turn back than to make herself known to Hepsibah. She looked toward the river shimmering in the dusk and saw the shadows of canoes where their owners had left them on the shore. It would not be difficult for Wood Pigeon and her to take one of these canoes and place themselves beyond the sound of what was about to happen.

Shindas had risen to his feet by the time she recovered her courage. He spoke a word to the Tall Man and advanced toward her. He seemed to have expected her, and pointed to the tepee. Ah De Bah did not look at her as she entered. Neither appeared to notice Wood Pigeon or the dog.

She found Hepsibah stretched out like a dead man, and knelt on the earth at his side. He was scarcely conscious of her presence until she touched him. She felt the buckskin cords at his wrists; then her hand found his sightless face.

Bending low over the doomed man she whispered:

"*Hepsibah—Hepsibah Adams—I am Toinette Tonteur*"

Shindas waited with Ah De Bah as the gloom thickened about them. After a time, they saw Wood Pigeon going toward the circle of fires. Shindas stopped her, and in answer to his question she told him Toinette was weeping beside the white man and that the dog was with her.

The fires beyond the oaks grew larger and stars began to show themselves in the sky. Tiaoga was talking to the people in the blazing amphitheatre, and Shindas and the Tall Man knew what it meant. Soon the order for the prisoner would come. Ah De Bah watched the fires, but Shindas paced back and forth as if the nearness of torture made him restless. In his face, hidden by the darkness, was the tenseness of one who listened as he waited. It was the Tall Man who broke the silence, wondering why Tiaoga did not send for the prisoner.

A fresh outcry told them that at last the time had come, and Ah De Bah went to the tepee and held back the flap. He spoke to Toinette, calling her Soi Yan Makwun. There was no answer. He spoke again and entered. After a brief interval, his voice rose in a demand for Shindas, and the young Seneca answered it. Ah De Bah was hunting like an animal in the blackness. The tepee was empty. Toinette and Hepsibah Adams were gone.

Shindas did not speak. There was no light to reveal his face as he went to the edge of the river and saw that a canoe was gone. He grunted his wonder when the Tall Man joined him. The canoe had been launched within fifty paces of them, and they had not heard a sound. Words of self-abasement fell from Ah De Bah's lips. He and Shindas were like two children, and every man and woman in Chenufsio would taunt them be-

cause of the ease with which the escape had been made.
But the missing canoe could not be far distant. They
would overtake it quickly, and setting his thought to
action he thrust a second canoe toward the water.
Shindas interposed by calling to Ah De Bah's distressed
mind the fact that Soi Yan Makwun was Tiaoga's daughter, and since she had brought upon herself the tribal
penalty of death, it was Tiaoga who should command
their action. The fugitives, one of them blind, could
not possibly succeed in their flight. The night would
see the white man given to the stake, and now that
Silver Heels had proved herself a serpent in the tribe
and a traitor to Tiaoga, she would probably die with
him.

Ah De Bah made queer sounds in his chest as they
ran to Tiaoga and the expectant people. He was not as
calm as Shindas when they arrived. It was Shindas who
announced the deception of the stranger whom they had
accepted as the true spirit of Soi Yan Makwun. He
spoke clearly so all could hear him. For a few moments
the desire for vengeance was quieted by the knowledge
that this was the greatest blow which could befall Tiaoga, who had given to the white girl the most sacred of
his possessions—the soul of his lost daughter. He was
coldly and terribly still. His face changed before their
eyes. The furrows in it grew deeper, and it became as
hard as the stones in the fields. They waited for him to
speak, giving him time to fight what was in his breast.
Then words came weighted with the decision of death,
rising until they swelled in a passion that was like a fire
consuming everything in its path. He declared that his

honour and the honour of his people lay in his hands. He called on Shindas and Ah De Bah to go with him to recapture the fugitives, for this was a duty imposed on him first of all. Before the night was much older, the fire stake should have its triumph. He had forgotten the blind man, for a man without eyes was already dead. *He would give to the flames the white girl who had betrayed them.*

A new sensation possessed Chenufsio after the three had gone. The white girl was to be burned! The thought travelled in whispers from cautious lips, for this which was about to happen was not a vengeance of the flesh: it was the spirit of Soi Yan Makwun calling for justice, a command from the dead before which Tiaoga had not dared to hesitate. The Silver Heels whose body had died in the pool was watching them. She was moving among them, listening to their words, filling their souls with a presence that dulled grief and chastened the frenzy of hatred. Even Wood Pigeon, who loved Toinette, could not cry. Those who were white drew away in horror. The fires burned down until they were eyes in the night. Hours passed, and the Senecas listened in the stillness as if oppressed by fear.

At last they heard the chanting of a voice coming nearer as fast as a canoe could travel. It was the death song with which Tiaoga had grieved for his daughter, and the savages were moved by it as leaves are moved by a wind. The suspense was broken, for in the song of grief was also a note of triumph which brought the message that Tiaoga had been successful in his pursuit. Fresh fuel was piled on the fires, and the flames leapt high. When Tiaoga and his companions came from the river, they brought no prisoner with them. Yet a fierce light shone in their countenances as they entered the illumination, and beginning his death song again Tiaoga snatched a burning brand and flung it into the midst of the pitchy material about the torture stake. In a moment a winding sheet of flame licked its way up the pole, and around this Tiaoga danced, finishing his song to the crackling of the pitch. He flung himself into a greater passion as he told his people what had happened. He described how they had overtaken the fleeing ones at the edge of the Great Rocks beyond which the water thundered in a maelstrom. The blind man had fought with a hatchet he had stolen from Ah De Bah's tepee until another blade was sunk in his brain to quiet him. He was a devil in his blindness, and Tiaoga pointed to Shindas, who held back his buckskin shirt to show a long and bleeding gash. The white man was dead, and his body, weighted by the darkness of his soul, was gone forever in the deep waters beyond the rocks.

But the unclean one who had tricked them, the girl whose evil spirit had come to bring dishonour upon them and to desecrate the soul of Soi Yan Makwun, *they had taken alive*. Tiaoga's face grew livid. His eyes were a madman's as he shrieked his anathema against her. Had he not taken her to his bosom? Had she not worn Soi Yan Makwun's treasures? Had they not given her a place in their hearts? And she had become a snake! His own soul had gone so black when they caught her that he could see only death, for he heard his daughter's voice crying to him for vengeance. *So he had killed the treacherous one.* He had killed her at the command of Silver Heels, whose spirit was singing to him. Shindas had heard that song. Ah De Bah had heard it. It was like the sweet music of water rippling over white stones in the springtime. He had killed the white girl with his own hands and had flung her body to disappear with that of the blind man.

Suddenly Tiaoga drew from its hiding place next his breast a thing which brought a gasp to the lips of those about him. All recognized it as Toinette's beautiful braid of hair streaming from the bleeding scalp the savage held above his head. Wood Pigeon gave a piercing cry. A score of times her little brown fingers had plaited those lustrous tresses for the one she had worshipped.

Tiaoga became more than ever a fiend in the flesh as he danced about the stake. Flecks of blood from the red scalp struck his face. At the height of his madness he flung it into the heart of the pitchwood fire.

Soi Yan Makwun was avenged and the demand of his people answered.

CHAPTER XX

AT NOON of the second day of his journey Jeems came to the village of Kanestio, whose chief was Matozee, or Yellow Bear. He had travelled the seventy miles in thirty hours, and was determined to return as quickly, for he was troubled deeply by the thought that Toinette was alone at a time when the sentiment of the Indians was turning against them. Why he and not a tribal runner had been sent to Yellow Bear puzzled him, and the fact that he bore a message of small importance increased his uneasiness. That Tiaoga, returning at the ebb of his fortunes, should trouble himself to forward by Shindas a command intended only for him added another doubt to those in his mind. These doubts would have assailed him more heavily had he known that a runner had preceded him, a young man called Na Swa Ga, or Feathered Arrow, who carried a more significant message from Tiaoga to Yellow Bear.

He had scarcely reached Kanestio when his weapons, a knife and a hatchet, were taken from him and he was brought to Matozee. This individual, who was killed at Lake George the following year and who was a boy in appearance though the French held him among the bravest fighters of the Six Nations, informed Jeems that he was a prisoner. He said Tioaga had defaulted in a payment of corn that was due, and Jeems was to cover part of the obligation. Matozee tersely explained the agreement between the chiefs. If Jeems attempted to escape and was caught by his warriors, he would be killed; if by any chance he succeeded in getting back to Chenufsio, then he would answer to Tiaoga with his life. A dead line was drawn encircling the tepee in which he was to live, and he found himself under a surveillance little less strict than that accorded to a prisoner whose fate was to be torture or death.

Dismayed by the change in his fortunes, Jeems could conceive of no reason for Tiaoga's perfidy except that it must vitally concern Toinette. He accepted Matozee's explanation as a falsehood, and thought Shindas and not Tiaoga was at the bottom of the plot which had been made to prey upon his freedom, though he had believed Shindas his best friend among the Senecas. His alarm increased until, on the second day, he made up his mind to escape and return to Chenufsio even if his life were the price of the act. His uneasiness must have betrayed his purpose, for the third day found him more closely watched than before, and at night half a dozen young warriors slept about his tepee in such positions that he could not move from his shelter without disturbing at least one of them.

The fourth afternoon he perceived an excited gathering of women and children some distance from him but paid no attention to it. Depressed by fears which had become unbearable, he was determined to gain his freedom before another dawn. Increasing cloudiness during the afternoon and a promise of storm with the beginning of evening added to his hopes for success.

Thunder and rain came with darkness, and he feigned sleep at an early hour. It was almost midnight when he sat up and listened to the downpour. He was about to rise to his feet, certain that no Senecas would be lying in the deluge, when he heard the sodden rustle of the skin flap to the tepee as it was drawn back and someone entered.

In a moment a small voice whispered his name. Cold hands found him as he held out his arms. He felt a child's drenched form.

Then came choking words half smothered in the heat of the storm: "*I am Wood Pigeon. I ran away from Chenufsio three days ago. I have come to tell you Silver Heels is dead.*"[1]

Lightning flashes which accompanied the storm that night revealed a solitary figure hurrying through the wilderness toward Chenufsio, a figure which sped until it was winded and then continued at a slower pace with a persistence no beat of rain or blast of wind could halt.

The traveller was Jeems. Had another come to him with the tale of horror Wood Pigeon had borne, he would have disbelieved, but truth in its simplest form had fallen from her lips. What one might partly have concealed, she had told with childish candour, and every lightning flash became a pillar of flame in the glare of which he saw Tiaoga dancing with Toinette's streaming hair.

---

[1]Wanonat, then in her ninth year, made this seventy-mile journey from Chenufsio to Kanestio late in May, 1756. Ten years later, the heroic little Seneca maid married a Frenchman named De Poncy and lived in the valley or the Richelieu.

Wood Pigeon had repeated the message Toinette entrusted to her a few minutes preceding her flight with Hepsibah Adams, and no blackness was so thick that it hid from Jeems the tortured faces of his wife and his blind uncle as they beckoned him to vengeance.

That he did not lose the narrow trail in his haste was one of the inexplicable phenomena of chance which are frequently a part of a somnambulist's adventures. Instinct more than the guiding marks he could feel and see kept his feet in the path, and not until the thickness of the rain-filled night gave way to a gloomy dawn was he conscious of the obstacles which he had overcome.

Light, though accompanied by sombre clouds and steady rain, served to bring his soul out of the chaos into which it had fallen. Toinette was dead, and the depressive horizons became walls of a prison which held but that one thought. She was murdered as his mother had been murdered. She was gone, with her father, with his own people, leaving him alone at last.

Even vengeance seemed futile and inadequate. Hope did not rise in his breast. He had hoped when he knew his mother was dead, he had hoped as he sought for life among the ruins of Tonteur Manor, he had never quite given up hope that his uncle was alive. But now it was impossible for him to find that saving grace within his mental reach. As he went on, he was slowly dispossessed of the power to hate, though every sinew in his body was bent with implacable resolution in its mission of death. He would kill Tiaoga. He would kill Shindas. There would be only justice and no gratification of the flesh or the spirit in his act. A greater and more encompassing thing than the impulse which had sent him from Matozee's village began to choke him with a force that was sickening. It was his aloneness. The vastness of the world. The sudden going of the one who had remained to make it habitable for him. Without Toinette there was no reason for its existence, no reason why it should continue to give him the warmth of life. Toinette was dead. It was a fate predestined from the beginning, something he had always feared vaguely. Nothing counted now; to kill Tiaoga and Shindas would not cause a rift in the hopelessness which lay ahead of him.

He advanced with a speed which would have exhausted him at any other time. As the hours passed, an explanation for this haste gathered in his consciousness. *He was going home.* That in all of its significance was the cabin in which Toinette and he had lived. *Their home.* A thing that had not gone with her body and yet was a part of her which he would find as he had left it when he came to the end of the trail, unless Tiaoga had destroyed that, too.

The rain fell all through the day. It was still raining with the dusk of evening. The earth was drenched, his footprints were wiped out. The sky cleared toward midnight, and the full moon came up. A little later he reached Chenufsio. The place gleamed with pools of water. Suspicious dogs appeared to identify him, but the people were asleep.

He found his cabin with the door closed as it would have been if Toinette were asleep inside. He could feel her presence when he entered. But she was not there. He made a light cautiously and screened it so that eyes outside could not see. The floor, the walls, the room were illumined faintly. He began to put his hands on things, to gather them here and there, making a bundle of his treasures on the table—*her things*. When he had prepared the bundle he armed himself with a knife and a hatchet and his bow, then extinguished the light and went out, closing the door behind him.

He sought Shindas, for his plan was to kill him first. Then he would kill Tiaoga. Shindas was not in his tepee. The place was empty and his weapons were gone, evidence that he was away on a journey. For a few moments after this discovery, Jeems stood in the shadow of an oak looking at Tiaoga's dwelling place. The urge to destroy was not strong in him. The gentle whispering among the trees and the drip of water from their foliage combined in a melody of peace which struggled to turn him from the thought of death. It might have won if a tall figure had not come out of the tepee he was watching. Jeems knew it was Tiaoga. The chieftain advanced toward him as if an invisible fate were leading him to his execution. Then he paused. The moon was bright. It lit up his features thirty yards away as he gazed into a mystery of distance which his eyes could not penetrate. What had brought him, what he was thinking, what the night held for him, Jeems did not ask himself. He strung his bow and fitted an arrow. Then he called Tiaoga's name in a low voice to let him know that retribution had come. The bow twanged and a slender shaft sped through the moonlight with the winged sound of a humming bird. He heard the arrow strike. Tiaoga did not cry out. His hands clutched at his breast as he sank to the earth and lay there a motionless blot.

Jeems went down the river. For many days he hid along its shores seeking for Toinette's body. He saw Senecas pass and repass, but as he travelled almost entirely in the water he was successful in evading them.

When he reached Lake Ontario, he turned eastward, still carrying his bundle. At night he slept with it close to his face, breathing the precious incense of Toinette's things. Sometimes he held to his lips the piece of red cloth she had worn around her hair.

As weeks followed his escape, he grew stupidly dull in some ways. He lost desire. He found himself without a motive in everything he did. For periods of time he remained in hiding places. Concealment became a habit rather than an intelligent act. No spring of action encouraged him to return to Forbidden Valley or the Richelieu, and it was chance and not a definite purpose which brought him to the place on Lake Champlain called Ticonderoga by the Indians. This was late in the summer of 1756. The French had occupied a point of land and were building Fort Vaudreuil and Fort Carillon. Jeems seized upon these activities with the avidity of one who at last had found something to assuage a killing hunger. He joined Montcalm's forces and was given a musket and a spade in place of his bow and arrows.

He entered now an apprenticeship of digging and building in the earth where the forts were going up. The work and its environment, the excitement of war, and the ever-increasing news of French victories were a relief to his broken spirits, but they did not thrill him. He fought against this apathy. He tried to hate once more. He repeated to himself many times that the English and their Indians were responsible for the tragedies which had befallen his loved ones. But he could not rise to the passion for vengeance. He wanted to fight, he wanted to see the English and their allies overwhelmed, but his emotions were as dull as they were implacable. They burned with a fatalistic evenness which neither triumph nor defeat could raise to great heights or lower to the depths they had plumbed. Death could never stir him again as it had already stirred him, no shambles could sicken him and no victory bring to him the remotest gladness of the song he had chanted in the firelight at Chenufsio. When the English stronghold of Oswego was laid in ashes and every church in New France sang Te Deum in gratitude and joy, he was not deeply moved. But the same day, when a newly arrived militiaman from Quebec spoke a familiar name, his heart leapt as if it had been roused from sleep with a blow, and after that the comradeship of the Lower Town man whose sister's name was Toinette meant more to him than the victory at Oswego or the concentration of French forces at Ticonderoga which followed it.

He made no confidants, and no one knew his story. An officer found he was acquainted with the country, and he was made a Lake George Scout in time to be captured by Rogers and his rangers on Christmas Eve of 1756. He escaped in January and was back at Fort Carillon early in February, when he learned that Paul Tache had been one of the French officers at Oswego, and that he had been killed. Jeems felt a pang of regret. Lately he had been thinking of Paul Tache and of Toinette's mother, wondering what their attitude would be when some day he told them what had happened after the massacre at Tonteur Manor.

There is no letter or information which covers the lapse in Jeems's military history between February and August of 1757, at which time he was present at the cap ture of Fort William Henry, or Fort George, and wit nessed the massacre of its English garrison by uncon trollable French Indians led by the Abenakis. Here Jeems must have experienced an unusual shock, for soon after the killing, when in their madness some of the Indians were cooking English flesh on spits and in kettles, he came upon the black-frocked priest who had accompanied the Abenakis and found him to be the Jesuit, Pierre Roubaud, who had made Toinette his wife at Chenufsio. Father Roubaud was even then pre paring that eyewitness document which was destined to become a valuable part of Jesuit and French-English history, and whose hundred or more age-yellowed pages, written mostly by torchlight amid scenes of horror, one may read in the Jesuit archives at Quebec. The priest saw Jeems, but so intent was he upon his task and so great were the changes wrought by sixteen months that he did not recognize him, and Jeems left his presence without making himself known.[1]

---

[1] It is recorded that Jeems Bulain was one of the few who dug the two long trenches in which the massacred English were buried. Signs of these trenches with almost the spade marks left by Jeems's hands are clearly visible to-day in the hollow below the ruins of the old fort.

After Fort William Henry and the brilliant French successes which preceded it, Jeems began to feel the inevitable pressure which is bound to crush the life from a country that is enormously outweighed by its antagonist. The English colonies had put an end to quarrels among themselves, and a million and a half people were set in motion against the eighty thousand in New France, and behind this inundating force were powerful English armies and a still more powerful English navy already inspired by Pitt and Wolfe. As Te Deums were sung because of his victories, Montcalm knew that New France was hovering at the brink of ruin, but at no time did the outcome of his heroic contest press with greater certainty upon himself than upon Jeems. While one fought on with the inspiration of God and mother and wife in his soul, struggling to shield the nation from its death blow, the other fought doggedly in the ranks but saw the end with equal if not clearer vision. For with Jeems there were no moments in which he placed such faith in God that hope rose above the darkness of environment as was the case with Montcalm even in his blackest hours. Through the lives of his wife, his mother and his father and his Uncle Hepsibah, Jeems could see and feel the impending catastrophe more than one who measured it in the counting of ships and guns and soldiers.

As the captured cannon were rushed from Fort William Henry to Ticonderoga, Jeems surrendered himself, as Montcalm was doing in another way, to the last chapter in his fate. There was no goal at which he could aim, nothing for which he could pray; winning for Canada, should the miracle of ultimate victory come, could hold no more of solace and happiness for him than defeat at the hands of the English. There were times when his French and English body was divided against itself, when his mother and Hepsibah Adams and all they stood for looked upon him questioningly from out of the past as if he had turned traitor to some precious part of them, yet in such a way that they could not condemn him. In hours like these, the spirit of Toinette came to his side and placed her hand in his, and he knew it was for her he was fighting, for the home which would have been theirs, for the country she would have made a paradise for him. She grew nearer as the sureness of an approaching end crept upon him, and he felt the beginning of a comfort he had not known before. It was the consolation of something about to happen. Something that was tremendous and final. Something that would have to do with her and with him. He knew what it was and waited patiently for it as another year passed.

Then came Ticonderoga, that July 8, 1758, when over a space of a hundred acres one could not walk without staining the soles of his shoes with French or English blood—that red day in history and heroism when three thousand toil-worn, harassed soldiers of New France faced six thousand British regulars and nine thousand American militiamen; the day on which Jeems and his comrades drove back the waves of scarlet and gold and a thousand kilted Highlanders of the Black Watch led by Duncan Campbell of Inverawe, until, as Montcalm wrote to his wife, even the bullet-scarred trees seemed to be dripping blood. Through hours of tumult and death, Jeems loaded and fired, and stabbed with his bayonet, and the thing for which he was waiting did not come. Men fell around him, tens and scores and hundreds of them, as the day wore on. He saw whole ranks shiver and crumble before blasts of fire. But when it was ended and the English dropped back in a last smashing defeat, he was unscathed except for bruises and powder burns on his flesh.

The day after the victory, when Abercrombie and his English and Colonials were in flight, Montcalm caused to be planted on the battlefield a cross inscribed with these lines:

Soldier and chief and rampart's strength are nought;
Behold the conquering Cross! 'Tis God the triumph wrought.

Jeems helped erect this cross. His feet stamped the earth about it, and its words burned themselves as deeply in his mind as they were carven in the timber. God! Yes, God must have hurled back the enemy which had outnumbered them almost five to one. But what had God against him? And why had this God destroyed Toinette? He heard Montcalm pray. He listened as he told the bleeding remnants of his troops that New France was saved in spite of the tragic fall of Louisbourg. But Montcalm retreated, and this puzzled Jeems. The army began to learn the truth as, weary and footsore, it turned toward Quebec. Rapacity, folly, intrigue, and falsehood had fed at the heart of New France until it was honeycombed by the rottenness of dissolution. Montcalm was its one star of hope, and as autumn came, then winter, it seemed to Jeems that

Montcalm's God had deserted him. The St. Lawrence was filled with British ships. The harvest was meagre, and a barrel of flour cost two hundred francs. Even Montcalm ate horseflesh. Still he did not lose faith in God. A thousand scoundrels headed by Vaudreuil had fattened on the nation's downfall, and he prayed for them. "What a country!" he exclaimed. "Here all the knaves grow rich and the honest men are ruined." A fighting man, a man of sword and death, he kept his faith to the end. "If we are driven from the St. Lawrence," he wrote to his wife, "we will descend the Mississippi and make a final stand for France among the swamps of Louisiana."

Thus planned and prayed the man whose bleached skull is now shown to visitors in the Ursuline Convent at Quebec. Through the spring and summer of 1759, Jeems watched the spiders as they wove their web ever closer about Quebec, the last French stronghold in America. It was in May of 1756 that Toinette had been killed, and it was in May of 1759 that he first saw from the Montmorenci shore the mighty rock which so long had been the mistress of the New World.

Four months later, on the most eventful September 13th of written history—that "To-morrow Morning" which will never be forgotten—he stood on the Plains of Abraham.

Montcalm's God was about to complete an immaculate elegy which hung in the air like a mighty chorus waiting for a whispered command to begin. To Jeems Bulain, facing the sun and the thin red line of the British across the meadows where Abraham Martin had grazed his cattle, fate was bringing an end to uncertainty and chaos. It had missed him at Fort William Henry, at Ticonderoga, at Montmorenci, but here he could feel its presence—an escape—a release from bondage—something greater than iron or flesh—as the crimson lines drew nearer. He felt the spirit of what Montcalm had said to his doomed heroes a few minutes before, "*God is surely watching over the Plains of Abraham to-day.*"

CHAPTER XXI

IT WAS ten o'clock, the hour of the crisis. At dawn it had been foggy; at six showers had fallen; now it was hot. It might have been July instead of September. In darkness twenty-four British volunteers had climbed the steep height from the river, hanging to bushes, digging their fingers into crevices of rock, crawling with their faces against the earth, making their way foot by foot. "I am afraid you cannot do it," Wolfe had said, looking at the pitlike blackness above. But they did. Nameless in history, they destroyed the old map of the world and put another in its place. In that hour twenty-four men ruined France, gave rise to a greater England, created a new nation.

At the top, Vergor, the French officer, slept soundly with his guards. To him fate might have given the glory of keeping the old map intact. But he was killed before he could wipe the daze of slumber from his eyes. Wolfe's Path was made, and like a thin stream of red ants the British continued to ascend the trail which had been blazed for them.

Vaudreuil, the governor, the arch-villain who lost half a continent for France, lay in his cozy nest of iniquity a short distance away dreaming of sensual days with the faithless Madame de Paean and planning a future with the King's own mistress, La Pompadour.

Across the St. Charles, expecting the British in a different direction, sleepless, worn, robbed of every chance to win by the weakness and imbecility of this favourite of a king's mistress, was Montcalm.

Jeems was with the battalion of Guienne which had come up from its camp on the St. Charles at six o'clock in the morning, its white uniforms thronging the ridge of Buttes-à-Neveu, from which it beheld the British molehill growing into a mountain.

About him Jeems saw the Plains of Abraham, and a strange song was in his heart as he thought that Toinette had been of this soil and that her great-great-grandfather had given name to the earth soon to run red with blood. The Plains were wide and level in most parts, with bushes and trees and cornfields dotting them here and there. They were the front yard to Quebec, a field of destiny lying between the precipitous descents to the St. Lawrence on one side and the snakelike, lazy St. Charles on the other, with a world of splendid terrain spreading in a panorama under the eyes.

As he lay watching with the men of Guienne, Jeems could scarcely have guessed that this scene of pastoral beauty was the stage upon which one of the epic tragedies of all time was about to be enacted. A feeling of rest possessed him, as if a period had come to mark the end of the confusion and unhappiness which had held him a victim for three years, and he felt mysteriously near the presence of influences he could not see. He was a product of times when faith in the spiritual guidance of the affairs of men was strong, and it was not difficult for him to conceive that Toinette was close at his side, whispering in words which only his soul could hear *that he had come home.*

Six o'clock grew into seven, seven into eight, and eight into nine. In front of him England was forming. Behind him, tricked and outgeneralled, Montcalm was rushing in mad haste across the St. Charles bridge and under the northern rampart of Quebec to enter the city through the Palace Gate. At the edge of the Plains of Abraham the boyish Wolfe, poet and philosopher, was preparing for glory or doom. In the quaint, narrow streets of the town were gathering hordes of Indians in scalp locks and war paint, troops of starved and cheated Canadians ready to make a last stand for their homes, battalions of Old France in white uniforms and with gleaming bayonets, battle-scarred veterans of Sarre and Languedoc and Roussillon and Béarn, fed on meagre rations for weeks but eager to fight for Montcalm. Ahead, where Jeems was looking, were quiet and order and the stoic sureness of England's morale. Behind were courage and chivalry and the iron sinews of heroes in the throes of excitement and undisciplined rush.

Jeems saw none of this and nothing beyond the distant red lines. The Plains lay in sunshine, with bird wings flashing, crows feeding in the cornfields. The earth was a great Oriental rug warm with autumn tintings, the woods yellow and gold in a frame about it. The guns of Samos, of Sillery, of the boats in the river made sleepy detonations, and on the rise of Buttes-à-Neveu Jeems might have slept, lulled by that never-ending monotony of sound, the warmth of the sun, the blue of the sky, the stillness of the Plains. He closed his eyes and the silver and gold mists of sunsets rose about him, the ends of days in which he saw the Plains peopled again, first by Abraham Martin and his cows a hundred and thirty-four years before, then by Toinette, his father and mother, Hepsibah Adams—and himself. Here was a place he had known, a place his feet had trod, his soul had lived. He heard the earth whispering these things, the earth which he held between his fingers as if it were Toinette's hands.

In the town, priests and nuns were praying, and a bell sent forth its melody, a cheer to man, another appeal to God. New France was on her knees, and Montcalm was on the Plains, some of his men coming through the gate of St. Louis and some through that of St. John, breathless and eager, to where the banners of Guienne fluttered on the ridge.

Tartans waved and bagpipes screamed defiance as Montcalm waited for reinforcements which never came, and the bushes and knolls and cornfields were taken by fifteen hundred Canadians and Indians whose guns answered with a roar. Back and forth the battle raged, and France began to crumble.

Then came ten o'clock.

Something must have broken in Montcalm's heart. His judgment wavered, and he gave the fatal command which raised England to the supremacy of the world.

The French had formed with bayonets fixed in five short, thick lines, four white and one blue; the English stood with double-shotted guns in a long, six-jointed, thin red line. Level ground lay between. Had England advanced, history might have written itself differently. But England waited. France advanced.

Jeems went with her. He was already hit. A shot had caught him in the shoulder, and blood ran down his arm and dripped from his fingers. He felt no pain, but a slumberous feeling was creeping over him as he staggered on with the lines. He saw Montcalm ride along the front of his men, cheering them on to victory; he noted the gold-embroidered green coat he wore, the polished cuirass at his breast, the white linen of his wristband, and he heard his voice as he asked, "Don't you want a little rest before you begin?" The answer, "*We're never tired before a battle!*" rose about him. Jeems's lips framed the words which were repeated like increasing blasts in a storm. But the sun was growing less bright to his eyes.

An advance of forty or fifty paces, then a pause, another advance, another pause, in the way regulars fought at that time on flat and open battlefields, and Jeems measured the distance between himself and the red line of the British. At each halt he fired with his comrades, then loaded and advanced. The red line had broken precedent. It made no move to play its part in the prescribed routine of war, and continued to stand like a wall. Openings came in it where crimson blotches sank to the ground, but those who remained were unmoved and steadfast as they waited with their double-shotted guns. A tremor ran through the French, a thickening of men's breaths, a quickening of their heartbeats, a crumbling under strain, while the melody of the bell stole softly over the Plains of Abraham.

They halted again less than a hundred paces away, and still England's thinning line did not fire. A man close to Jeems laughed as if nerves had cracked inside his head. Another gasped as if he had been struck. Jeems tried to hold himself erect. The weird sensation came over him that the armies were not going to fight, after all.

Then he heard his name. It was his mother calling him. He answered with a cry and would have swayed toward her if hands had not dragged him back. "*Mad!*" he heard a voice say. He dropped his gun as he tried to wipe the blindness from his eyes. Things cleared. There were the red line, the open space, sunlight—something passing. Those who lived did not forget what they saw. England took the story home with her, France gave it a little place in her history. For a few seconds men were not looking at death but at a dog. An old, decrepit dog who limped as he walked, *a dog with one foot missing*.

Jeems made an effort to call.

"*Odd—Odd——*"

Then came Montcalm's command—"*Forward!*"

He marched with the others into the jaws of death, blind, groping, straining to make the dog hear words which never passed his lips. There was no longer a day. No sun. No red wall before him. But his ears still caught the tramp of feet and the melody of the bell. These died in a roar, the roar of double-shotted guns. England fired at forty paces, and France went down in a shapeless mass of dead.

With the front line fell Jeems.

CHAPTER XXII

I T WAS a long time before Jeems again heard the melody of the bell. When he broke through the blackness which had overtaken him on the Plains of Abraham, he found himself in the General Hospital under the care of the nuns of that institution. It seemed as if only a few minutes had passed since the crash of the English guns. But it was the middle of October. Montcalm and Wolfe were dead, Quebec lay in a mass of ruins, and England was supreme in the New World, although the battle of Sainte Foy had not been fought. From then until late in November, when he was strong enough to take advantage of the freedom of movement the British gave to French soldiers who had been wounded, he thought frequently of the three-legged dog that had passed between the French and English lines. He said nothing of the incident, not even to Mère de Sainte-Claude, the Superior, who took a special interest in him, nor to any of her virgin sisters who cared for him so tenderly in the dark hours of his struggle for life and the more hopeful ones of his convalescence. Each day of increasing strength added to his suspicion that what he had seen and heard were the illusions of senses crumbling under the effects of hurt and shock, and he kept to himself whatever faith he had in them.

When at last he was able to mingle with the disarmed populace and the crowds of soldiers in the streets, he was strangely unlike the old Jeems. He had been badly wounded and realized that nothing less than a miraculous intervention which the nuns ascribed to the mercy of God could have kept him beyond the reach of death. A ball had passed through his shoulder when three others struck him at the discharge of the English guns. That they had failed to kill him he did not accept as a blessing. The impression grew in him that he had been very close to his mother and Toinette and that a fate not satisfied with his unhappiness had drawn him back from them. This thought established his belief that Odd's appearance as well as his mother's voice and the nearness of Toinette had been purely spiritual.

But whenever he saw a dog in the streets of Quebec he looked to see if one foot were missing.

His excursions were short and he wandered alone He saw a number of his comrades, but they did not recognize him and he did not feel the impulse to let them know who he was. Flesh had dropped from his bones until he resembled one approaching death instead of escaping it. He walked with stooped shoulders. His eyes were sunken, and his hands, in one of which he carried a staff, were emaciated to the thinness of extreme age. The small interest life had held for him seemed to have shrivelled with the strength of his body. The English rekindled the spark, his mother's English, the half of himself which he had tried to hate. They were not acting the part of conquerors. They were—unbelievably—friends. From the gallant Brigadier Murray to the commonest soldier, they were courteous, humane, generous, dividing their rations with the

starved citizens, sharing their tobacco with them, helping without pay to build up ruined homes, each day
working themselves deeper into the good will of those
who had been cheated and despoiled by Governor Vaudreuil and his degenerate crowd and by the weakness of
the King of France. Even the nuns and the priests wel-
comed them, men and women of God who for two
hundred years had fought indefatigably for New France.
Honour and chivalry had come to conquer Quebec and
had brought such friendship for its people that a British soldier was hanged in the public square for stealing
from a resident of the town.

Jeems felt this comradeship of his enemies. At first
he was taciturn and aloof and talked only when courtesy required the effort of him. He observed that many
eyes regarded him with a pity which added shame to
the burden of his distress, and at times when he was
struggling to hold his stooped shoulders erect, sympathetic hands came to help him in spite of himself. His
health returned slowly, but in the second week of his
freedom an incident occurred which sent a warmer glow
through his veins. He heard two soldiers talking on the
street. They were talking about a dog—*a three-legged
dog that passed in front of their line as they had stood
ready to fire upon the French.*

When he returned to the little room which he still
occupied in the General Hospital Mère de Sainte-
Claude thought fever had set itself upon him again.
The next day, he went out looking for the dog and found
others who had beheld what his own eyes had seen.
But he asked no questions except in a casual way, and

did not reveal the reason for his interest. He knew the dog could not be Odd, yet it was Odd for whom he was seeking. This paradoxical state of mind bothered him, and he wondered if his illness had left him entirely sane. To think Odd had escaped Tiaoga's vengeance and had wandered through hundreds of miles of wilderness to Quebec would surely be an indication that it had not. He continued to seek, trying to believe he was making the quest a diversion which was healthful for his body, and that curiosity, not hope or faith, was encouraging him to find the three-legged dog. As Lower Town was the home of most of the dogs, he spent much of his time among its ruins, but without success.

His search came to an unexpected end in St. Louis Street where many aristocratic families of the city lived. Nancy Gagnon, who had been Nancy Lotbinière before her marriage to Peter Gagnon, and a dearly loved belle of the town, described the incident soon afterward in a letter to Anne St. Denis-Rock, and this letter, partly unintelligible because of its age, is a cherished possession of that family.

I had come out of the house [she wrote] in time to see a strange figure pause near the iron gate which shut him out from the plot of ground where the dog was watching little Jeems at play with some blocks and sticks. He was a soldier in a faded uniform of France, with a hospital badge on his arm, and had apparently just risen from a terrible sickness. As he staggered against the gate with a strange cry, I thought he was about to faint and hurried toward him. Then a most amazing thing happened. The dog sprang straight at him, and so frightened was I by the unexpectedness of his attack

that I screamed at the top of my voice and snatched up one of
the baby's sticks with which I was about to beat the animal
from his victim when, to my still greater astonishment, I saw
that both man and beast were overcome by what appeared
to be a paroxysm of recognition and joy. The action of the dog
together with my scream set little Jeems to crying lustily and
my terrified voice brought Toinette and my father to the
door. Shall I ever forget what happened then? Toinette started first toward her baby, then saw the man at the gate, and
the cry which came from her lips will remain with me until
my dying day. In a moment she was in that poor wreck of a
soldier's arms, kissing him and sobbing, until, with the antics
of the dog and the fiercer shrieking of the child, to say
nothing of my own wild appearance with the stick, we were
beginning to attract the attention of the public. . . .[1]

In this way Jeems found his wife and boy. Their
story was destined to be remembered because it was a
marked incident in a transition of land, people, and cus-
toms which history could not regard too lightly. Manuscripts and letters were to bear it on, until, almost forgotten, it was to remain only a whisper among a thousand others of days and years whose echoes grow fainter
as time passes. The walls of the old Lotbinière home in
St. Louis Street, close to the residence of the beautiful
but infamous Madame de Paean, witnessed the piecing
together of the story and might repeat it to-day if
they could talk. For Jeems the few minutes after his
entry into the Lotbinière house, where he and Toinette

---

[1] The letter from which the above lines were taken bears the date of December 12, 1759, and was addressed to Anne St. Denis-Rock at Three Rivers,
which destination it did not reach until March, 1760, according to a note
on the letter.

were guided by Nancy and her father while a black servant brought up the rear with the baby, were nearly as
unreal as the last moments of his consciousness on the
Plains of Abraham. Inside the door, Nancy placed the
child in his arms, which had not relinquished their hold
of Toinette, and the discovery that he possessed a son
leapt upon him. He was so overwhelmed by the emotion
which followed that he did not see Hepsibah Adams as
he felt his way through the wide hall to find what the
excitement and crying were about. It was Hepsibah
with his round, sightless face and his voice breaking with
joy when he found Jeems alive under his great, fumbling
hands which added—as Nancy wrote in her letter to
Anne St. Denis-Rock—"a final proof that God does
answer prayer."

That this God who had seen New France sink into
ruin had guided their own destinies with a beneficent
hand Jeems devoutly believed when Toinette told him
what had befallen her after the flight from Chenufsio.
They were alone in her room. It was the eleventh of
December, and the afternoon sun shone from a sky
filled with the smiling warmth of autumn rather than
the chill of winter. A few hundred yards away, General
Murray was holding a review of the regiments which
were soon to face Levis in his attempt to retake the city.
The sound of martial music came to them faintly,
and with it the distinct but softer tolling of a bell which
marked an hour of prayer, and to this appeal Toinette
bowed her head and murmured words of adoration
taught her by the white-robed Sisterhood of Christ.
Three years had changed her. Not time alone, but

motherhood and the grief of hopeless waiting had made her more a woman and less a girl. At last she had believed Jeems was dead, and now that she had him again, an indescribable beauty suffused her face and eyes with its radiance as the mystery of the years was unveiled.

She told of Hepsibah's capture by the Mohawks in Forbidden Valley, of his escape, his recapture later by the Senecas, and of her appeals to Shindas and Tiaoga and of her failure to inspire their mercy when, blinded, he was brought to Chenufsio.

"Only God could have directed me after that," she said, "for I was so desperate that I scarcely know how events shaped themselves as they did. I feared what your action might be when you returned and found your uncle had been blinded and killed, and not until I entered Ah De Bah's tepee did it strike me as an answer to my prayers that a hunting knife should be dangling by its cord in the opening. With this knife I freed Hepsibah and cut a hole in the skin tent through which we crept to the canoes, after I had given Wood Pigeon my message to you. When we were pursued and overtaken my hope died, but the depth of my despair was no greater than the joyous shock which overcame me when I heard Tiaoga's voice telling us not to be afraid but to go ashore quietly and that no harm would befall us. Shindas explained what they were about to do, for as soon as we were ashore, Tiaoga went off alone into the darkness. He told us that three days before reaching Chenufsio they had learned, through facts which Hepsibah related, that their prisoner, already blinded, was your uncle and my own dear friend. It was too late for them to save him, for the warriors were in bad humour and demanded the sacrifice at the stake of the one who had killed several of their number. Shindas came ahead so you would not be in the village when the prisoner arrived. As Shindas talked to us I learned that hearts as kind as any in this world beat in savage breasts, for these three men had turned traitors to the Senecas that we might live. In the light of a torch, Shindas disclosed a long braid of hair which looked horridly like my own, and drenched its scalp in fresh blood which he drew from his breast. It was a scalp Tiaoga had taken from a French Indian he had killed, and I turned faint when I saw it gleaming in the flare of the pitch pine. Then Hepsibah and I went on in the canoe. Hours later, Shindas rejoined us and said that Tiaoga had danced with the scalp before his people and that they believed we were dead. Shindas stayed with us until we came upon French soldiers near Fort Frontenac, and each day I dressed the wound in his breast."

She paused, as if revisioning what had passed, then said:

"There were a few moments with Tiaoga—alone— that night we stood on the shore, while Shindas took the blood from his wound. God must have made Tiaoga love me, Jeems, almost as he had loved the one whose place I had taken. When I found him, he was so cold and still in the darkness that he might have been stone instead of flesh. But he promised to make it possible for you to come to me as soon as he could do so without arousing the suspicions of his people. And then he touched me for the first time as he must have caressed

Silver Heels. He held my braid in his hand and spoke her name in a way I had never heard him speak it before. I kissed him. I put my arms around his neck and kissed him, and it seemed that even my lips touched stone. Yet he loved me, and because of that I have wondered—through all these years—why he did not send you to me."

Jeems could not tell her it was because he had killed Tiaoga.

As the melody of the bell had fallen like a benediction over the Plains of Abraham, so peace and happiness followed in the footsteps of the conquerors of New France. At the stroke of a pen, half a continent changed hands, and from the pulpits of the Canadas as well as from those of the English Colonies voices were raised in gratitude to God that the conflict was ended. Even the beaten rejoiced, for during the months of its final agony the heart of the nation had been sapped by corruption and dishonesty until faith had crumbled in men's souls and British presence came to be regarded as a guarantee of liberty and not as the calamity of defeat. "At last there is an end to war on this continent," preached Thomas Foxcroft, pastor of the Old Church in Boston, for like a million others of his countrymen he did not foresee the still greater conflict for American independence less than fifteen years ahead. And the echo was repeated—"At last there is an end to war." Again the sun was golden in its promise. Men called the days their own, the frontiers slumbered, the most vengeful of the savages retreated to their fastnesses, women sang and children played with new visions in their eyes. These were the days of a nation's birth, when the Briton mingled with those whom he had defeated, and transformed New France into Canada.

In the spring of 1761 Jeems returned to the Richelieu. Madame Tonteur, her spirit subdued and her malice chastened, placed into his hands and those of her daughter the broad domain of Tonteur Manor which it was her desire never to see again. That the home of their future was to be built amid the scenes of a tragedy which had brought them together, and where they would feel the presence of loved ones who had found happiness there as well as death, brought to Toinette and Jeems a joy which only they could understand. For the charred ruins of Tonteur Manor and of Forbidden Valley were home, even to Hepsibah Adams; and when Jeems reached the hallowed ground he had left five years before, he wrote Toinette, who waited in Quebec, telling her how the hills smiled their welcome, how green the abandoned meadows were, and that everywhere flowers had come to bless the solitude and the resting places of their dead. Then he set to work with the men who had come with him, and in the golden flush of September he went for Toinette and his boy. A haze of smoke drifted once more from the chimneys of cottages in the valley lands, and with another summer the lowing of cattle and the bleating of sheep rose at evening time, and the old mill wheel turned again, and often Toinette rode beside Jeems toward Forbidden Valley, sometimes with her hair in curls, with a ribbon streaming from them.

It was in this second year, when the chestnut burrs were green on the ridges, that strangers came down the trail from Tonteur Hill one evening, two men and a woman and a girl. The men were Senecas, and the miller, who met them first, eyed them with suspicion as well as wonder, for while the girl was pretty and the woman white, the men who accompanied them were fierce and tall and marked by battle. They were also extremely proud, and passed the miller without heeding his command to make themselves known, stalking to the front of the big house, followed by the woman and the girl, where Toinette saw them and gave such a cry that the miller ran back for his gun. In this way Tiaoga came to Tonteur Manor to show Jeems the scar his arrow had made, and with him were Wood Pigeon and Shindas and Mary Daghlen. For many years after this, until he was killed in the frontier fighting which preceded the American war for independence, Tiaoga returned often to the valley of the Richelieu, and as time went on, the pack of soft skins and bright feathers he brought with him grew larger, for another boy was given to Toinette, and then a girl, so that, with three children always watching and hoping for his arrival, the warrior was kept busy accumulating treasures for them. Once each year Mary and Shindas visited Tonteur Manor, and with them came their children when they grew old enough to travel through the wilderness. Wood Pigeon did not return to Chenufsio. Tokana, her crippled father, had given up his valiant struggle the preceding winter and had died. She lived with Toinette and Jeems until she was nineteen, when she married a young

French landowner named De Poncy, whose descendants are still to be found in the valley of the Richelieu.

From one of a sheaf of yellow letters may be read these lines, dated June 14, 1767, written to Nancy Lotbinière-Gagnon by Marie Antoinette Bulain.

MY OWN DEAR NANCY:

Sadness has fallen over us here at Tonteur Manor. Odd is dead. I no longer have a doubt that God has given souls to the beasts, for wherever we look we miss him, and a fortnight has passed since we buried him close to the chapel yard. It is like missing a child who loved us, or, more than that, one who guarded us as he loved. Even last night little Marie Antoinette sobbed herself to sleep because he cannot come when she calls him. I cannot keep tears from my own eyes when I think of him, and even Jeems, strong as he is, turns from me when we pass the chapel yard, ashamed of what I might see in his face. Odd was all we had left to us of other days—he and Hepsibah. And it is Hepsibah for whom my heart aches most. For years dear old Odd has guided him in his blindness, with a cord attached to his neck, and I believe they knew how to talk to each other.

Hepsibah now sits alone so much, keeping away from others, and every evening we see him groping about the gate to the chapel yard as if hoping to find someone there. Oh, what a terrible thing is death, which rends us all with its grief in time! But I must not moralize or unburden my gloom or you will wish I had remained silent another month.

It is a glorious June here. The roses . . .

One wonders if the misty spots on the yellow page are tears.

THE END

CPSIA information can be obtained at www.ICGtesting.com
Printed in the USA
LVOW08s1110080514

384946LV00001B/1/A